UNVEILED

A DARK ARRANGED MARRIAGE MAFIA ROMANCE

BRATVA KINGS

JANE HENRY

Unveiled: A Dark Arranged Marriage Mafia Romance

ISBN: 978-1-961866-47-8

ACKNOWLEDGMENTS

I would love to thank the people who helped bring this book to life and in your hands!

- First, The Book Brander Boutique for bringing my vision of Semyon Kopolov to life on the alternate cover edition of *Unveiled*, as well as Jason O'Bannon for creating the discreet cover edition of *Unveiled*.
- To my amazing editor Steph at KLS Literary Services for your humor, feedback, and patience helping me work through this story and my endless questions.
- To Becca Mysoor, the "Fairy Plot Mother," for her indispensable feedback during the writing process of this book.
- To my street team for their tireless support, encouragement, and feedback!
- And as always, thank you to Jessie and Michael for having my back and doing all the things so I can focus on what I love to do most of all — tell the stories.

To my husband, Mr. Henry, who reminds me every day that love doesn't require sameness — it flourishes in understanding, acceptance, and seeing each other fully. This hero, with all his quirks, is for you... and my sacral chakra thanks you.

SYNOPSIS

Semyon Kopolov.

Gorgeous and formidable.

My childhood crush and brother's best friend.

They call him the Ice King—cold, ruthless, unforgiving.

He's the reason my mother's dead.

Now he's my husband.

Once he was my protector.

The boy who carried me when I fell and swore to shield me from monsters.

Until he became one.

Forced into marriage, I'm trapped with the man I swear I'll never forgive.

But the harder I try to escape, the harder I fall.

My body betrays me, and my heart whispers lies.

I tell myself he's not the boy I once loved,

Yet I'm forced to face my greatest fear:

I'm falling for my enemy.

CHAPTER I

SEMYON

I SHAKE my head and exit the warehouse, the relentless bite of a Moscow winter hitting me. I pull my coat tighter and check my watch.

Behind me, I hear the telltale sounds of Rodion cleaning up the mess I left—the heavy scrape of a body being dragged across the floor, the dull thump of a weapon hitting the ground, and his unmistakable carefree whistling. Like one of the fucking seven dwarfs.

Only my brother would whistle while running the cleanup crew.

But he's impeccable, reliable, and takes pride in what he does.

I wasn't planning on delivering an ass-kicking right before the huge benefit I'm supposed to attend, but here we are.

Sliding into the driver's seat, I flip down the mirror to check myself. My hands are clean, my suit is immaculate, and not a speck of blood mars the fabric. Good.

My phone buzzes, the ringtone unmistakably Rafail's. "Where the fuck are you?"

"Took longer than I thought." My jaw tightens as I start the engine. The dickhead had more fight in him than I expected, and I wouldn't let Rodion intervene. I fight my own battles.

"How'd it go?"

"As good as can be expected. The job's done." I blow out a breath and glance at the time. "Got ten minutes to show up fashionably late."

"Good." There's a pause. Too long. I know immediately something's wrong. He didn't call to make sure I handled a job. Rafail knows better than that.

"Rafail. What is it?"

My older brother and I are tight and have been since he became our legal guardian after our parents' deaths. He's ruled our family with the proverbial iron fist, and as second-oldest, I'm his right-hand man. We don't waste words or time explaining things to each other.

"I've got bad news."

In the background, I hear Polina, his wife, murmuring in her low, soothing voice. She whispers something in Russian, and Rafail mutters back before speaking to me again.

I grit my teeth. I hate showing up late to anything. I plug the address into the GPS and throw the car into reverse. Rodion will get himself there.

When Rafail doesn't tell me right away, my patience begins to wane. "You wanna tell me, or do you and Polina need to have a little pillow talk first?"

"Semyon," Rafail says warningly. He'd take any shit I'd throw at him, but bring his wife into it, and he gets his hackles up. Fair.

I put the car into drive and ease onto the road before gunning the engine. "I just kicked someone's teeth in while making sure I didn't get any blood on this fucking white shirt, Rafail. Patience? Fresh out."

Rafail sighs heavily on the other end of the line. "Elizar Borozov was sighted on a plane heading to Costa Rica twelve hours ago. He fucked you over. We've had two shipments ambushed and our backup safe house exposed because of him."

I grip the wheel tighter, a haze of red clouding my vision. Eli. My fucking friend. The kid I grew up with. The one I trusted. Gone, betraying us in the process.

"Are we positive he left?" My best friend has as many enemies as I do.

"Yes."

I glance at the GPS. Ten minutes out. My voice drops, cold and venomous. "So I'm boarding a plane to Costa Rica tonight."

I'm already mentally combing the streets.

"No. I wanted to talk to you first."

"What's there to talk about? Eli was supposed to give us the details on the shipment and the harbor security leak in exchange for pardoning his fucking debt. That was literally all he fucking had to do to keep him off our shitlist. And now you're telling me he's gone? Vanished, still owing us four mil?"

This one's personal.

We spent every afternoon by the creek in Zalivka, the city outside of Moscow where we both grew up, throwing rocks and climbing trees, swearing that nothing would ever come between us.

He was the one I cried to when my parents died. As teens, we bought each other condoms and borrowed each other's weapons. We shot weapons by the creek until Rafail caught us and kicked both our asses. We didn't stop—we just got more discreet.

But the liquor came too easily. The lies were harder to detect. I should've seen it all coming.

I shoot Eli a text, watching the message hang before failing to deliver.

After all these years, after everything we've been through, he fucking *betrayed* me. All of us.

As if his family can fucking afford it.

"The problem's bigger than that, Semyon." My pulse beats hard and fast. I blow out a breath as he explains. "Eli's father couldn't pay back the Irish, so he put up his daughter as collateral. If the Irish take her and the bakery, they get access to the harbor—dangerous for us."

I know Rafail cares about the fucking harbor, but I'm stuck on *Anya*.

The Irish. Fucking *The Irish.* Our rivals, always looking for an opening.

Rafail continues. "When he couldn't pay, he put Anya down as cosigner on the loan."

Silence. Then, a roaring in my ears. My vision tunnels. The steering wheel creaks under my grip.

Anya. Christ.

I slam my fist against the dashboard, the plastic groaning under the force. My breath comes in sharp, short bursts. They think they can take her? They think they can fucking touch her?

Rafail keeps talking, but I barely hear him. My heart pounds, my pulse racing. Anya, in the filthy, bloodstained hands of the fucking Irish. They'd rip her apart. Break her.

Rafail continues. "And in the eyes of the Irish..."

"A contract is a contract," I finish through gritted teeth.

The Irish have been circling like vultures. If they get to the Borozov first and take the bakery, they claim access to the harbor... and Anya.

Anya Borzova. Elizar Borozov's younger sister.

The girl who used to chase fireflies by the creek, the glow of them catching in her wild hair, her laughter making me smile when the world seemed dim and hopeless. The girl who would look at me with such wide and trusting eyes, it would make my heart ache. She'd blush furiously and run whenever she caught my gaze.

I watched her grow from a shy, freckle-faced kid into a headstrong woman with too much light, too much innocence for this world. I kept her at a distance.

I *had* to.

She was off-limits. Untouchable. I told myself it was to protect her, but the truth was much worse: I wanted her too much. She didn't belong in this world—my world—and the closer she got, the more I knew I'd ruin her. I knew how easily I'd corrupt her. In my mind, if she was still my best friend's little sister, she would stay *safe*.

If I could just pretend—if I could freeze her in time, hold her in my memory as the innocent kid who loved books more than people and dreamed of worlds bigger than ours— maybe she'd stay untouched by this life.

By me.

My mind quickly slides everything into place like the pieces on a chessboard.

"We have an option, Semyon, but I need your buy-in."

"What's that?" I curse under my breath, gripping the wheel tighter.

"We clear Borozov's debt in exchange for his daughter's hand in marriage." A pause. "She's an option."

She could never be a fucking option.

"She's a fucking child."

"She was when you knew her. She isn't now. Marriage to Anya secures the bakery and with it, the harbor. It strengthens our family's power and cuts the Irish off at the knees."

I shake my head, grateful he can't see me right now. I'm supposed to protect her, not use her in this endless game.

I'm silent for long moments, unable to respond.

Anya. Beautiful, headstrong, willful, and brilliant. I remember her sitting in the corner of her room with her freckled nose wrinkled in concentration, reading book after book while ignoring her chores, when she wasn't risking her neck down by the stupid fucking creek.

I grind my teeth together as Rafail continues. "You marry her. Inherit the bakery, and it becomes ours. We pull that pawn right from under The Irish's greedy hands, and from there, we control the routes they've been sniffing around. Tighten our hold on the region."

I barely hear him. All I can think about is Anya.

Marry her.

A sharp rise of blood pulses through my temples as my hands tighten around the wheel. My teeth grind together. "Anya's grown up, her brother's made enemies ours and others—and she's out there." I swallow hard. "Alone. And the Irish are about to take her."

"Yes."

"Call her father," I snap. "And Rafail?"

"Yeah?"

"Make him an offer he can't refuse."

I hang up and gun the engine.

CHAPTER 2

ANYA

I YAWN SO WIDELY that my eyes water, then shake myself awake. I was up before the sun rose and made my way to the bakery in the dark to discover one of our ovens broken and a notice about the increase in the cost of flour. Now Stefan needs help with his homework.

My head is pounding, and my vision blurs. The relentless grind makes a good night's sleep seem like a pipe dream.

But my family needs me.

"I can't remember how to do this," I admit with chagrin as I drop the pencil on the table. The numbers on the page swim in front of my eyes, mocking me. I was a good student once—good enough to make my teachers proud. My mother. But now, the weight of keeping the family afloat has turned my brain to mush.

Why is this so much harder than it was back then?

"Anya." Stefan sighs. "I have to figure this out!" His eyes blur with unshed tears. He sighs again. "C'mon. You're smart."

I lean over and ruffle his hair with a wry smile. "Thanks. Let's work on the spelling practice next and come back to this. Maybe something will click."

I can't help but look into the living room, past the peeling wallpaper and stack of dishes in the sink I haven't done yet, to where my father is slumped in a chair with an empty bottle of vodka.

He's not helping with homework tonight.

"Where's Eli?"

"Who knows," I mutter, shaking my head, and bite my lip before I blurt out *who cares*? Eli can go fuck himself for all I care. He's become no more than a younger carbon copy of my dad. I don't say that out loud though. Stefan hero-worships him.

Stefan crosses his arms over his chest. "*He* knows how to do this."

"Well, he's not here," I snap, pushing to my feet as guilt gnaws at me. It's not his fault. I turn to him and squeeze his shoulder. At only eight years old, it isn't his fault.

I sigh. "I'm sorry," I whisper. "I brought you cookies home from the bakery."

His eyes light up. "Chocolate?"

"Mmm. Keep working on the rest of the problems. Sometimes, you have to leave the part you can't solve and work on what you can." Before I turn to the dishes, I take the white paper sack and put it in front of him. "Here. Maybe this will help your concentration."

He grins, forgiving me for my short temper, as he gleefully plucks a cookie out of the bag and takes a massive bite, crumbs flying everywhere. I sigh and walk to the washing machine. I'll toss in a load of laundry and let that run while I tackle the dishes.

My father mumbles something unintelligible under his breath. I look at him curiously. I swear I heard something like, "Take her."

Take who?

The remnants of my paycheck sit on the counter, stretched thin between rent, food, and clothes for Stefan. I'm lucky enough that I can still fit in my mother's old clothes, but I swear Stefan grows an inch a day.

I grab the load of clean towels out of the dryer and pile them in a basket. I draw in a cleansing breath and release it. A stolen moment of quiet. I need to put Stefan to bed soon so I can get to bed myself. Four o'clock comes way too soon.

Where is Eli? He said he'd be by the bakery before close, but he never showed. He's been vanishing for hours lately, sometimes days, and always comes back apologetic and exhausted. I half expected him to be here with my father, throwing back the vodka, but the silence feels heavier than usual.

Something is wrong. *Very* wrong.

I frown, staring down at the basket of laundry. Eli's clothes are in a basket of his own since I won't do his. I shove it out of the way when something clatters to the floor.

I stare at it as the hair on the back of my neck pricks. It's Eli's mobile.

Something's... not right about this. I pick it up, holding my breath. Eli never leaves his cell phone behind.

"Anya! Did you want the other cookie?"

"Take it," I mumble absentmindedly as I lift the phone.

Why did he leave this? It makes no sense...

I type in his birthday and see it spring to life. Predictable. I frown at the blinking battery—almost dead—and plug it into a charger in the corner of the tiny laundry room.

There are thirteen unread text messages and as many missed calls. A chill skates down my spine when I see the name *Semyon*.

My stomach churns as I scroll through them. It doesn't make sense. If Eli left, why hasn't he tried to contact me? Or is it because... he can't?

I stare at the name on the screen again.

Semyon Kopolov.

My brother's best friend. My mortal enemy. The man who destroyed my family and is responsible for my mother's death.

My vision blurs. My fingers tremble. I shouldn't open it. I should throw this damn phone across the room and smash it all to hell.

And yet, with a breath I can't seem to catch, I click on the messages.

> **Semyon**
> Four fucking million. I don't give second
> chances. I'm coming to collect.

> **Semyon**
> You betrayed us. I won't forgive that.

> **Semyon**
> Pay up or I'll take more than the bakery.
> You won't like what's left

I stare, my chest tightening, the words sinking in like a blow. *More than the bakery?*

What the hell else could he take? We don't *have* anything left—just this crumbling apartment, a failing business, and each other. My heart pounds with fury. Semyon *knew* Eli couldn't pay him back, and he let it spiral until it reached this point.

He planned this. And now my family is caught in the crosshairs.

I tuck the phone in my pocket as my heart aches. Elizar pisses me off, but he's my brother. I have no idea where he is, but based on the fact that he left his phone here, I can only assume he ran.

Unless he's hurt...

Rage simmers in my veins. First, at my brother for leaving us in this position to begin with. Next, at Semyon, who let my brother accumulate this staggering amount of debt.

I haven't talked to Semyon in *years*.

Years.

But now... I can find him. I have to find him. I shouldn't—god knows I shouldn't—but Eli's phone burns in my hand like a loaded gun. If I don't do something, we'll lose what little we have left. The bakery, the apartment, Stefan's future—gone. All gone.

I promised my mother I would protect Stefan no matter the cost. It was my last promise to her before she died.

I take a shaky breath and type the words that seal my fate. I lift my brother's phone, my fingers trembling as I type out a message to Semyon.

Where are you?

CHAPTER 3

ANYA

WHEN I WAS LITTLE, my mother used to call me her little firefly. Because I was so tiny, I practically flew about the house or yard, skipping rocks by the creek or climbing one of the huge maples that overlooked our backyard. But if I got angry—usually at my older brother or the injustice of a situation—my temper would *flare.*

"Be careful, my little firefly," she'd say after another one of my tantrums, running her hand down the back of my head over my hair. "One day, that temper might get you in trouble. And I won't always be here to save you."

Her voice still echoes in my mind, each word a ghostly reproach as I tug her threadbare coat tighter around my shoulders and brave the biting wind.

She's gone, and I failed her.

It's so frigid I feel like my nostrils are sealed together when I breathe; any bit of exposed skin aches when the wind touches it. But we haven't had a car in years, and I don't have the money to hire a ride. The wind knifes through me, stealing the air from my lungs, but it can't compete with the storm in my chest.

Every step toward the pub is a battle—against the cold, against the pain in my legs, against the fury that tears me apart.

Each frozen breath is a vow: *I'll make him listen.*

Maybe the mile-long walk to the pub will cool my raging temper.

His response was immediate.

Iron Birch. Come now and come alone.

Oh, I'll come alone alright. Who else will I bring, me and my battery of alliances and besties? Ever since I had to quit college and work in my family's business, my time with friends has dwindled to nearly nothing. Ophelia's the only one left. And while I know she'd pick up if I called her at any time of day, I also know she'll do her best to talk me out of what I'm about to do.

Rage and desperation are powerful fuel.

I have to confront him.

"Hey, gorgeous. Need a ride?" I shiver and keep my head down, ignoring a man standing in a doorway. I'm so desperate for warmth that I almost entertain the thought but manage to keep some semblance of self-respect.

I look at the number on the building to my left. Only fifty more to go.

"Hey," he calls after me but doesn't follow. I pick up my pace.

By the time I get to the Iron Birch, I'm shaking, disheveled, and angrier than before I left. How *dare* he and his stupid family come after mine? After all he did to us?

How *dare he?*

I shove open the bar door. It swings on its hinges, the overhead bell jingling. Chatter dies down, but when the people inside see it's just me, it quickly picks up again. I'm short and slight and hardly someone any of them would be concerned with. But I don't care. My mother always said good things come in small packages, and Semyon Kopolov is about to meet his match.

I hate him.

I hate him for ruining my family. I hate him for dragging my brother into the depravity of his world, for ignoring my mother's pleas to keep my brother out of it. I hate him for pulling the trigger that caused my mother's death.

And I hate him now for putting my family in this position.

So I march straight to the bartender, who eyes me with mild curiosity. A man in his early fifties with short, salt-and-pepper hair, he holds a beer mug in his hand as he dries it. "May I help you?"

I lean in, bracing myself on the shiny lacquered bar top. "The Kopolov family is expecting me."

His bright blue eyes widen as he processes my request. Leaning in closer to me, his voice lowers to a whisper, and he gestures for me to come closer. "Are you sure about that? If you're in trouble... if you need help..."

I lick my lips and swallow, completing the sentence. "There would be nothing you'd be able to do about it. Would there?"

His response is all I need. I blow out a breath and blink back tears. I wasn't expecting kindness in a moment like this, and it almost undoes me. "Tell me where they are, please."

Placing the glass down on the bar top, he nods and points to a hallway behind him. "Down that hall, third door on the left." He blows out a breath. "Be careful."

My heart pounds as I storm down the hallway. The door isn't even shut, wide open for any fool to see. I take in a deep breath. I conjure up a picture of my mother and take a quick moment to brush my palm against the fabric of the coat she once wore, a fleeting anchor to steel my nerves. I lift my head high. I march straight into the lion's den.

The sharp, synchronized clicks of guns being cocked pierce the air. It seems every weapon in the room is trained on me, the cold metal mirroring the ruthless eyes of the men who hold them.

The room itself feels like a loaded gun, the weight of every man's stare pressing down on me. My heart pounds like a war drum as the silence stretches. And then I hear him, his voice sharp enough to cut diamonds.

"*Guns down.*" They instantly obey.

I don't flinch under the weight of his stare. I take a step forward. I will *not* back down.

Semyon sits at the head of the table, his ice-blue eyes locked with mine. Gone is the warmth I remember, and in its place, nothing but piercing and unrelenting cold.

For a moment, I forget the danger. I forget the guns, the men, the risks, and my errand. Because there he is—the boy I used to know, now the man I hate.

How can he still make my heart ache after all he's done, after all that's happened?

I forgot how mesmerizing he is, how his presence makes my heart seize in my chest. How my mind goes blank when he's near, just as it did when I was a child. For one fleeting moment, I'm the little girl by the creek again, watching him bask in the golden heat of a summer day. I wished then that he would smile at me, but Semyon never smiles.

When I was a child, he was a superhero in my mind. He even looked like Clark Kent with his black hair and ice-blue eyes, as cold and unforgiving as a Siberian winter. I imagined when he took off his glasses he became Superman.

Even seated, he commands the room with an effortless dominance. His sleeves are pushed up just enough to reveal inked forearms, the dark lines of tattoos twisted over taut, hard muscle. Every movement is controlled, precise. The tats on his hands are a quiet, lethal promise. He looks like a man who never raises his voice...because he never needs to.

He lifts one dark brow curiously.

"You," I spit out, my voice shaking with fury. "You sit here on your throne of lies and power, manipulating everyone around you for your own gain. How *dare* you?"

The room falls silent, the tension crackling like electricity, finally broken by a low whistle. I look over to see Semyon's younger brother Rodion, a few years older than I am, shaking his head. Rodion is the family wildcard, defined by his athletic build and charm, a perpetual smirk on his face.

He's Semyon's opposite in every way.

"This her, brother?" he says, shaking his head. "You've got your work cut out for you."

What the hell is he talking about? Semyon shakes his head once at Rodion, who quickly clams up. I turn back to him.

"*You're* the reason my mother is dead. You're the reason my brother is drowning in debt. You ruined us." My voice shakes with fury. "And now you threaten to take away our only means of survival?" I'm shaking with fury as Semyon's icy blue gaze settles on me. Before he responds, he takes a long, slow sip from his drink.

"It's been a while, Anya. How nice to see you. It seems you've forgotten your manners."

Rodion stifles a snort, and someone in the back morphs a laugh into a cough.

I stare at him and don't respond. I expected anger, outrage, a scathing remark—anything but this cool, collected indifference.

"I'll allow your disrespect to go unpunished this once," he says coldly. Holding up a hand, he gestures for someone in the back, who immediately rushes forward to refill his drink. "If you tell me the truth, please. It wasn't your brother who texted me, was it?"

I shake my head.

"So you lied to me," he states, his cold voice dropping a few degrees. I swallow hard and stifle a shiver.

"I didn't *lie* to you. I texted you from my brother's phone."

"Pretending you were him, knowing full well, I wouldn't have disclosed my location to you."

My temper flares. The goddamn *nerve* of the insensitive prick. "Because I'm a woman? Because I don't deserve to be in the presence of men like you?"

"No," he says without a trace of dishonesty. That's one thing about Semyon—he never lied. To a fault, even. Sometimes it hurt that he didn't. "Because I would never have allowed you to come out alone into a dangerous place like this unaccompanied. You ought to know that."

I can't help but scoff at him. "As if my safety's any of your concern."

He lost that privilege a *long* time ago.

He rises slowly. I swallow. Semyon's bigger than I remember, bigger than when he was a boy. Stronger. Taller. Even from here, I can see the corded muscle at his neck, the veined strength of his hands. The room falls silent as he draws himself to his full height. He wears a black button-down shirt. Even in my fear and anger, my eyes are drawn to the way his rolled-up sleeves reveal the dangerous mark of the Bratva, every deliberate movement like the clanging of a warning bell.

"You'll see very soon that it's of my utmost concern."

What?

I don't understand what he's saying—it's incomprehensible, infuriating. The anger that simmered like molten lava inside me as I stormed up here erupts, scorching through reason, and the final thread of self-control snaps, as fragile as fishing line pulled taut under heavy weight.

I somehow find myself standing inches away from him, unaware of how I got here, fueled by desperation and fury. I'm blinded to the danger around me, only dimly aware of six strong men who rise to their feet and Semyon's flip of a palm that holds them all back.

"*You,*" I seethe, a flash of memory causing tears to well in my eyes. My mother, thin and frail, pleading with Semyon at the worn table in my kitchen. "You pretend as if you care anything about me... as if you didn't turn your back on my family. As if my mother's death isn't your fault!"

I jab my finger at his chest.

He lets me.

"You act as if you're the one in control—as if you need the fucking money my brother owes you—when you own this entire city and half of Moscow. You act all calm and collected when *I* know the truth." I blink, hot, fat tears rolling down my cheeks. I swipe them angrily away. "You've already destroyed the only good things I had left in this world and plan on taking the last of it? You're a *monster,* Semyon Kopolov, and the men in this room might lick your goddamn feet to get a crumb from your table, but *I* remember." I jab another finger at his chest, irrationally angry that he isn't stopping me. "I remember when you were still human."

Something I can't quite read flickers behind his glasses in his cold blue eyes. Regret? Guilt? I can't tell, and it doesn't matter because all that stands before me now is the heartless monster who abandoned my family who loved him for the coldhearted Bratva.

"Just sayin', I am not licking anyone's feet," Rodion mutters, which earns him a few snickers and a sharp backhand to the head from a thick guy sitting next to him I don't recognize.

I can't stop seething, can't stop fuming at him. "I came here to tell you," I hiss, my voice breaking, "that no matter how much power you have, no matter how untouchable you think you are, I know better." My lower lip wobbles, and my voice drops. "And I *hate* you. You want my family's bakery? You want to come in and destroy what's left of my family? Kill me first, Semyon."

He wraps his hand around my finger and presses my hand down as he speaks in an unnervingly calm voice. "Finished yet, sweetheart?"

Tacking on a term of endearment? The absolutely condescending *asshole*.

How *dare* he?

I ignore the warm feel of his hand on mine.

"Nope," I seethe because I'm just warming up. "I came here to tell you that no matter how untouchable you are, you'll never be anything more than a coward who preys on the innocent. You can take everything from me, and you'll still have to live with that."

Rodion mutters something under his breath, but the guy

sitting next to him—I can see it's his cousin now—smacks him again.

Semyon's frigid stare rests on me with mild curiosity. "Are you done?"

I stare at him. "So you don't deny it, then? None of it?"

The cold look in his eyes is unwavering. "You'll be quiet now. I gave you your turn to speak, which was more than you deserved. Now it's my turn."

Strong fingers encircle my wrists, his grip unyielding yet controlled as he effortlessly restrains both of my hands in a single one of his.

Damn.

My chest heaves, and no matter how hard I fight it, heat ripples across my skin. He may be a monster, but he's a beautiful one.

Up close, he's overwhelming, every inch of him exuding raw alpha male and unfettered masculinity. The faint shadow of stubble along his jaw only sharpens the angles of his face. I can see that though his eyes are distant, there's a smoldering fire in their depths behind his fortress of control.

In seconds, I take it all in—the black fabric of his shirt clinging to the broad expanse of his chest, his strong arms and torso, the way heat and power radiate off him like a predator ready to strike.

I open my mouth to tell him off again when he taps my lips with his free hand. "I said it's my turn, little Anya. You'll be quiet and listen to me now and not speak again unless I give you permission. If you do, I'll gag you and give my men a show. Understood?"

My mouth drops open in outrage, but he continues. "You came in here uninvited. Disrespected me in front of my men. You think you know all about my world and who I am, do you?"

Leaning in so close. I stare at his perfect white teeth that he bares at me like a wolf with barely restrained energy. My eyes dip down. His hands are clenched.

He's holding himself back. My heart thumps.

"Let me tell you something, Anya," he says, low and calm. "First, behavior like this will never go unpunished. You crossed a line, and there will be consequences."

Fear claws at my chest when the grip on my wrists tightens to painful. I can see the scar that runs across his hand from the night his parents were killed, and he tried to save them.

"And second. You really don't understand anything about my world. But you're about to learn."

I shake my head as if I can deny it and somehow make him hear reason and fall to his knees, repentant.

What did I actually expect from him? I didn't think that far ahead.

"Call Rafail," he snaps at someone to his left, who leaps to his feet, his phone already at his ear. "I want him to know what I'm doing next."

Oh god. Rafail is the family *pakhan*, his oldest brother, the beast that rules his family and Moscow with an iron fist.

"There's only one way to ensure your family's safety and settle this debt, Anya."

I stare at him. So he'll consider it, then? I may have lost my temper and come barging in here, but maybe he's actually listened to me? Maybe he has a shred of humanity in him after all?

"You mean there's a chance?" I ask, unable to keep the hope out of my voice.

"A chance to keep what's left of your family intact?" His words are sharp, laced with condescension that cuts deep. I hear the insult loud and clear but force myself to ignore it. I have to. I won't get a second chance.

He nods, his gaze unreadable. "Yes. But a chance your outburst and disrespect will go unpunished? No."

Fear skates down my spine. I hold his gaze, but his expression remains stonelike, a mask of calm authority that makes my stomach twist.

His voice drops, each word deliberate and heavy. "You'll marry me."

For a moment, my world tilts. I blink once, twice, my mind scrambling to catch up. Surely I misheard him.

I'm... stunned. Marry my mortal enemy?

"Marry you?" The words tumble from my lips. It doesn't make sense. It *can't*. Why? Why would he say this? Why would he even want this?

He doesn't answer right away, and the silence stretches. The weight of his gaze and his words keep me rooted in place.

Leave my baby brother to the mercies of my alcoholic father and whoever decides to take advantage of him?

"I..." My voice falters, and I make myself swallow the lump rising in my throat. "You can't be serious."

But deep down, I already know the truth. Semyon Kopolov never says anything he doesn't mean.

"Marry you? Give myself to the man who single-handedly destroyed my family? You can't force me into this. And I can't imagine you'd actually want to be wed to someone who hates you." I shake my head. It isn't computing.

He lazily drags his gaze down the length of my body, lingering on my neck, lower to where my mother's jacket has slipped down, revealing the threadbare top that barely covers my shoulders. Without a word, he bends as if he's going to kiss me. My heart races, and I'm so confused by my intuitive reaction that I freeze. But he doesn't kiss me. Instead, he closes his eyes and inhales as if he's in the presence of the world's most precious flower. I stare in disbelief.

He opens his eyes. "Are you able to pay the debt or not?" he asks, the cruelty in his voice telling me he already knows I can't.

"Of course I can't." Even if I gave him every penny of the bakery's earnings for years, I could never repay him.

"You have no choice, then. Your family has nothing else to offer." He leans in, his tone chilling. "This isn't about what you want, Anya. This is about survival."

A voice booms from the doorway. "A good solution, brother. Let her earn her family's safety the hard way." I turn to see Rafail Kopolov, Moscow's most wanted and Semyon's eldest brother, leaning casually against the doorframe, his steely gaze fixed on me.

Semyon clears his throat. I turn back to him.

"I'll give you until tomorrow to decide. But know this. If you refuse, your brother's blood and the fate of your family are in *your* hands." He turns to Rodion and jerks his chin at him. "Take her home."

CHAPTER 4

"You're not bothered by this at all?" Rafail sits next to me and pours me another shot of vodka.

I frown. When people expect an emotional response from me, I try to understand why.

"Bothered? By what?"

"What she said to you."

I scoff and polish off the shot Rafail poured me. "No. It only helps me to understand her better."

"I didn't know you two had so much history, Semyon."

Of course he doesn't. It's not something I'd share with anyone. But hell, I didn't know she hated me as much as she did.

"Growing up, I spent years at her home," I say with a shrug.

"I was best friends with her brother. I didn't know she even remembered me."

It's just as well. I'm not someone cut out for love, and her hatred will make our arrangement much easier... though it'll probably take some time to teach her to behave.

Still, her words battered the air around me. I cataloged every movement and fluctuation of her voice. The way her hands trembled and her chin tilted in defiance. The sharp intake of breath before her accusations. I slot every detail into the mental framework I use to understand the world, yet somehow... her raw emotions were unexpected.

Anya. Standing in the doorway, fire in her eyes, defiance etched in the straight line of her spine. It's been years since I've seen her, but my body reacts instantly.

The freckles. The stubborn little chin. The mouth I've dreamt about but sworn I'd never touch.

My fingers flex against the rough wooden edge of the table, grounding myself in the sensation of lacquered wood. Familiar. Solid.

Why are humans so unpredictable?

I need patterns, logic, reason, and control.

I pinch the bridge of my nose and go over the details again.

The way her voice cracked when she talked about her mother—a data point. I lock it away in my mental catalog.

The tremor in her tone left an unfamiliar, uncomfortable warmth in my chest.

When she jabbed her finger at me, the physical contact was jarring. I felt the press of her fingertip and can still feel the exact spot where her touch lingered. I normally hate uninvited intrusion, yet I allowed it from Anya.

Why?

Her words should've made me angry or defensive, I guess.

Coward, monster. Hate.

They repeat in my head, reverberating, not because I believe either of those to be true, but because *she* does.

Another note.

Interesting.

Did she say those things out of fear and desperation, or does she truly believe them to be true?

Does it matter?

What I know is that her family has a debt to pay, and I aim to collect.

"She can think what she wants, Rafail. You know it's in our family's best interest for me to marry her, and after that little outburst—I'm more invested in this than I was before."

He huffs out a laugh and shakes his head. "She's wrong about you being a coward. You're the bravest person I know. But monster?" He shrugs and winks at me. "Jury's still out on that one."

I shrug and register that too. He might be joking. He might not be. Neither impacts the truth: Monstrous behavior is relative, and how one defines a monster is highly influenced by emotion.

Emotions aren't functional. They cloud judgment, slow decision-making, and weaken people. My memory holds onto details with ease.

I remember the bold little girl who never backed down, even when the odds were stacked against her. She would stand her ground, whether it was against Eli's teasing or an adult's dismissive tone.

I remember the way her hair glowed in the sunlight when she skipped rocks by the creek. I remember the way her tongue stuck out as she practiced until the sun set, and her mother scolded her because she wouldn't give up until she succeeded.

What I don't like is the unpredictability of her emotions and the chaos they bring. My world is ordered and predictable, and I won't let even the most beautiful woman I've ever met change that.

I replay the way she looked standing before me—her auburn hair in a messy bun, her hazel eyes flashing at me. She's so much smaller than I remembered, but I guess I'm bigger now. Still, her presence filled the room like a tempest.

My tempest.

I remember the way heat rose in my chest and my hands acted of their own accord. She has the ability to make me behave in a way no one else ever has.

I call my sister Yana. She answers on the first ring. "We have a wedding to plan. Nothing fancy, Yana. I want it brief and businesslike, only our family and associates."

"So I heard. Are you sure?" she asks, her voice, as usual, dripping with sarcasm. "Because I was just about to book the Kremlin and order matching tiaras for everyone. You're killing my vision here, Semyon."

"Yana."

"Alright. I'm on it."

I'd planned my encounter with Anya with surgical precision, and her storming in here tonight wrecked those plans. Yet something about her passion and fury... I'm fighting the urge to... feel.

And that's what scares me most of all.

CHAPTER 5

I BARELY PROCESS how I get home. I don't really know Semyon's brother Rodion. He was young when his parents died, and I always got the impression Rafail kept him close to home. Semyon was the only one in their family who came to our house.

I know Rodion got married to a woman from the States. But everyone knows when a man of the Kopolov Bratva marries.

I suspect I might like Rodion if I talked with him—he seems the softer of the three brothers, though I should know by now that my first impressions of people *suck*.

But I'm numb right now. I don't return his chatter and don't answer his questions, and eventually, he stops talking to me. He's a big guy, as tall as Semyon but bulkier, so no one even thinks about bothering us on the way back. When we get to my place, his brows lift in surprise before he masks his expression.

I know. It's a total shithole and probably looks even worse to a wealthy, powerful man like him.

"You need... help packing or something?" he asks, his expression almost boyish, as if he doesn't know what to do in the presence of a distraught woman.

I catch the gleaming glint of gold on his finger and flash him a glare. "I haven't agreed to marry your brother."

This time, he doesn't bother to hide his reaction. "It would be a grave mistake not to, Anya."

"That's what you think."

He shakes his head. "You don't understand. Semyon is cold, I know. Sometimes, I wonder if he's really human. He doesn't... feel things the way others do. But if you married him, he would make sure you had what you needed. I know he would."

I turn away from him to mask the raw emotion in my chest. "What do you or your brother know about what I need?"

He sighs. "You'd be dumb as fuck not to take him up on this offer."

Of course I'm going to take him up on his offer. Do I have a real choice? I just don't want to give him the satisfaction of caving so quickly when I haven't even had a chance to process this myself.

I grit my teeth, slide the key into the wobbly lock that Rodion side-eyes without bothering to pretend he isn't, and push it open. "Thanks for walking me home and the unsolicited advice," I say with a forced smile before I shut the door in his face, trying to ignore how much he looks like his damn brother. A mean trick from the universe, making monsters so beautiful.

Argh!

I press my forehead to the cool door to quell the trembling. It doesn't work. I clench my hands into fists to stop the tears that *will* come now that I'm alone. It doesn't help. I sink to the floor in a heap and give way to sobs. They rack my body, my shoulders shaking, deep, heavy tears that feel as if they're torn straight from my heartstrings. I give in to all the fears and anger I've been holding onto for so long.

I'm furious at my father for being a weak asshole who cares more about his next bottle of liquor than he does his own children. I hate my brother for being no better than my father, for betraying his family and leaving us to fend for ourselves when he could've done so much better.

He used to be my best friend.

Gregarious and charming, he could talk a candlestick into falling in love with him. I swear Semyon and I are the only ones who see him for who he's become.

I'm so angry at Semyon for using my family's misfortune for his own personal gain, for refusing to back down and compromise. For pushing me to the brink of breaking.

A fresh sob escapes me. I wipe a hand across my snotty nose as hot tears plop onto the floor because I hate myself for the next person my anger settles on: my mother. I'm angry at *her* for dying and leaving me to bear the burden of this alone.

I cry until the well of hurt, anger, and fear inside me begins to dissipate. Until my eyes are swollen and scratchy, my head feels two times its normal size and aches, and I'm too stuffy to breathe out of my nose. It's tolerable when weeping leaves you feeling relieved as if a pressure's been lifted. But when you finish a good cry and still feel as desolate as before you began... it isn't a good cry at all.

I pull myself to my feet and look around me. My father's knocked out in his chair, a line of drool hanging from his lips. I'm glad. The only thing worse than losing my shit is losing my shit and knowing he doesn't care.

The dishes I left are still piled in the sink. The light under Stefan's door is out.

I close my eyes, a lump forming in my throat, and reach for my phone. With trembling fingers, I dial Ophelia. It goes to voicemail.

I put my phone down. I've never felt so alone in my life. I push to my feet when the phone begins to buzz. I reach for it, hope rising in my chest, and stifle a sob when I see Ophelia's name.

I answer immediately. "Are you alright? What's wrong?" she asks, her voice still tinged with that lisp she's tried to fix for years.

I let out a sob. "*No.*" I tell her everything. Like the good friend that she is, she gasps, screams, curses, and moans at all the right parts, and when I'm finished, she blows out a shaky breath.

"Oh my god. *Anya.* What are you going to do?"

"Do I have a choice?" I ask, sniffling through a fresh wave of tears. "But I can't leave Stefan here."

Ophelia is quiet for a moment before her voice picks up, filled with her usual misplaced optimism. Normally, I like it, but tonight...

"Listen, maybe you don't have to actually marry him. Maybe... stall. Tell him you'll think about it, and then maybe we can figure something out. You can—get a lawyer! Or... or maybe you can take Stefan, leave your useless father, and run. Change your names, move to another country. Canada? No one would look for you in Canada. It's so cold."

I laugh through my tears, but it sounds bitter and desperate. "Girl, I don't even have enough money for bus fare, never mind fake passports and whatever I'd need. And how long could I hide from them? He'd find me before I even left the city."

She didn't know Semyon like I did. She doesn't know how laser-focused he was when he wanted something, how determined he was when he set his eyes on a target.

I do.

"I can... I can loan you some money. I've got a little stashed away, I could—"

"Babe. I love you," I say, swallowing a fresh sob. "I love you so much. But no. Running isn't an option."

I can't tell her that leaving the bakery my mother started would break me. I couldn't do that to her. I was there the day she opened her doors. I was the one who sat on the kitchen counter, swinging my feet, as she taught me how to proof bread, showed me the perfect color of creamed butter, and when she taught me the intricacies of making the perfect loaf of sourdough.

It would feel like burying my mother all over again.

"What if you... What if you pretend to be really sick? Maybe under that stern exterior, the man actually has a heart." In my mind's eye, I see his cold, expressionless eyes.

She has no idea.

"Maybe if he knows you're like... dying of cancer or something, he'll show some mercy. You could fake it?"

"Ophelia," I say patiently. "He's one of the most powerful men in Russia. You know that."

"Which is why I think you're ballsy as *fuck*," she interrupts.

Ugh, where did ballsy get me though?

I finish, "...and he would have access to doctors who would make it very clear I'm not on my deathbed. Then what?"

She sighs. "Right. God."

Her voice trails off. It's rare she's at a loss for words.

"How long did he give you?"

I look at the broken clock on the kitchen stove that's missing half a digit and squint.

"I have twenty-three hours left."

I know Semyon well enough to know he meant that literally.

Her silence stretches for long moments before she finally

whispers, "Anya, all I can tell you is... I'll take care of Stefan. I won't let your father neglect him."

I swallow the lump in my throat. Stefan can hold his own with my father; I know that much, as he's had enough hours without me here to fend for himself. And while my father is a selfish, useless asshole, he doesn't hurt him.

"Thanks," I whisper. The word hangs in the air between us. "I have to go."

Maybe I can get some sleep, and when I wake up, the universe will magically present me with the answers to my troubles.

Maybe not.

I can't run. I know it's futile. Semyon's reach is too far, his control too absolute.

That's exactly what I'm afraid of.

I go to bed, burying my childhood dreams of actual love. Of freedom. Of hope.

I only have a few hours before I have to wake and go to the bakery.

In my dreams, I nearly drown in the little creek by my house. I'm screaming for someone to help me.

No one does.

I wake, gasping for air, to the faint trickle of morning light filtering in through my window.

My head pounds with a headache. My stomach burns with nausea.

I ease myself with the knowledge that my biggest fear—not having a caretaker for Stefan—will be eased with Ophelia's help.

"I'll marry him," I mutter to the empty room. I shake my head and make a vow. "But I'll have conditions. And he's going to live to regret agreeing to this."

CHAPTER 6

SEMYON

"She won't wear the dress, Semyon."

I stand in front of the mirror and straighten my tie. My sister Yana stands in the doorway behind me, her slender frame pushed against one side, her arms crossed. "I tried." Her tone is sharp, clipped. Not her usual.

I turn to face her. "What the hell is she wearing?"

"A dress," Yana says coldly, her lips pursed. "Simple. Plain."

I blow out a breath, adjusting the cuffs of my shirt. "As if I care." I know my words are dismissive, and I want them to be. What difference does it make what she wears? What matters is the agreement—the structure it cements.

But Yana doesn't move, doesn't respond at all. Her silence feels charged and pointed. I catalog her reaction like I do everything and turn to face her.

Why do I care about Anya's dress?

The only thing she'll be wearing *tonight* is my ring.

I look away from Yana when unfamiliar discomfort presses against my chest. Anya—beautiful, headstrong Anya—is going to be my wife and all that entails. She won't be able to run from me anymore.

"Is there a problem?" I ask, fully facing her. I keep my tone calm, but it's direct and calculated. If there's an issue, I'll address it, fix it, and move on. Like I always do.

Yana's eyes narrow, and her arms tighten as she lights into me. "My *problem*, dumbass, is that you're treating her like she's one of your stupid fucking chess pieces you can push around your damn chessboard."

I blink, taken aback. "That's because she *is*. Have you been reading those romance books Zoya's always talking about? Have you forgotten who I am? This marriage is a strategic move, and honestly, I think you, of all people, would understand that. If anything, I'm being kind to her."

Her jaw tightens. "Do you even hear yourself? She's not just a move on a board. She's a *human being*, Semyon."

My mind races to dissect her reaction, but the pieces don't align. Yana doesn't usually act this way. "I'm ensuring her family's survival. It isn't personal."

"Exactly my *point*," Yana says, making a noise of disgust. "Marriage! Not personal? Have you ever considered the fact that maybe it should be?"

What the fuck does she want from me?

I shake my head. "What would you have me do, then?"

Yana stares at me. "You're serious right now."

"Deadly."

"Try to understand her. Try to bring a thread of compassion to the table. Maybe, just maybe, you're more than Rafail's cold shadow." Her voice lowers and softens, along with the gaze she levels at me. "*I* know you are. You were the first person I told when I knew the truth about myself. You were the one who listened when I was confused and scared. You were the one who helped me bridge the gap with Rafail. I know deep down inside you aren't as cold as everyone says you are." She shakes her head. "I know there's more to you than what everyone thinks. But does she?"

More than... everyone thinks?

I care?

Rafail comes to me next. "What was all that about?"

I make a sound of disgust. "A fun wedding day lecture on compassion and humanity. I told her she was reading too many romance books, and that didn't go over so well."

Rafail snorts and gestures. "She's here. I heard the details about what happened last night. Do you have a plan?"

"For what?"

He reaches out and adjusts my tie, which is strange, considering he never does shit like that, and I wouldn't have left the room if it wasn't already perfect.

"For what you're going to do with her after you marry her."

I frown at him. "Consummate the marriage, obviously."

Eventually. I have no interest in an angry fuck.

Or several.

"Jesus," he mutters. "Do you always have to be so literal?"

I blink at him and shrug. "Yes."

"Case in point." We walk down the stairs toward the small gathering of our family dressed in formal attire, ready for the wedding, but Yana's words ring in my mind... *Rafail's cold shadow.*

Doesn't she know I'm marrying Anya because I'm as committed to our family's stability as he is?

Rafail continues. "I mean... have you given any thought to *after* the wedding?"

"Yes. I'll move her into my house. Establish her hours at the bakery with an armed guard with her at all times. Look over her family's finances and see where the fuck they went wrong and fix that shit. Make it well known she's mine now."

Rafail nods. "Interesting."

I blow out a breath. If people would only state what they actually think, it would be easier. "Why?"

"Because based on what the men said she was like last night, it seems you might have your work cut out for you."

"How so?"

"She's defiant as fuck."

I nod and stifle a grunt. I don't have time for this shit. "Right. Teaching her her place is a given. Would be boring if she didn't push back."

Rafail doesn't respond at first but finally nods. "Of course you'd say that."

I told my sisters to keep it simple, and they listened. The living room in The Cottage, the large, sprawling family home we inherited after my parents' death, looks untouched. It looks like our home, not a venue.

The wedding party is stripped down to essentials: an officiant who stands by the window, the armed guards stationed outside, visible through the wide plate glass. Rodion's wife, Ember, holds her camera and gives me a reserved wave when I enter. The family photographer, she has an eye for detail. I crook a finger at her.

"Yes?" she says in a low voice when she reaches me, trying to keep our conversation private. A hard task in a large, nosy family like ours. She tucks a stray strand of bright-red hair behind her ear and blinks up at me, obviously scared. "What?"

"None of these pictures get leaked until I look at them first. Take many. Show no one."

Her jaw tightens, and her lips press tight. I catalog that too. The girls aren't happy with me today.

Maybe they'll be fucking happy with the stability of our family and the credit limits on their fucking credit cards.

Rafail stands stoic and proud beside his wife, Polina, the Romanova family princess. Her long blonde hair spills down her back, and her light-blue eyes meet mine with cold detachment. When I look back, she averts her gaze.

I see Anya standing in front of me and come to a standstill. She came to me, wrapped in an old coat, her hair in a sloppy bun. She wore no makeup, but her fury made her cheeks blush pink and fire spark in her eyes.

Yana told the truth. Anya wears a simple dress, probably borrowed or handed down, its modest lines doing nothing to hide the soft curves beneath. My gaze drags over her, noting the way her neckline exposes the delicate line of her collarbone. Her hair's loosely tied back, no makeup or jewelry. I note every detail—the way she lifts her chin in defiance as if expecting a reaction to the way she's arrived.

Sorry to disappoint you, Anya. I don't care.

The way she looks over her shoulder at the guards by the doorway. The way she meets my baby sister Zoya's eyes as if reaching for reassurance.

The way she doesn't meet mine.

The ceremony is short and sterile. Vows. She finally glares at me, and her tone is venomous, but I ignore her the way I'd ignore a toddler having a tantrum. She can fall to the floor and pound her little fists for all I care.

But the truth is... she's beautiful when she's furious and completely unaware of the power she holds in that moment. I clench my jaw, barely suppressing the urge to grab her and show her exactly what it means to defy me.

I slide the ring onto her finger, my thumb brushing over her soft skin. She shivers, and I tell myself it's because she's cold, that it has nothing to do with me. Maybe she feels this, too.

Her breath hitches before she can stop herself, a sound so soft I might have imagined it, but for the way her cheeks flush. For a fleeting second, our gazes lock, and the room and its hollow applause fade.

Then she wrenches her hand back.

My heart beats against my ribcage like a warning.

Anya's my wife.

She's mine.

Standing before me in a dress.

And she fucking hates me.

Good. She should. If she knew how much I really wanted her, she'd run.

"Congratulations," she says through gritted teeth as we turn to face the camera, as stiff beside each other as cardboard cutouts.

"For what?"

"For winning the game," she whispers.

"Oh, sweetheart," I whisper back. "That's cute you think the game is over. It's only just started."

Her sharp intake of breath tells me I rattled her, but she masks it quickly. She can't hide the flush that creeps up her neck though.

My gaze sweeps the room for an exit. I said no reception for the two of us. They can party all night long for all I care.

"This way." I take her hand roughly in mine and tug her along so she trots to keep up with me.

"Where are we going?"

Ember takes pictures, and Rodion watches, an unreadable expression on his face.

"Home, Anya."

I tug her into the foyer and march with purpose toward the door. Our men open the double doors for us and stand aside amidst formal wishes of congratulations. I nod, barely acknowledging them.

"You don't have a driver?" she asks when I lead her to the car parked and waiting by the curb. "I thought you'd practically have hired people to wipe your ass."

I don't bother to reply and only click the key fob to unlock the door when Rafail calls from behind me.

"Semyon."

I turn around to face him. He nods at me, his hands tucked into his pockets. "You sure you don't want to stay and at least have a drink?"

Why would I do that? I have my favorites at my own house.

I shake my head. "Not tonight."

"Congratulations," he finally says. "We'll be in touch."

We will.

I'm surprised to hear the click of a car door being opened behind me. When I swivel to face her, Anya's opening her own fucking door before sliding into the passenger seat with a scowl.

I let it go this time, but she has to know that won't fly. I lean against the car door, taking up her space and caging her in.

"Don't ever do that again, Anya," I say, my voice soft but laced with steel. "Or we'll have a problem."

The air between us is charged, electric. For a second, it

seems she's confused when a look of genuine curiosity crosses her face. "Do what?"

She really doesn't know?

"Open your own car door. That's *my* job." I lower my voice. "Do we have an understanding? If you do that again, you and I will need to have a talk."

She blinks, disarmed. I wish I knew what I was doing that causes her to look at me like that. For one moment, she's put her armor down.

I like that. I want to tell her to do it again, but I don't know why she did it.

"Okay," she finally whispers, swallowing hard. "Right."

I nod. "Patience. Be patient if I'm occupied." I wonder if she needs more explanation. "You're mine now."

Doesn't she know the rules? The expectations? She can hate me, fight me, defy me all she wants—but she'll never be unsafe. As mine, she will be protected in ways she doesn't even realize. I'll walk on the outside of the street. I'll open her car door. When we're in public, I'll know every exit, every potential danger, I'll note every man whose gaze lingers on her too long. She doesn't have to like me, but she'll be safe, whether she wants my protection or not.

I have to remind myself she didn't grow up like I did. Her father's an asshole drunk, and her brother's a selfish prick. Now, anyway. He wasn't always.

I remember watching her mother work her fingers to the bone to keep that bakery afloat while her husband pissed away their profits.

No. Anya doesn't understand my expectations, but she will.

I close her car door and take the driver's seat. We drive in silence for the first five minutes. I'm acutely aware of her beside me—the subtle rustle of her dress when she shifts, the faint scent of citrus and peonies and something distinctly *her*.

For the first time, I allow myself to fully own the fact that she's my wife. It stirs something deep and primal in me. I grip the wheel to ground myself.

"Wait, so you don't live at The Cottage anymore? I thought we'd live there."

"No. I moved into a place of my own a few years ago, so I don't live there anymore. I spend a lot of time there though. It's still my family home."

"Oh."

She shivers in the passenger seat beside me, pulling her thin coat tighter. Without thinking, I reach for the temperature controls, adjusting the heat for her.

She notices. Her lips part slightly, as if she wants to say something, but she doesn't.

A beat passes. She reaches to turn the car radio on, but I swat her hand away. "Leave it."

"I like music."

"Not while I'm driving."

"*Not while I'm driving*," she huffs out, mimicking me under her breath in a petty voice with a sour expression on her face. My hand shoots out and grabs her wrist. The sudden contact freezes her, her pulse fluttering under my fingers.

Is she scared? Did her father hurt her? I'll murder him.

But I don't let her go. "Do you enjoy testing me, Anya?" My one-hand grip on the steering wheel tightens. "Do you enjoy trying the limits of my patience, or is sarcasm just a talent of yours?"

She scoffs. "If sarcasm burned calories, I'd be skinny as a rail."

"Thank fuck it doesn't."

She casts a sidelong glance at me as I take a left and head home. We're not far.

"What does that mean?"

"It means I like my wife with curves."

Anya makes a sound of disgust, crosses her arms, and sinks into her seat. "Do you even know how to lie?"

"I could learn anything if it was useful. Lying is a waste of time and energy." She doesn't respond as I park the car. "Welcome home."

"This will never be my home, Semyon."

I turn to face her. "Patience isn't something I've cared to cultivate, Anya. But keep pushing, and you might see exactly how little I have left."

Her breath stutters, her defiance flickering as she leans toward me before she catches herself and pulls away.

I'm not finished.

"I won't demand much, but your respect is nonnegotiable."

"Respect!" she fumes. "*Respect?* You don't scare me, Semyon. And respect isn't demanded but earned."

"Cute thought. Also, inaccurate."

I open my car door and pause, looking over to make sure she doesn't disobey me and open her own damn door. I watch as her fingers grasp the handle, and she turns to look at me.

"Are you that immature and petty?" I shake my head but won't warn her again. "If you behave like a child, I'll treat you like one, Anya."

Color floods her cheeks. She opens her mouth to protest, then slams it shut as if second-guessing her response. And when I exit the car, taking my time walking to her side, she sits obediently, waiting for me.

Good girl.

I open her door, watching the way her narrowed eyes are fixed on me. She doesn't like submitting to me. Makes me fucking hard knowing that, knowing I'll be forced to punish her.

Fire courses through my veins like molten lava. I'm not a man who could ever love, so a thought like that isn't even on the table. It isn't in my chemistry. I know that.

But lust? I've been lusting after Anya since before it was right, when we were still too young for anything even close to a relationship. I blinked one day, and my best friend's baby sister wasn't a child anymore but a woman with full, curvy hips, a soft belly, and tits that begged to be weighed in my palm, her nipples lonely for my mouth and teeth.

I watch her delicate hand grasp the outside of the door as she moves to exit the car, but I clear my throat with a *tsk* and sharp shake of my head. Her beautiful eyes are narrowed on me.

"I didn't open my door," she says in a tight voice as she ignores my warning and gets out of the car.

I close the small space between us. Her back hits the side of the car. In one swift move, I lace my fingers around the edge of her throat, my palm so much bigger than the slender column of her neck, engulfing her easily. I hold her there, braced against my palm, her back pressed against the door.

"We've only been married for a short time, Anya," I whisper in her ear. "But we've known each other much longer, haven't we?"

Her gaze sweeps over my hand, my arm, and up to my eyes. She's doing her best to hold onto her anger, but she can't hide the fear that flashes in her eyes.

"No," she whispers. Her answer takes me by surprise.

No?

"I knew who I thought you were, Semyon. But the boy I knew is long gone. I don't know you at all."

Clever. She's wrong though. Men like me don't change.

I shake my head slowly. "The only thing that's changed between us is how you see me. I've always been exactly who I am. The difference now is the balance of power between us."

"Always the master manipulator of words, aren't you?" she snaps, her tone cutting.

"Not at all. I don't manipulate anything. There's no need. I speak the truth and don't bother to sugarcoat." I lean in, my voice in her ear. "So listen well, little Anya."

She shifts uncomfortably. Good. I want her uncomfortable. Questioning. Off-kilter.

I need control.

"You took your vows to me in the presence of my family to save yours. That took courage, but you didn't have much of a choice. I've allowed you to push back. I haven't punished your disrespect. *Yet.*"

Her pulse flutters beneath my hand, and my dick springs to life.

"But we're at *my* home now. I have people who work for me. Staff. Men under my control who've sworn their lives to me. Here, little Anya, you do not disrespect me. I promise you, if you do, I *will* punish you. I know you haven't been well-schooled in the expectations of my world, so consider this your first lesson."

I flex my palm and lean on my forearm, caging her in as I hold her gaze.

Her fiery gaze locks onto mine, challenging me in a way no one has ever dared. She's smaller, fragile, yet she stands as though she's made of iron and steel. A goddamn queen in her own right.

"And what exactly does that mean, Semyon?" Her voice is low and cutting. "Punish me how? What else can you take from me?" She can't hide the way her lower lip trembles.

I catalog every breath, every micromovement. I imagine her tied up in my bed, handcuffed and vulnerable. I imagine her kicking her legs over my lap while I teach her manners. I imagine her screaming my name and begging to come while I hold back pleasure and make her earn her climax.

I sigh and brush my finger along the curve of her lower lip. It's dry, a little chapped. She's worked long hours at the bakery and tabled her self-care.

Noted.

"You don't seem to fear me, little Anya."

Her voice is small but her stance immovable when she responds. "What is there to fear when you've already lost everything?"

Oh, she hasn't lost everything.

"So dramatic. I thought better of you." I take my hand from her neck and place it on the other side of her head so she's caged beneath me. "But you forget something."

She doesn't take the bait. Doesn't respond. Only stares at me, trying desperately to hide her fear.

"I don't play by the rules."

CHAPTER 7

ANYA

I TRUDGED *up to the house, rubbing the heels of my hands into my eyes. I didn't want anyone to see me cry. Crying was a sign of weakness. My mother was at work—she had just opened the bakery—and my father... I hoped he wasn't home.*

The sun filtered through the trees, half blinding me because, at twelve years old, I was still too short to see much of anything. I just needed to get home, find a bandage, and I'd be fine.

Voices came from the back of the house, and I immediately recognized them. Shit. It was too late to turn around—they'd already seen me. Semyon and Eli. I turned and made my way toward the front door, but they were scrambling with something, hiding it under a pile of books. I didn't care what it was—a cigarette, a dirty magazine, could've been anything. All that mattered was that they didn't see me.

"Anya?" My brother's voice traveled the short distance. I didn't reply and kept walking. I heard Semyon say something to Eli in a low voice, and Eli gathered a bunch of things and ran to the back of the house. It was Semyon who came for me.

"Anya, what did you—" He froze when he saw me—my knees bloody, abrasions on my arms, tears welling up in my eyes. I looked away.

And then he ran. He ran to me. No one had ever run to me before.

"Who did this to you?" I knew by then he was part of the Bratva, so of course Semyon thought somebody had hurt me.

I shook my head. "No one did this to me."

I told him the truth, but I could tell he didn't believe me by the way his eyes darkened with doubt. His body language spoke louder than words.

I swallowed hard, caught in the intensity of his gaze, in the storm behind those glacial blue eyes. It seemed in those few seconds that passed between us he was weighing his options. I stared, half-frozen in place.

"Let's get you cleaned up." He bent, coming nearer to me than he ever had before, and scooped me into his arms effortlessly.

I opened my mouth to protest but was so taken off guard nothing came out. This was Semyon. So near. So strong and unyielding. Protective.

His grip was steady and firm but surprisingly gentle as he carried me like a baby, his chest firm and warm beneath my cheek. When had he grown into this? Semyon wasn't the scrawny boy who trailed after his older brother, shadowed by grief and duty.

He was a man now. A real man, older than me, bound to duty and family... and now holding me like I mattered.

"Semyon—" I began, but the words died on my lips. His face was closer than it had ever been, and the intimacy of the moment completely rattled me.

"What happened, Anya?" he asked in a dangerous whisper.

"I fell," I said, not meeting his eyes.

"Off what?" His voice was a low growl. He sounded angry. Why was Semyon angry? I was hurt, I was crying, I was bleeding, and I thought my leg might be broken—and he was mad?

"Off my bike," I told him honestly. "I just went for a ride down by the train tracks, and I was going fast, and my bike hit a rock. I don't really know what happened, but it went out from under me, and I just..." I sniffed, turning my head away. He shook his head gently.

"It's all right now." He looked at me awkwardly, like he didn't know what to do with me, as he brought me into the apartment. With a gentleman-like determination in his eyes, he sat me down at the kitchen table and propped my leg up, lifting my ankle tenderly in his large hands.

"Not broken," he said quietly. "Sprained, probably. You'll need to wrap this."

"Where did Eli go?" I didn't want my brother here. I didn't

want him to intrude on us. This moment felt private, special. Sacred.

"He had to run an errand," Semyon said cryptically. Now I was the one narrowing my eyes.

"My mother asked that you not involve him, Semyon."

Semyon's eyes flashed to mine before he schooled his features. "I don't know what you're talking about."

"You know exactly what I'm talking about!"

He shook his head. "I had nothing to do with this, Anya. If you only knew—"

"Knew that you're Bratva? Do you think I'm so dumb that I don't know?"

A muscle ticked in his jaw. "No, of course you know that. I mean, if only you knew how hard I was trying to get your brother out of trouble—" He stopped, his mouth snapping shut like he had said too much. What?

"Now, back to your injuries. I'm only going to ask one more time." His blue eyes held mine captive, and my heart ached under the intensity. "Are you telling me the truth?"

I swallowed, and for one crazy, wild moment, I imagined telling him that somebody had hurt me. That I was bullied. No one had ever looked at me like this before, and it satisfied a strange desire in me that I didn't understand.

I wanted to see how he'd respond.

"I'm telling you the truth. I fell."

"If you're lying to me, Anya—" My heart thumped madly. But he didn't finish the sentence.

"I'm not," I said quietly.

It was then that I noticed how his jaw had firmed and how the stubble on his chin had grown darker. Up close, I could see the shift in the color of his eyes—brilliant at times, lighter at others, framed in dark, thick lashes that would've been almost feminine on any other man.

I had never noticed any of those things before.

I did now.

"I'm not lying," I whispered vehemently. "Are you?"

"I'M NOT HUNGRY." I pick at a slice of plain bread, my appetite gone. I haven't eaten and need to, but the reality of my situation and the pang of loss hits my belly.

It's exhausting keeping up with my anger toward him. I'm not an angry person. I rarely lose my temper. My mother used to say I had the longest fuse of anyone she'd ever met, but when someone finally got to the end of it, watch out.

Maybe she was right. I don't want to think of my mother now because the most painful memories I have of her involve the man—or monster—sitting right across the table from me.

Semyon prides himself on telling the truth, no matter how brutal, but he lied to me outside his home before we came inside. He said he hadn't changed. That couldn't be further from the truth.

Because I remember.

I remember lying by the creek, side by side, when we were kids. It was the only time I ever saw him relax, surrounded by the hush of wind in the trees above us, my brother lazily casting his fishing line time and again and never catching a bite. I can still hear the sound of the water trickling and birds singing and fluttering past us.

He says he hasn't changed, but I know the truth: Semyon was a boy I trusted and grew into a man I hated.

"Eat," he says, pushing a platter of food toward me. Unsurprisingly, everything in his home is sharp lines and muted tones—steel, glass, and dark, varnished wood. Everything is cold and precise. Immaculate. There isn't a shred of warmth or personal touch to be seen.

Semyon frowns, considering me. Likely trying to decide whether or not this is a hill to die on. Finally, he shrugs. "Suit yourself."

He might see this as a silent rebellion against his wealth and control, but I'm tired, and it's late.

Stefan would have come home from school. He meets me at the bakery and tells me about his day, swinging his legs while sitting on the counter, messily eating whatever treat I let him pick from the day's seconds. He loves to look over the trays of baked goods and find the ones with imperfections before he stuffs them in his mouth.

I feel a little guilty looking at the lavish display in front of us. The spread is a feast of Russian tradition—bowls of borscht, their rich, ruby tops crested with sour cream, golden pirozhki stuffed with savory fillings, and plates of blini filled with smoked salmon and caviar.

Stefan would whoop with delight at this and eat until he couldn't stuff another bite in his mouth.

My heart aches.

I look down at my plate, the little appetite I had gone.

Ophelia looked after Stefan today and checked in on the bakery. Galina, our only employee and my mother's best friend, sells our wares with gusto but doesn't know how to bake the way I do. She can hold down the business for a day, but I'll have to come up with a plan to get back.

"I need to work," I say. "I can't just sit around looking pretty."

Semyon shrugs. "You can sit around looking petulant. It's worked for you so far."

"Oh fuck *off*," I snap before I can stop myself. As soon as the words leave my mouth, I regret them. Someone on his staff behind us gasps, and the cold flicker in his eyes tells me I've crossed a line.

"Excuse me?"

I open my mouth to respond but don't know what to say. "I-I didn't mean that."

"Did you already forget our conversation outside?"

My cheeks color, and I look away.

"Look at me."

My eyes fly to his, cold and merciless behind his glasses. I stifle the need to squirm under the heat of his glare.

"I told you if you behaved like a child, I would treat you like one. How might you punish a child who was disrespectful?" He leans forward before taking a sip from his drink. "I'll tell you what Rafail would've done. What he *did* do. You know all about Rafail becoming guardian to us, don't you?"

I nod uncomfortably. "Yes."

"And do you know how he would've responded if any of us disobeyed or disrespected him?"

I swallow hard and shake my head. "No," I say, shifting in my seat. There's a prickling awareness in the room now, an invisible weight pressing down as Semyon watches me with his ice-cold eyes.

He leans back in his chair, yet every movement seems calculated. It feels strange looking at him now, like visiting a ghost that's come to haunt you because I still see him, still hear him, still imagine the boy who was strong and powerful, the one who feared nothing. And in front of me now is a monster. A stranger.

"Rafail believed in swift, memorable lessons. Humiliation. He never yelled. Never raised his voice."

"Sounds lovely," I mutter.

"Sounds effective," he counters.

I look away. "So that's what you have planned for me? If I don't behave, you'll have 'swift, memorable' lessons?"

Semyon shakes his head, cuts a large bite of chicken, and

chews it methodically before answering me. "Not at all. I plan on taking my time and enjoying it thoroughly."

Gah.

"Enjoying punishing someone?" I shake my head.

Semyon shrugs. I'm fixated on his large, inked hands tearing the bread in half. "If it's done right," he says with a note of something dark and wicked in his voice. "You might enjoy it too."

I stare at him, my mouth agape, but I can't help the way my body responds. I don't like it. I hate him.

I look away.

"Even if you devise whatever punishment you think I deserve," I begin. My voice wavers no matter how hard I try to keep a lid on my temper. I look away from him. It feels like he's made a move on the board and put mine in jeopardy. "You won't win, Semyon. You'll only make me hate you more."

He sips his drink before he replies. "Hate me all you want. But your family is alive because of this."

Despite my anger, I can't help but recognize the truth in his words. I can't help but be confused by his motives.

I shake my head. "I don't understand. I have nothing to offer you."

His cold, hard eyes drag down the length of my simple dress before he meets my eyes again. "I need a wife."

I shake my head. "You could've had your pick of anyone in Zalivka. You're wealthy and attractive. Why *me*?"

For the first time, he looks almost perplexed. "Isn't it obvious?"

I blink in surprise and shove a crust of bread in my mouth. I shake my head.

"I didn't want anyone. I didn't want a wife who would use my family or my wealth for her own gain. I didn't want some pretty little thing taking selfies by my pool with her manicured nails and flaunting them or someone who'd go behind my back and seek the affection of someone who'd give it to her when I knew full well I couldn't."

I feel as if he's doused me in ice water. I stare. He goes on.

"I wanted a wife dependent on me. I wanted a wife who had no choice but to be faithful because the price of infidelity cost her too much." He took another sip of wine. "I wanted a wife who wasn't seeking love or affection or anything else I couldn't give but was desperate enough to take what I could give her, so there was no backing out."

Leaning forward, his gaze is so chilling, I actually shiver.

"I wanted a wife who knew that marriage to me was forever. And just like always, Anya... I got exactly what I wanted."

I open my mouth to tell him off, to snatch back some scrap of dignity, but I don't know where to begin.

"Here. Look."

With a scowl, he takes his phone out of his pocket and shows me the screen. With deft movements, the blunt tips of his rough fingers slide over it. I stare, not sure what I'm seeing. "Come closer, Anya."

I rise out of my chair, curiosity getting the better of me. I stand close enough to see the phone but not close enough for him to touch me. Numbers swim in neat rows on the screen.

"This is your family's debt to me." I stare at the numbers, a sick feeling growing in the pit of my stomach.

With a few swipes, the screen of red goes white. My shoulders feel a bit lighter. I let out a breath.

"And this," he continues, tapping a few more things with cold precision, scowling at the screen, "is what I've deposited in your business bank account. I've settled your outstanding debts, and on Monday, I'll introduce you to Claude, your new business manager. Do you know what this means, Anya?"

I shake my head slowly.

"A few things," he says, his voice low and his eyes blazing into mine. He doesn't look cold right now but as fiery as a stoked furnace. "Your family is no longer in debt. Not to me, nor to anyone. That would be a liability I won't take on."

"Thank you," I say in a tentative whisper as I stare at him because it feels like the right thing to say, even though I know this isn't the end.

"Don't thank me. I didn't do this to save you. I did this because I'm a businessman, and I know ensuring your reliance on me will mean you stay. You have no choice. It also means I'm now the cosigner on your bakery. The next move is to bring your business back in the black."

Cold fear trickles down my spine.

That was my mother's bakery. It feels like the worst form of betrayal to know he's co-owner.

Hate me all you want, but your family is alive because of this.

He puts his phone away and turns back to his dinner. "Are you done with your meal?"

"I told you, I'm not hungry."

"Then I'll excuse you from the table," he says. "I haven't forgotten your punishment from earlier. Your room is at the top of the stairs on the left. Go."

He looks away, excusing me.

"You're punishing me by sending me to my room?" I shake my head.

Your room?

So we aren't sharing a bed?

His fork raised to his mouth, he looks up at me. Why does he have the face of a vengeful angel? "Would you rather have a spanking?"

My cheeks flush as I stare at him. I consider flouncing away and storming out, but that feels petulant and childlike.

"I'm your wife," I say inanely as if that somehow dulls the roaring in my ears and the swoop of arousal between my legs. I'm so angry at myself because it seems like every time I make any headway with him at all, he takes back control with hardly any effort.

"Your point? Yes, you're my wife. It seems we have different ideas of what that means."

"Oh, do we? What does that mean to you? I'm just a figure-head to you, Semyon."

I note the flare of his nostrils and the flash of his eyes before he's calm and in control again. What was that all about?

"No, Anya. You're wrong about that."

My cheeks feel hot, my pulse ragged. I swallow and stand straighter, as I remind myself to hold my own. He might be older and more powerful, but he doesn't own me.

He continues. "In my world, that means I expect respect and obedience. It's a husband's job to protect and care for his wife. And it's your job to allow me," he says as if it's obvious.

It isn't in *my* world. When I don't respond, he continues, a note of finality in his voice. "Top of the stairs on the left, Anya. *Go.*"

I scoff, even though it sounds weaker than I want it to. "Obedience?" I echo. "What am I—a dog?"

"No," he says simply. I wonder if he gets sarcasm. He's so literal and matter-of-fact it's maddening. "I would have had a dog trained better than this by now."

My cheeks burn, and I want to lash out at him, do something, anything that would take him by surprise and break through that absolutely maddening, unshakable calm. But instead, my throat tightens. "You're unbelievable," I whisper.

"And you're still here," he counters, shaking his head. "Do you really think it's wise to push me right now?"

I open my mouth, then close it again because I don't have an answer. Why *am* I still standing here when I can go collect myself and get some time alone?

"Your room, Anya," he says, softer this time. "I'm not going to ask you again. I'm a patient man, but I have my limits."

His words hang in the air, a promise and a threat rolled into one.

I want to see him snap. I want to see him lose control. I want to dismantle him as thoroughly as he does me. I hate how he twists my resolve into something that feels dangerously close to... submission.

I hate him for it. I hate myself for the glimmer of something like hope that still flickers in my chest.

Top of the stairs. On the left.

His words ring in my head. I make it to the top of the stairs and slam the door behind me when I hear a *ping*.

I look up in surprise to see my phone on a fancy charging station next to the bed. I walk to it and check the notifications.

> **Ophelia**
> I'm sorry to bother you, Anya. I hate to do this. I can't find Stefan.

CHAPTER 8

SEMYON

I ᴋɴᴏᴡ the second she decides to run.

The shift is subtle, like a piece moving on the chessboard. A faint creak of the floorboards. The guards outside her window reporting nothing because she's clever enough to know they'll be watching.

I sip my drink and shake my head. Maybe she thinks she's outsmarting me. It's funny how she thinks she knows me.

I almost admire her audacity. I thought seeing me prove that she wasn't in debt anymore would change how she felt about things, but apparently not.

I open the security feed on my tablet and stare at the screen, flipping through the cameras until I find her. I want to see where she'll go and why. She's moving with purpose, slipping through the hallways, her expression a mix of determination and desperation. She swipes at her eyes and doesn't look back.

What does that mean? She can't think she'll be able to just slip away, does she? Or does she fear the punishment I promised her?

I tap the comms button, signaling the guards stationed inside the house. "No interference. Let her go."

There's a pause at the other end of the line. They know better than to question me and know better than to talk back. "Yes, sir. Understood."

I watch as she makes her way to the side door. She's found the keycard—predictable. She's anything if not resourceful. She doesn't realize I left it there intentionally. I wanted to see what she'd do. I'm almost disappointed she took the bait so easily.

If I really wanted to make sure she didn't run, it would've been laughably easy. But you can tell a lot about a person based on two things: how they react when cornered and where they go when they get a chance to run. So far, I've learned a few things about Anya: She's a fighter. Doesn't crumble under pressure. Her pride won't let her admit defeat. She values autonomy.

I almost smile to myself. Others might see her as rebellious, but I see her in a different light—Anya's a challenge to me.

I adjust my dick, hard as fuck.

God, I love a challenge.

I watch on the feed as she steps outside, straight into the pouring rain. God, she couldn't grab an umbrella? They're lined up in the front hallway.

I'm paces away from her, my keys in my hand. I'll take the Lexus because it's quiet and dark.

Her steps quicken, her pace picking up as she gets closer to the edge of the property. I open the side door that takes me to the garage and slide into the driver's seat, still watching her.

A car waits for her on the street outside the gate. It's hard to see in the rain, but I zoom in—Ophelia. She looks at the exit as if half expecting that my guards will stop her, but they're standing down as ordered. The taillights disappear, and she drives off. I wait a beat before taking off after them.

I won't storm her; that's not my style. I follow slowly and curse to myself.

Her friend drives like a fucking lunatic. This will be the last time my wife gets in a car with Ophelia in the driver's seat.

I hold myself back, intentionally making sure I don't allow them to see that I'm following. I want to see where she's going.

Work? Is she so concerned about the bakery that she has to go see to it? It's late at night, and the shop is closed by now, but making sure my business was taken care of would be one of the few reasons I would be out alone at night, so it's the first one that comes to my mind.

Is she trying to escape? She's too smart of a woman to do a thing like that, my reason tells me. I made it abundantly clear that her family's best interest would be for her to marry me, and she has to know that if she's planning something stupid like an escape, I won't make any promises about protecting them.

No. I don't think she's trying to escape.

Then a thought occurs to me that makes me grip the steering wheel so tightly my knuckles whiten.

Is there a man?

A red haze clouds my vision momentarily when I entertain the thought.

That would make sense. She's given herself to another man. Normally, we'd run a background check on a woman like her before a major step like marriage, but I bypassed some of the more usual methods because I reasoned that I knew her.

I don't, not really. I knew the little girl who grew up along-side me. I don't know the woman who stared daggers at me in the middle of my goddamn dining room.

No. I don't know her at all.

What if she has a lover?

What if she's given her heart to a man she can't have because she's married to *me*?

She won't like it when I kill him, but her only chance at keeping him alive would have been to stay far, far away.

I shake my head. I wouldn't have chosen to start things off this way.

I try to lighten my grip on the steering wheel when my fore-arms ache, but it's anchoring me right now. I breathe in through my nose and out through my mouth the way Yana taught me when I was younger. It works, sometimes.

Not now.

They take a sharp left, and I almost give myself away when I have to take the corner hard to keep up. I let off the gas, even though it takes all of my self-control not to drive the pedal to the floor and go after her. I take in another deep breath and let it out slowly when the red brake lights flash ahead.

I slow down. Thankfully, the street isn't that well-lit, and I'm driving a black car.

We're near her family home. I follow at a steady pace, staying far enough back to avoid recognition or spooking them. In the dark, I can't see her face well, but the occasional streetlight illuminates her through the window. Even from here, I can see the worry written in her features.

Is she worried I'll catch her? Or worried about something else? She *should* be worried I'll catch her. If she isn't, I haven't done my job thoroughly.

I'll fix that.

She shoves a finger in her mouth and gnaws at the nail. A nervous habit. She's like a bird flapping its wings against the metal bars of a cage.

Desperate. Stubborn. Futile.

What is it about her that brings out the worst in me? Most people bore me. They fall in line like predictable little soldiers, and the few that don't, keep things occasionally interesting. They're easy to read, easy to understand. Once you put your mind to truly understanding human nature, it isn't as hard as one might think. People like what's precious to them. They don't like change. They don't want anyone to upset the apple cart and cause too much distress. They appreciate praise and money, and one of the easiest ways to ensure compliance is to give them one or both.

Anya though? Every move, every breath, every sentence she utters is a seeming contradiction. She's defiant yet loyal, independent yet tethered to responsibility.

And then there's the way she looks at me like I'm the villain in every story she's ever read.

I tighten my grip on the wheel, the leather hot under my palm. It's not admiration, no. Not attraction or anything even close to resembling infatuation or *love*. It's nothing more than curiosity.

Love.

The one word that men and women alike toss around like confetti. "Love you!" "Oh, I love this chocolate." "Hello, love!"

No, no, *no*.

Love is a weakness, a liability, and I know what it does to people. I know how it makes people crazy.

Hell, look at Rafail, the sternest of our family, our fearless leader. One minute, he's ruling Moscow with militaristic precision. The next, he's courting sleepless nights and cooing over the way his precious infant burped.

And my father... no. I won't think of that now.

Love is a fucking leash, a tether, a poison disguised as a gift. It robs you of control, and control is the only thing I trust.

I glance in the car ahead and watch as Ophelia says something to her, gesturing wildly, but Anya only shakes her head as if lost in thought. Her gaze is fixed out the window.

I wonder what she's thinking...

As soon as I find myself wondering that, I stop myself, irritated. It doesn't matter what she's thinking.

Unless she's thinking *I shouldn't have run away from my husband*, her thoughts are irrelevant.

This is a game. I feel like a cat playing with a mouse, letting it run just until it gets to a point of near safety—before I smack my paw on its little tail and drag it back to me, squealing, before I feast.

You can run, little mouse.

Run as fast as you can.

My dick throbs, and my mouth goes dry.

I'll catch you.

And when I do...

Their car comes to a stop ahead. They're getting out.

I wait a few blocks behind them before I follow.

CHAPTER 9

ANYA

"Are you sure no one followed us?" I ask Ophelia. I don't trust that I got away that easily from Semyon.

I don't trust anything to do with him.

"Babe, no one followed us. Did you see how fast and recklessly I drove? That was on *purpose*."

She actually looks offended when I huff out a laugh.

"*This* time, alright? That way, if anyone was following us, we lost them."

I look behind me and see nothing but inky darkness. At this point, I don't care if he had me followed. All that matters is that Stefan is safe.

As soon as I got the news from Ophelia, I sounded the alert with the small group of tight-knit friends I've made in my neighborhood. We're all just trying to make ends meet, each of us navigating our own struggles while watching each other's backs.

Lena, the local grocery store owner with a houseful of kids and a huge heart, responded first.

> **Lena**
> I'll look around. I'm so sorry I haven't seen
> him. Is the story of what I heard about you
> true? Everyone knows someone, we'll
> find him

Marco, the bartender who knew half the city's occupants, poured drinks, and collected whispers like currency.

> **Marco**
> Don't worry, we'll find him. Little kid like him
> would stand out. Hang in there.

FINALLY, it was Viktor, the barber whose shop was adjacent to mine, who gave me a tip.

> **Viktor**
> I think I saw him in the shop earlier? Not
> long ago. I think he was hiding out but
> needed a place to get out of the rain.

So to the shop we went. I cast one last look into the sheets of rain behind us before I opened the door.

"If he's here, I'm going to shake him til his teeth rattle as badly as mine do." Ophelia shivers, tugging her soaked sweater tighter around her curvy frame. She wouldn't harm a hair on Stefan's head, but I didn't blame her. "And will you stop looking around like your Bratva batboy's gonna come out like a vampire and suck your blood? God."

I shake my head. "You don't know what he's like," I mutter, my hands trembling as I slide the key into the lock. It's crooked and freezing, so it takes a full minute before I'm able to unlock the door and head inside.

To anyone else, this place would look vacant. But I know the telltale signs of a sneaky little boy who has a penchant for trouble and a taste for sweets.

The front display case is open, and a row of cookies is missing. I never leave the display case open, and I always fill it before we close for the night.

I narrow my eyes and look around the shop.

"Stefan?" I ask, flicking my phone's flashlight on. I don't want to alert anyone outside that we're in here. "Are you in here? The sooner you confess, the less trouble you'll be in."

No answer. But the fridge door is slightly ajar, and a wad of napkins still sits on the steel top of the kneading table.

"Stefan," I say warningly.

"Hey!" Ophelia yells into the store. "We know you're in here. Don't tell me I risked my life kidnapping your sister and driving in a storm just so I could make myself fat on your sister's cinnamon rolls and drown my grief in vanilla icing!"

I snort and shake my head.

"Drown your grief?" I mouth, still panting from running in here.

I turn my head sharply, straining to listen. Did I hear something? What was that? I scan the shop, but there's no sign of movement. Still, my brother is young and clumsy, and I know he's in here.

"Stefan," I call, my voice low and warning—the tone I use when he's in trouble and I need to sound motherly. I hate when he makes me do this. "If you don't come out…" I trail off, unsure of what to threaten him with because I never like making threats.

Finally, the door to the large freezer creaks open.

"Stefan!" I can't keep the shock out of my voice. He knows he's not allowed in there. It's an old freezer, and if the door shuts from the inside, he could freeze to death. That's been drilled into his head a hundred times. He's never been allowed in there.

Barely able to catch my breath, I grab him by the shoulders and shake him hard enough to make him stumble.

"What were you thinking? You can't run away like that and in the *freezer?*" My voice cracks, fear cutting through my anger. "Don't you know what could've happened if I didn't find you?"

"I didn't lock it," he mutters, lifting his chin with false bravado. For a moment, he looks like our oldest brother—the arrogance is the same, that's for sure.

"Do you know what would've happened if the wrong person caught you?" I press, my words coming out sharper than I intended.

His eyes widen, guilt shadowing his expression. "I just wanted to come find you," he whispers. "I thought... I thought eventually you'd come back here. I only stepped into the freezer just now. I didn't want anyone to see me—I thought it might be him. You know, your new husband."

"You thought wrong," I snap, pulling him into a fierce hug, holding him tightly for a moment before shaking him again. "You should've stayed hidden, and you should've never gone in that freezer. Don't you ever go in there again, Stefan."

The door to the shop jingles open. Moments later, heavy footsteps fall. My stomach drops, tightening into a knot.

I don't need to turn around to know who it is.

Semyon's imposing shadow spills into the light of the doorway as he steps inside. His icy-blue eyes burn with fury, and his jaw is clenched tight. He looks as if he's been carved from stone—his face rigid and controlled, every line etched with precision. But I can feel the storm beneath his surface. He's barely hanging on to his self-control.

"You thought you could leave without telling me?" His voice is low, calm, far more dangerous than if he'd yelled. I understand now why people fear him when his voice lowers.

My instincts roar to life, and I shove my brother behind me. "I'm not leaving him here," I snap.

Ophelia, standing behind me, makes a little squeaking sound and curses under her breath. I can feel Stefan trembling as he clutches my arm, but I don't move.

"He needs me," I say firmly.

Semyon's gaze flicks to Stefan and then back to me, a glimpse of something—surprise?—crossing his face.

"Who?" he asks, his tone colder than ice.

"Stefan. My younger brother," I reply, my voice steady despite the lump rising in my throat. "Who do you think?"

For a moment, Semyon's expression is unreadable. Then he speaks, blunt as ever. "I thought you came here to find another man."

"Another man? What are you talking about?"

His eyes dart away, and for an instant, I think I see something like shame in his expression. But it's gone just as quickly, replaced by the cold, calculated mask that always makes my skin crawl.

"You were forbidden from leaving," he says, stepping closer, his words snapping like a whip. "And at the first opportunity, that's what you did."

"Ophelia couldn't find my brother!" I protest.

Semyon steps even closer, crossing his arms over his broad chest. He crooks a finger, his command sharp and precise. "Come here," he orders.

I instinctively take a step forward, but he shakes his head.

"No, Anya. Not you."

Panic rises in my chest. Oh god. Stefan?

Before I can stop him, Stefan steps out from behind me, standing straight. There's a flash of arrogance in his expression, the same kind our oldest brother used to wear like armor.

Semyon's eyes widen, just slightly, before narrowing again. "And this is…"

"Stefan," I reply quickly, stepping forward protectively.

"I knew you had a brother," he says coolly, his voice like steel. "Because your other brother owes us four million, Anya."

"You didn't know I had a younger brother?"

"My records say your brother is in a boarding school, sent there by your uncle," Semyon says, his tone flat.

"Well, maybe it's time you update your records," I snap. "My brother hasn't been in that school for over two years—not since my father spent the tuition money."

Semyon's expression softens, his voice dropping. "I'm sorry," he says quietly. "I had no idea you have a younger brother at home. You should have told me."

He shakes his head, the faintest trace of frustration flickering across his face.

"You should've come to me," he continues. "You should've told me why you were leaving. I would've brought you here safely instead of…" He gestures vaguely at me. "This wreck of a situation."

His eyes sharpen as his voice hardens. "Your life belongs to me now, Anya."

Stefan's eyes flash with defiance as he steps forward, his

small fists clenched. "You can't own someone's life," he says, his voice trembling but firm.

Semyon's icy gaze snaps to him, narrowing. "Watch your tone, boy," he warns. Instinctively, I pull Stefan closer, wrapping my arms protectively around him.

"He's right," I say, my voice steady despite the tightening in my chest. "You don't own me. I won't let Stefan think this is how things work—that this is normal. I owe him more than that."

Semyon's lips twitch into a faint, almost amused smile, baring his teeth. "Don't I?" he murmurs, his voice a low growl.

I don't know what shocks me more—his words or the certainty with which he says them. It's not even a question; he speaks it as if it's a simple fact. And yet, beneath the icy detachment in his tone, there's a hint of something... something I hadn't expected. For one fleeting moment, I wonder if I've misjudged him.

But then, as he straightens, the mask snaps back into place. His next words are clipped, unyielding. "You're going to pay for this," he says, shaking his head.

The fire in my chest roars back to life. His gaze locks on Stefan, cold and calculating, like a headmaster sizing up a defiant student. "But I won't have any loose ends—or liabilities. You'll come with us," Semyon says to Stefan. "You will not run. You will not disrespect my family. You will come, and your sister will take care of you in our home. Is that clear?"

I blink, stunned by his words, my breath catching in my throat. "Wait—Stefan's coming with us?" I ask aloud, unable to hide my shock.

Ophelia gasps. Semyon and I both look over at her. We forgot she was there.

Semyon's ice-blue eyes meet mine, unwavering. "This wasn't part of my plan either," he admits. "But it was an oversight. I should have done a background check. And don't even ask me about your father." His lip curls in disdain. "That man can drown in his own piss for all I care."

"Me too," I murmur. For a brief moment, our eyes meet in unexpected solidarity—a fleeting connection that vanishes almost as quickly as it appears.

"Just so we're clear... he can live with us?" I ask, disbelief thick in my voice.

Semyon's gaze doesn't falter. "Do you think I would leave him here with that deadbeat father of yours?" He shakes his head. "I thought your brother was in school. I didn't know you'd been taking care of him all this time. I don't tolerate weakness, Anya, but I'm not a monster."

Conflicting emotions churn within me: anger at his arrogance, confusion at this unexpected act of kindness, and an unsettling sense of gratitude. Is this truly kindness? Or is it just another calculated move, another piece on the chessboard that will eventually lead to my downfall?

No...

Semyon doesn't love. He doesn't choke on kindness. This is just another move to keep me occupied.

My brother, Stefan, in that cold mansion? Yes, I can make sure he's well-fed, that his clothes aren't threadbare, and his socks don't have holes in them. We'll have adequate light to do homework, and I won't have to worry about the heat being shut off.

But Stefan is headstrong, and I fear what will happen to him under Semyon's cold fury.

I open my mouth to argue, but nothing comes out. What am I supposed to say? "No, I don't want my brother subjected to your severity—I'd rather he starve to death or wonder if our drunken father will backhand him?" Yeah, no.

Ophelia stares at Semyon, then at Stefan, and back to me. "I don't know about you," she says, tucking a strand of hair behind her ear, "but I think this might work out pretty well for both of you."

"It definitely won't," Semyon says, his voice cold and precise.

Ophelia's eyes widen. She looks at him, unable to hide her fear, then backtracks awkwardly. "Oh, I didn't mean you two. I meant... them." She gestures between Stefan and me. "Those two."

Her voice falters, and she tilts her head to the side with a forced smile. "Semyon, have you tried these delicious baked goods?" she asks, gesturing wildly at the half-open pastry case.

I want to bury my head in my hands. Semyon's eyes narrow into slits, and he actually lets out a low growl—a real growl, like an animal.

"You two," he snaps, pointing at Stefan and me, "get in the fucking car outside." Then he turns to Ophelia. "And you—go home. Do not contact my wife without my permission again."

Ophelia's face flushes with justified outrage, but I silently will her to stop provoking him before he snaps.

"Just do what he says for now, okay?" I mutter.

"Not for now," Semyon cuts in, his voice sharp. "Do what I say. Period."

I step closer to Ophelia and whisper, "I'll call you later. Thank you."

She hesitates but nods before retreating, muttering under her breath as she marches to the door.

"I'm not going with him," Stefan says stubbornly, his small shoulders squaring as he glares up at Semyon. "Someone has to be home when... when Eli comes back." He trails off, his voice faltering.

"Eli isn't coming back," Semyon says coldly. "And I'm out of patience. It's the middle of the night, Stefan." Semyon's voice softens. "Don't you have school tomorrow?"

Stefan flinches but says nothing.

"Your sister and I will set rules for your time in my house. We'll discuss them after everyone's had some sleep. For now, gather your belongings and go with Anya to the car."

When neither of us moves, Semyon's nostrils flare. His voice cracks like a whip. "Now."

Then he turns back to Ophelia, his tone icy. "Leave. I don't want to see you again."

"For God's sake!" I snap, unable to stop myself.

Semyon levels his gaze at me, his voice dropping dangerously. "If I were you, I'd be quiet right now. You're in heaps of trouble. You left without my permission, snuck away, and got into a car with a reckless driver who could've killed you."

I ignore Ophelia's indignant huff as she slams the door behind her.

"You disobeyed me," Semyon continues, his tone cutting, "and you're already on thin ice."

Semyon steps closer to me, dragging his fingers along my wrist. His thick thumb presses against my pulse, and his eyes glint coldly. "Just as I thought," he murmurs, cataloging my every reaction with unnerving precision.

It's hard to believe men like him exist. I've known men like my brother—selfish, reckless, charming as hell. And men like my father—selfish, addicted, too broken to take care of the people they should love.

But Semyon is different. Responsible. In charge. Yet as cold as an ice king. And he's my husband.

I made a decision long ago that I would never fall in love. I've seen how it wrecks people—how it destroyed my mother. Women lose their self-respect in the futile hope of earning love in return. That will never be me.

Maybe, in a way, I'm almost thankful. Being married to an ice king makes it easier to keep that promise.

"You're soaking wet," Semyon says suddenly, shaking his head. "Were you so afraid for your brother's safety that you had no regard for your own?"

I glance down, only now realizing I'm still wearing my old, faded dress, soaked through and clinging to me. The wet fabric reveals more than I'd like—the dusky outline of my nipples, the curve of my breasts.

Before I can move, Semyon shrugs off his coat and drapes it over my shoulders.

"Zip that up," he orders curtly. "No one looks at you but me. No one, Anya."

He jerks his head toward Stefan. "Have you eaten?"

"I had some cookies," Stefan mumbles.

"Grab a paper bag and pack some things for breakfast," Semyon says, his tone softening just slightly. "You'll eat at home and in the morning before school." He shakes his head.

Stefan hesitates at the pastry case, then asks nervously, "Do you... want anything?"

The surrealism of the moment nearly knocks me off balance —my little brother, my dangerous husband, and me standing together in this strange, fragile truce.

Semyon glances at the case, then points. "Two of those," he says, pointing to a pair of pirozhki. It's not indulgence he's after, but practicality. A quick, filling meal, chosen with the same cold efficiency he applies to everything else.

It's a small gesture, but it feels almost human.

"Lock the shop behind you," Semyon says brusquely.

I hold up the bent key.

"Are you serious?" he mutters, rolling his eyes. "Forget it. We'll handle this tomorrow. For now, everyone needs sleep."

He leans down, his voice dropping to a whisper. "And you and I will discuss every detail of your disobedience... when we get home."

CHAPTER 10

ANYA

THE SKY HAD TURNED *a deep shade of gray before it split open, rain pouring down in furious sheets, turning the dirt path beneath my feet into mud. Lightning forked across the horizon, followed by a peal of thunder so loud I screamed. I was soaked to the skin by the time I stumbled into the shed— an old, rickety thing at the edge of the woods, with its rusted metal roof and broken planks that groaned against the wind.*

My breath came in gasps as I fought the rising panic. I hated storms. Ever since I was trapped in my bedroom as a child during one, they made me feel like the world was unraveling around me. Panic would sweep through me, and I'd have to force myself to breathe.

Seconds after I stumbled into the shed, a figure loomed in the darkness, yanked the door open, and ducked inside, not seeing me.

I flattened myself against the splintered wall. *Semyon.* My god.

Semyon was right there, in the small space of the shed that didn't seem big enough to hold both of us. He hadn't seen me yet and stood just a few feet away, grabbing the bottom of his shirt and wringing it out with quick, efficient movements, giving me a wide-open view of the hard, bare planes of his chest. My eyes were riveted on his lower abdomen, on the line of barely visible dark hair that sunk low into his waistband.

I swallowed hard.

"Semyon," I whispered, not wanting him to be caught off guard. His head jerked up at the sound of my voice, his sharp blue eyes locking on mine, wide with surprise for a second, before his expression shifted back to something controlled and unreadable.

The shed was barely big enough for the two of us, and his presence filled it, steady and unshakable, like an anchor. Larger than life.

I tried to stop shaking, wrapping my arms around myself. The fabric of my dress clung to me. Now that Semyon was here, I became viscerally aware of every sensation. The cold drops of rain down my spine felt heavy as I tracked them falling between my breasts and trailing between my thighs. But it wasn't just the cold that had me trembling now.

"Anya," he said, his voice low and firm, cutting through the howl of the wind outside the flimsy shed, as if saying my name out loud made my presence here more solid. I loved the sweet lilt of my name in his rough voice. I wanted to record it *and play it on repeat as I fell asleep at night. "What are you doing in here?"*

I glared at him. "The same thing you are, obviously."

He looked away, shrugging off his coat with practiced ease, his movements, as always, methodical, deliberate. "You're freezing," he said bluntly.

I shook my head. "I'm fine," I lied, but my teeth chattered, betraying me.

"Your lips are blue." Without another word, his piercing gaze didn't leave mine as he stepped closer. My heart leaped, excited panic sweeping through me. Was he—no. I stood frozen as he draped his coat over my shoulders. The outside was still damp, but the inside was warm and soft and carried his scent. The smell of him was sharp, masculine—woodsy and clean. I was instantly wide awake, my blood heating under my skin.

I clung to his jacket, a lifeline.

"You're soaked too," I whispered, looking up at him, admitting too late that I was, indeed, freezing.

His hair, jet black and usually meticulously groomed, was plastered to his forehead, droplets of rain trailing down his sharp jawline.

I realized with startling awareness how I wanted to lick them off.

I was startled by how quickly my thoughts turned sexual, but I was eighteen years old, lonely, and irrevocably in love.

"I'm fine," he said simply, his tone calm, unbothered. But there was something about the way he stood—his shoulders

tense, his eyes scanning the tiny space as if searching for threats. He wasn't afraid of the storm. In my mind, Semyon wasn't afraid of anything.

I sank to the floor and pulled his coat tighter around me. "Do you think it's safe in here?" I asked, my voice barely above a whisper as thunder boomed and lightning lit up the sky. "If lightning hits—"

"We have a better statistical chance of that happening than we do winning the lottery three times in succession." His voice was quiet, but there was a certainty in it that made me believe him. Some people poked fun at him for his analytical brain that clung to data and facts, but there was something about it I couldn't explain that made me swoon. "Anyway," he continued, "storms don't last forever."

I clung to that line and made it mine.

Storms don't last forever.

Your father won't always be a drunk.

Your brother won't always be stealing from him.

You won't always have to fight for food for your younger brother or hold it together so your mother doesn't cry.

As for Semyon—you won't always have to be the strong one, the guardian, the big brother.

Please don't always be the big brother.

The air between us felt charged, heavier than it should have been, as electric as the lightning outside the shed.

His knee brushed mine.

I wondered if it was accidental. But the spark I felt jolted straight through the fabric, and he didn't move away.

I tried to focus on the storm—the rain pounding against the thin roof, the wind rattling the tree branches outside, the clouds moving like soldiers prepared for battle. But I couldn't help it. My eyes were glued to the way Semyon's chest rose and fell in slow, steady breaths, visible under his soaked shirt. The way the fabric clung to his body, outlining the muscles beneath. When lightning struck again, it illuminated the glorious tattoos inked across his arms and neck.

"Thank you," I whispered, my voice barely audible over the storm. He turned his head and locked his gaze on mine. For a long moment, neither of us spoke. The space between us seemed to shrink, and I almost forgot about the raging storm outside.

"It's nothing," he said softly, his eyes searching mine.

Was he talking about the coat?

I didn't know what to say. I just stared at him, my breath catching. Was it my imagination, or was he leaning closer? No, he was definitely leaning closer. His hand came up, brushing a strand of wet hair away from my face. His touch was gentle, almost hesitant, but it left a trail of undeniable heat in its wake. My body came alive, electric.

"Semyon," I whispered, a warning and a plea. I didn't know what else to say. His eyes dropped to my lips, and when he swallowed, my heart slammed against my ribs. Maybe I wasn't just his best friend's little sister anymore.

Maybe I wasn't the only one nursing unrequited affection— or was it more? Maybe I wasn't the only one burning inside, aching to be closer, every nerve alive with the possibility of what could happen.

"Anya," he murmured, his voice rough, almost pained. "Are you alright?"

No. I wasn't okay.

I'd run into the storm after my father screamed at me because I had the audacity to question how much he drank. And when he threw his cup of coffee halfway across the room, where it shattered against a wall, I left.

But I couldn't tell Semyon that. I knew I couldn't. He'd do something drastic and violent. Kill my father, probably. And then my father's death would be on my hands.

My pulse thundered in my ears as he leaned closer, his breath warm and minty. The outside world tilted. It could've ended, and I wouldn't care. But just as his lips were about to touch mine—or so I thought—the shed groaned violently, the wind slamming into its walls. We both stared at the door as if expecting Eli to find us.

I jumped, and the moment shattered. He pulled back, his jaw tight, his expression unreadable.

My brother would kill him. We both knew that. Bratva or not, Eli would absolutely destroy him. And Semyon would lose the only friend he had.

"We should wait it out," he said, his voice hoarse, as if nothing had happened.

And in my small, self-deprecating mind, I told myself it wasn't because of the tension between us. It was me. I was too much. I was always too much. It was me. I was the problem.

As we pile into the car, the silence between us feels suffocating. Stefan sits in the back seat, clutching the paper bag, his eyes darting between me and my... *husband.*

Predictably, Semyon insisted I sit beside him, and because I didn't feel like testing my luck, I let him open my door.

Now he sits in the driver's seat, his jaw locked, tension radiating off him in waves. He hasn't spoken since we left the shop, but the white-knuckled grip on the steering wheel tells me everything. I want to poke him, to push him, to say something to break the silence, but I don't. Not yet.

"Anya," Stefan whispers from the back seat.

Semyon's eyes flick toward the rearview mirror almost imperceptibly before returning to the road. I turn in my seat, leaning toward my brother.

"What is it?" I ask softly, my voice gentler than I feel. My stomach twists as I look at him, still unsure how I feel about him being here. He isn't safe at home but bringing him into this world isn't much better. The first day I trusted Ophelia to watch him, she lost him. Granted, Stefan didn't make it easy, but still.

"Are we... really staying with him?" Stefan asks, his voice small. "Are you serious? All my stuff's back at the house..."

I shake my head, too tired to explain the truth. It feels too heavy, too complicated. I glance at Semyon, but he answers for me.

"Yes, you're staying with me. If you have belongings you need, I'll send someone to retrieve them." He shifts his gaze from the road to the rearview mirror, locking eyes with Stefan. "I'm not letting either of you out of my sight."

Stefan flinches at his tone, and I glare at Semyon. "Might be nice if you tried not to terrify him," I snap.

Semyon's cold gaze swings to me. "If I were trying to terrify him, he'd wet his pants."

I stifle a growl.

"Am I a prisoner?" Stefan asks, his voice trembling slightly.

Semyon doesn't respond, but I see the corner of his mouth twitch in the mirror. I hold back a smile, though it's more out of exhaustion than amusement.

I cock my head and look at Semyon sweetly, in a way I know annoys him. "Is my brother a prisoner, husband?"

"Yes," he says without hesitation. "If you want to label it, neither of you will leave without my permission. Neither of you will roam this house freely until I know you're trustworthy. I won't have you ruining things, leaving fingerprints on my table, touching things that don't belong to you, or making me lose sleep because you're impulsive."

I cross my arms, making a sound of disgust. "Do you think treating us like this will make us warm up to you?"

Semyon growls, his voice dangerously low. "Do you think I

care? Do you think I wanted to run out in the middle of the night, in the rain, dragging your brother into this mess?"

I flinch slightly at the rawness in his voice, but his words keep coming, sharp and cutting.

"I don't," he snaps, his tone softening only slightly. "But it's my responsibility. I take care of what's mine."

My chest tightens at his words—*what's mine*.

I don't want to be his. I don't want Stefan to be his responsibility. But some traitorous part of me, the part that's so damn tired of fighting, clings to the word responsibility like a lifeline.

"Fine," I say, crossing my arms. "But if you think treating us like this will make us trust you, you're in for a rude awakening."

A muscle in his jaw twitches, but he doesn't respond.

We drive in silence. I glance back at Stefan, whose eyes are closed. He's snoring softly.

When we arrive at the house, Semyon parks and turns off the engine. I kneel on the seat to gently shake Stefan awake. "Honey... we're home."

He doesn't stir.

"Watch your foot," Semyon barks at me. "You're going to scuff the—"

Something inside me snaps. I plant my muddy shoe on his pristine console and smear it across the surface.

In one swift motion, his palm slams against my ass. My breath catches in shock.

"What did I tell you about acting like a child?" he snaps, his voice low and lethal.

"Hey!" I gasp, my cheeks flaming. Something dark and unfamiliar flares in my chest.

Between my thighs.

My body betrays me, heat pooling in places I want to ignore. His gaze pins me in place, his tone leaving no room for argument, a promise there's more where that came from.

Oh god.

"Anya, turn around and sit properly before I spank you again," he growls. "And clean up the mess you made."

I huff indignantly but grab the tissue he hands me to wipe the console. It *was* childish. Still, I hate the smug look on his face as I obey.

"I need to wake him up," I mutter.

"No," Semyon says, his tone clipped. "He's a child and exhausted. I'll carry him upstairs."

And then he's out of the car, pulling Stefan into his arms like he weighs nothing. I want to hate him—I *do* hate him—but the way he holds my brother, careful and steady, breaks something inside me.

Stefan looks so small in his arms, so fragile. He's always been too thin, no matter how much I've tried to feed him. He grows like a weed, but there's never enough.

Semyon carries him toward the house with his back straight, his movements precise. I feel an ache in my chest born of grief and relief, opposing feelings but holding the same space somehow.

"I'll put him in the second room on the right," Semyon says, his voice cold. He glances back at me, his eyes sharp and half-lidded. His voice drops an octave as if trying not to wake my brother.

"When you come upstairs," he murmurs, "I want you waiting in your bedroom." I stare at him.

"I want your clothes off, Anya."

I stare at his retreating back before I somehow make it up to my room.

Semyon is so cold, so detached—like a machine, ruthless and efficient—but today, he brought my little brother home. He carried Stefan into this house like he was something precious. That's not something I can forget.

Earlier, when I first walked into this room, I hadn't even looked around. Now, as I stand here trembling, I force myself to take in every detail.

He's coming back for me.

I can barely begin to process everything that's happened in the last few hours. It's all too much, too fast, and every time I try to piece together my fears of what happens next, my thoughts dissolve into chaos.

The room itself is larger than anything I could have imagined. It's more lavish than I expected too. A massive king-sized bed dominates the center, draped with a heavy ivory duvet, soft and inviting. Ample pillows are propped neatly against the headboard, and the room is accented in polished silver and glints of warm gold. Somehow, it feels simultaneously impersonal and beautiful.

I expected a prisoner's confines. But this? This is anything but.

In the corner stands a large white desk, solid and heavy, paired with a sleek standing lamp. On its surface, brand-new accessories are arranged in perfect order—pens, pencils, even a tape dispenser and scissors. My bag sits empty beside a closet door, an incongruous reminder of home.

Tentatively, I walk over and push the door to the closet open. My breath catches.

The closet is enormous, a walk-in space larger than Stefan's entire room back home. Shelves line the walls, displaying rows of shoes so pristine they look like works of art. Heels, boots, flats, all arranged by style and color—black, nude, and red blending into softer pastels and bolder choices. Dresses and skirts hang neatly beside sweaters and coats, all perfectly organized. Everything is new, modern, expensive... and my size.

They all sit beside my mother's clothes, in such stark contrast it makes my nose tingle.

The two pairs of worn shoes and the few faded garments I'd packed sit awkwardly on a shelf. My cheeks burn at the sight of them. They don't belong here. They're relics of a simpler, poorer life, a life that feels a million miles away now.

I slam the light switch off and turn my back to it all. If he thinks he can buy my affection...

No. He won't win.

But he said he doesn't want my love. He doesn't care for my attention. So what is this game he's playing? I won't forgive him for what he's done.

And yet... it's getting harder to hold on to my anger.

I take a deep breath, willing the rising tide of confusion to settle. Stefan is asleep, safe down the hall in another room. I can almost picture Semyon laying him down. He wouldn't have left the coverlet on to get dirty—he'd have removed Stefan's shoes first, then tucked him in neatly.

Would he? Does he have that kind of softness in him?

Panic grips my chest. Is my brother really safe here?

I shake the thought away and move to the door, trying the handle. It doesn't budge.

Locked.

Oh god.

I whir around, scanning the windows for the first time. They're locked, too, with heavy steel bars framing every pane. He doesn't trust me not to run. And why would he? I already proved I would at the first opportunity.

My phone buzzes on the desk, a text lighting up the screen. It's Ophelia.

Ophelia
Are you all right?

I grab the phone but hesitate. Semyon's cold words echo in

my mind: *You're not allowed to contact my wife without my permission.*

The sound of footsteps outside the door breaks my thoughts. My stomach drops, and I shake my head, denial flooding my mind.

What is he going to do to me?

I scramble, stripping off my wet dress and tossing his jacket onto the pile of discarded clothes. But then I pause, staring at the heap on the floor.

Which is worse—disobeying him by not undressing as he ordered or leaving a mess in his pristine room?

Semyon is always precise. Impeccable.

I scoop up the clothes and toss them into a nearby hamper, stripping the rest of my garments as quickly as I can. My gaze catches on the full-length oval mirror in the corner.

For a moment, I freeze, staring at my reflection.

My cheeks are flushed, my hair wild in soft waves over my shoulders. Standing naked, I take in what I haven't seen in years. My body is unfamiliar, the curves of my full breasts and the flare of my hips foreign after years of not looking. My belly is soft but flat, and my thighs strong. My hands trail down my sides unconsciously.

Semyon's voice echoes in my mind: *I like my wife with curves.*

I swallow hard and avert my eyes, wrapping my arms around myself. What is he going to do?

The door handle clicks. My heart leaps into my throat. I stand frozen, my breath shallow. I have never felt more vulnerable in my life.

"Good," Semyon says, his voice tired and taut. "For once, you did something I asked you to." He steps into the room and removes his tie, unloosening it with his large, thick hand. I watch, mesmerized. I cross my arms over my chest, but he only shakes his head sternly at me.

"No. Don't cover up. You're my wife. Hiding accomplishes nothing."

"I'm your wife, but I hardly know you."

He doesn't respond because he's too busy staring at me.

"You're beautiful," he whispers, his voice softer than before, as if testing the words aloud. Nodding, satisfied, he repeats himself. "Beautiful."

I blink, caught off guard. "What?"

His clinical gaze lingers. "A simple observation, but it's true." It's the first time I realize he's soaked to the skin like I was.

"Are you trying to manage me with compliments?"

The furrow of his brow hints at confusion. Frustration? "No."

He's standing before me, wearing nothing but the white T-shirt clinging to his skin, tucked into a pair of soaking-wet pants. He walks over to me, and I stand stock still. I don't know what to expect.

"Your hair is wet." He strokes it out of my face—not like a gesture of tenderness, but as though he needs to see my eyes. "Where did you get that dress?"

I swallow hard. "It was my mother's."

"I thought so." Wordlessly, he trails a finger over my shoulder and down the length of my arm.

"Your skin is so soft," he whispers.

I shiver.

"Are you cold?" His brow furrows.

Does he have no idea what he does to me?

"No." My voice is a husky whisper.

He circles me, staring as if I'm a work of art he's trying to understand. "Do you know the rule of the Bratva?"

I lick my lips. "Which one?"

"We have to consummate our marriage."

Heat floods through me. I nod. "No, but I figured as much."

"Why?" he asks.

"Because I assumed that if you treat marriage as a transaction, then you would also treat... sex the same way. If you need to be married, then you need to have children."

"Smart girl. Are you a virgin?" His eyes darken, daring me to answer anything but yes.

I lick my lips and nod. "Of course I am."

It isn't a lie. I don't know when I would have had the time for anything else.

Dragging his knuckles across my collarbone, he whispers, "Then I'll have to take my time with you."

I look at him curiously. "Are *you*?"

He shakes his head. "No. But I've never made love to a woman I... cared about."

Oh god.

"Why not?"

"Never took the time to bother figuring out how or why, but I suppose it has something to do with not having an emotional connection." He shrugs. "We do."

This whole discussion is making me nervous.

"I...I know how it's done."

"I would imagine so," he says, with a sound that's almost a laugh. "I don't mean sex, Anya. Anyone with access to the internet could figure that one out. I mean, I know how to make you enjoy it."

My breasts feel so heavy, my nipples taut. "You want a medal?"

Shaking his head, he only shrugs again. "No, Anya. Just your pleasure." He leans in a little closer and ever so lightly presses his palm to my lower back. "It's mine to give or keep."

I try to toss my head. "Sure. Yeah. You have a plan, do you?"

"Mmm, of course," he continues. "I do everything in my power to make you wet so that you're ready. Then I take my time."

A beat passes between us. I wonder if he can hear how rapidly my heart is beating right now. I wonder if I can.

"Do you know what you like?" he asks.

I shake my head. "I mean, I'm human. I know where my fantasies go when I'm asleep."

"Right. Unfortunately, there's a small matter of your punishment before we get to your pleasure, isn't there?"

"If you insist on being a barbarian," I snap, refusing to allow my voice to waver.

"Barbarian?" his ice-blue eyes hint at amusement. Couldn't be further from the truth. "You should know by now that I'm civilized to a fault, Anya. But I'm also a man of my word. This is my house, and it's important my wife understands how things work under my roof. Wouldn't you agree?"

"If you say so." My pulse quickens as tension crawls up my spine. I haven't been punished since my childhood. What the hell is he planning?

He mentioned a spanking earlier, but the look in his eyes now... god, it's like he's *waited* for this moment, and now he's savoring the tension before he uncorks the bottle and unleashes whatever he has planned.

"I'll go easy on you this first time." He tilts his head slightly, his expression inscrutable. "You're my wife, after all."

"How considerate." My voice cracks under the strain. I watch as his lips curl into a subtle, knowing smile. He clears his throat and jerks his chin toward the bed.

"On all fours, Anya. Lean on your forearms, ass up. Thighs apart." He runs his thumb along his lower lip and lowers his voice. "I won't ask twice."

Of course vulnerability is the first thing he demands. He wants control over me, wants to make sure this punishment gets him off.

But I'm not stupid enough to refuse him. Not with the stakes this high.

I move to the bed, swallowing my fear, and arrange myself as... directed.

I hear his footsteps approaching and feel him draw closer. "Good girl," he says. "Just like that."

I close my eyes as a rush of feelings floods me, feelings I can't decipher.

I hate how my body responds, how the silence that follows stretches taut, a thin thread about to snap. How I feel him watching me, assessing, like a predator savoring the moment before the strike.

I wonder if he sees I'm shaved. If he notes the way my thighs jiggle and my belly wobbles. If he cares that my toenails are unpolished and my hair askew and disheveled.

The tension between us snaps and crackles, sparks flying. I tremble in spite of myself. My breathing is shallow.

When he doesn't move immediately, the silence between us stretches.

When his hand grazes the curve of my hip—barely a whisper of a touch—and shockwaves course through me. I feel his heat, the deliberate control behind every move, and I shiver.

"You're trembling," he observes, his voice low and smooth, like the edge of a knife. "Are you afraid, Anya?"

I want to snap back at him, to deny him the satisfaction of seeing the effect he has on me. But I can't. I'm not just afraid—I'm undone. He strips away my defenses with every word, every look, leaving me raw and exposed.

"I don't know," I manage, my voice barely above a whisper.

I feel the tears before I realize they're falling. They slip silently down my cheeks, splashing my hands.

He leans down, his voice impossibly close to my ear, and when he speaks, it's softer, almost coaxing. "Good," he murmurs. "Fear keeps you sharp. But it's obedience, Anya, that earns rewards."

Before I can process his words, his hand slams down sharply on my bare ass. The sound is deafening in the quiet, the sting radiating across my skin, hot and bright. My breath hitches, and I let out a strangled gasp—not from pain, but from the unexpected wave of pleasure that surges through me.

My core clenches, and I hate the way my body reacts to him.

"You deserve a lot more than that," he says, his voice a dark purr. "To remind you who's in charge." His hand doesn't leave my skin. Instead, his fingers trail lazily over the spot he struck, soothing the sting in a way that only makes the ache inside me worse.

"You liked that," he says, and it's not a question. His voice is full of dark amusement, and I want to deny it, to fight him, but I can't.

I bury my face in the bed, trying to hide from the shame and vulnerability.

"Look at me."

Reluctantly, I meet his eyes.

They are sharp, unreadable, but his gaze burns into me. "I said, look at me, Anya."

"Do you want me to stop?" he asks, his voice a dangerous whisper, and I know it's not a question he asks lightly. He doesn't want to. And a part of him doesn't want to continue without my say.

Oh god.

I swallow hard, my throat dry, and shake my head.

"Good girl," he repeats.

My eyes flutter closed at the feel of his warm hand slipping between my thighs, his fingers grazing me where I'm already embarrassingly wet. I gasp, my hips jerking involuntarily at the contact.

"Jesus," he groans, his voice tinged with approval. "You're soaked."

His fingers slide over me again, teasing, never quite giving me what I want. It's maddening.

"Do you like this?" he asks, his lips brushing against the curve of my ear.

I nod, unable to speak, my body betraying every ounce of resistance I thought I had.

Chuckling softly, his fingers press harder, drawing a low moan from my throat before he pulls away entirely.

"Then maybe this will be your punishment, Anya," he says, straightening to his full height. "To want but not have. To feel what I can do to you and know it's mine to give—or take away."

I don't know how I feel about this. Part of me wants to tell him to stop, that I don't want his touch. But I couldn't do that right now if I tried. Because I *do* want his touch. Because I've wanted more than this, more from him, for so long—even back when it was wrong.

And now I'm his wife.

I try to bring myself back to the present, to tell myself that this isn't what I need, that it isn't what I want. But it isn't working. My body is desperate for relief. Desperate for *him*.

Why do I feel this storm of emotions—anger, confusion, and need colliding inside me?

"This is for storming into my office and disrespecting me in front of my men," he growls, his voice low and dangerous, before his hand comes down sharply against the full curve of my ass. I inhale at the sting but stay in place, unmoving.

"That's right. Just like that." His voice softens, almost approving. "My handprint on your ass pleases me so much, beautiful."

I swallow hard, unable to stop the shiver that runs through

me before his fingers slide through my wet heat, brushing where I crave him most.

My back arches instinctively, my body surrendering to the pleasure he offers.

It feels so fucking good—*so* damn good—that all my thoughts, my anger, and my pride dissolve into nothingness. Everything I've ever known or wanted could fit on the head of a needle.

"Does that feel good?" he asks, his voice low and probing, as though he genuinely wants to know and is cataloging this moment like he catalogs everything else.

"Yes," I breathe out in a hushed whisper, my voice trembling.

He speeds up his movements, circling my clit with precision, smearing my wetness over every inch of me. My body bucks against his hand, craving more.

"And this?" he asks, his tone almost clinical as he shifts the rhythm.

"It's... too much," I gasp, the sensitivity overwhelming me.

He slows, adjusting his pace to something deliberate and steady, coaxing moans from my lips that I can't suppress. The pleasure courses through me, taking over every rational thought I might have had.

"And then there's the matter of you running out," he says, his tone darkening as he slows his movements. "Leaving my home when you knew I wouldn't allow it."

Before I can respond, his hand presses firmly on the center of my back, pinning me in place. Then his palm slaps hard against my ass—once, twice, three times in rapid succession, never in the same spot. The sting is sharp, radiating heat through my skin. It hurts like fuck, but the pain only intensifies the ache between my legs.

What is wrong with me?

"Spread your legs," he growls, tapping the inside of each thigh with the back of his hand.

I obey, opening myself to him without hesitation. His fingers slide into me, thick and deliberate, stroking my most sensitive place. Oh *fuck, yes, please.*

"How does that feel, Anya?" he asks, his voice low and rough in my ear.

"So good." I breathe, my voice a barely audible whisper.

"Tell me you're going to obey me," he commands, his tone leaving no room for argument.

"Yes," I gasp, switching to Russian instinctively. "I'll obey you."

He rewards me with another perfect stroke of his fingers.

"Tell me you will never leave this house without my permission again," he growls, plunging more fingers inside me now, his movements unrelenting and precise. My breath hitches, my muscles tightening as pleasure coils within me, ready to snap.

"I won't," I cry out. "I won't leave again without your permission!"

"That's what marrying into the Bratva means," he says, his

tone colder now. "You will obey me. I will accept nothing less."

He removes his fingers before his hand comes down one final time, a sharp smack that makes me cry out.

"You've got a lot to learn, Anya. Is that clear, beautiful?"

The word "beautiful" sends a bloom of warmth through my chest.

My wife.

Beautiful.

"I asked if that was clear, Anya."

"Yes," I whisper, my voice trembling. "Crystal."

"Good." His tone softens, but the command remains. I ache for him, no matter how hard I try to resist. "Because I want you to remember this night. I'm taking it easy on you, Anya. You deserve my belt for what you did. If you ever do anything like that again, you won't sit for a fucking week. Is that clear?"

"Yes," I whisper again before I can stop myself. "Yes, sir."

His growl of approval makes my body melt like heated caramel.

"Spread your legs, baby. Come on my hand," he murmurs, his voice a low growl in my ear as he strokes me again, relentless and precise. His fingers bring me higher and higher, finding my clit, spreading my slick heat, and when I finally shatter, it's like lightning strikes through me, leaving my body trembling and boneless.

I'm dimly aware of him shifting behind me, of the sound of his own low groans as takes out his cock and fists it. My breath catches as I tense, thinking he's going to take me. I watch, half-drunk, as he strokes and pumps his hardened cock, tracing a finger over my heated ass, between my legs.

With a groan, his hot seed splashes across my back, marking me in the most possessive, intimate way. He muffles another groan, and I feel a wicked smile curve my lips.

I did this to him. Me. I made the ice shatter.

The thought sends another ripple of pleasure through me as I collapse onto the bed, barely able to move.

"Lie on your belly," he says quietly.

Too tired to argue, I obey. He cleans me off with his own soaking T-shirt, the act so filthy and possessive it sends a shiver down my spine.

My eyes grow heavy.

He bends down and presses a soft kiss to my cheek. "Get some sleep, Anya. We have a lot of work ahead of us."

The click of the door shutting behind him sounds as I close my eyes and begin to drift off to sleep, but a second later, my eyes fly open when I hear a series of clicks.

He didn't just shut the door. He locked me in.

CHAPTER II

SEMYON

I WAS eleven when I learned the true meaning of fear. Not the shallow kind that makes your stomach flip when you're caught sneaking out, or the faint distress in a dark alley, or facing someone bigger than you. Fear that claws at your insides and makes you immobile. Fear that sears through your chest like acid, making it hard to breathe.

I sit in my room and take another sip of whiskey. I drink too much; I know I do, but sometimes it's the only thing that grounds me.

I close my eyes and the memories rush to me, as vivid as the day it happened.

"Go!"

Rafail's voice is sharp, cutting through the chaos like a whip. I can see him, only eighteen years old. I can still feel him shove me with one arm as he picked up Zoya with the other and threw her into my arms, practically shoving us in a small closet in the back of the house—the tiny one no one would ever look in.

I remember shouting, even as I pressed Zoya's head into my chest so hard she couldn't see a thing. "No, Rafail!" My feet dug into the hardwood. "Poppa is out there—Mama—"

Rafail didn't let me finish. His grip was like iron as he shoved me into the closet along with Zoya, desperation pushing him to the edge. "What did I fucking say? Get in there. Now. Keep them safe!"

The door slammed, and he took out his gun. Even then, Rafail was a force to be reckoned with—looming over all of us, tall and commanding, barely eighteen years old. I thought he was unbreakable, untouchable. But through the gap in the closet door, I could see the faint tremor in his hand as he gripped his gun.

"What's happening?" Zoya whispered. "Semyon—" She was only six, too young to understand. Too young to know why our father had suddenly screamed at us to run when the shouting outside turned into gunfire. Too young to know why Mama's screams were abruptly cut off and ended in a gurgle.

I shook my head, unable to comprehend the horror of it all. But I understood it all. The metallic taste of blood that hung in the air. The low groan of my father as he tried fruitlessly to crawl to safety. And the utter hatred and fury of the man who ended it all—my mother's lover, coming to take what he said was his.

"You thought you could get away from me, didn't you?" he sneered, his voice slithering through the walls. "You thought I wouldn't find her. You thought I wouldn't take her back."

His voice made my skin crawl.

I flinched as another shot rang out, followed by the sickening thud of a heavy body hitting the floor.

Rafail pulled that trigger. If our enemies realized it was him, if there were more of them—

Rafail had told us to stay here, no matter what, but I had to help.

"Stay here," I growled to the younger ones. I glared at Rodion, bold and reckless, and put every threat I'd ever issued him into my command. "Don't you fucking move. Make sure they stay here, or I'll beat the shit out of you."

He paused a second as if weighing whether or not coming to their aid was worth an ass beating but finally nodded.

I crept out, unseen by everyone. Rafail stood over the dead body of the man he'd shot—the man we all knew to be my mother's lover. But it was too late. My father was bleeding out on the kitchen floor, his skin pale as he reached for Rafail.

"Hold them together," he said in a low voice. "Our family."

Out of the corner of my eye, someone rushed at Rafail.

I moved without thinking. I grabbed the butcher knife from the kitchen counter and flung it with all my might. I knew the second it hit—I knew it would. We'd practiced, over and over again, me and Eli down by the creek, throwing knives into the tree bark. Every time, I imagined it was my enemy on the bank.

Someone grabbed me from behind. Cold metal slashed against my skin as I pulled away, and pain exploded in my hand when they missed their mark.

Rafail leaped from the floor, his hand shaking as he pointed the gun and pulled the trigger.

Thud.

Another body.

The two of us stood, breathing heavily in the bloody aftermath, my father's eyes now vacant as our mortal enemies bled out on our kitchen floor.

I stared at Rafail. His face was pale and splattered with crimson. His hands trembled as he lowered the gun, crouched down, and took my father's pulse.

His eyes bore into mine with a fierceness that cleaved straight through me.

"You're safe now," Rafail said, his voice barely more than a whisper.

But it wasn't true. It wasn't true then, and it isn't true now. Nothing about that night had been safe. Nothing would ever be safe again.

I pour another drink and sip it again, welcoming the familiar burn. I flip on my monitor, arranged by my bed, and look at the sleeping form of Stefan in one room and Anya in the next.

I take a deep breath, let it fill my lungs, and then let it out slowly.

They're safe.

I didn't want this responsibility, but it's mine now, and nothing—*nothing*—will ever persuade me to allow my family to be in danger again.

Tomorrow, I move in on the bakery. Tomorrow, we make it brutally clear that she belongs to me—that no one will take over her family's business. Tomorrow, we make it clear that I've made the move I need to, to keep my family safe.

I look at the sleeping form of the woman who hates me, the woman who blames me for her family's ruin, and shake my head.

No matter the cost.

CHAPTER 12

ANYA

THE DIM ROOM *reeked of cigarette smoke and alcohol, with a faint tinge of body odor, the low hum of voices punctuated by the clink of coins and glasses. I hated this place. I hated this place and the people who frequented it even more, but most of all, I hated that my brother was sitting at the center of it, a grin on his face as he threw down another handful of cash he didn't have and had probably stolen.*

I stayed near the doorway, my chest tight with dread. When I followed him here, I had no idea this was where I'd end up. I just wanted to talk some sense into him.

But now, staring at the scene in front of me, I felt frozen in place. The place reeked of danger. And Eli wasn't going to listen to me. He was too far gone, drunk on adrenaline and whatever delusion of invincibility he was chasing.

The sound of a chair scraping across the floor made me jump. My breath caught when I saw him. Semyon. He moved like a shadow, noticeable even from a distance since he was the only one wearing glasses.

He looked out of place, wearing an impeccable, pressed shirt and suit among the other sweat-stained shirts and leather jackets. He looked sharp and untouchable among a roomful of older men who nursed potbellies, heavy jowls, and receding hairlines.

Semyon was a king among men. I glanced away for a moment, not trusting my heartbeat.

I'd had a little crush on him for as long as I could remember. It didn't help that the usual hum of conversation faltered as men noticed his presence. The way they deferred to him and spoke with respect and more than a little fear. He was just that powerful.

Others might say it was because he was Bratva that the palpable fear followed him like his shadow. But I knew better. I knew Semyon had a way of commanding the attention of everyone in the room.

Part of it was his Bratva-meets-Superman aura. But it wasn't just the way he looked—it was the way he carried himself, that air of not giving a fuck that could make a woman weep. Because who wouldn't want a man like that in her corner? Someone who would stop at nothing to protect her?

Even at twenty-one years old, he carried himself with a chilling authority that belied his age. I watched as he walked straight to my brother's table, his blue eyes narrowing.

"Eli," he snapped, his voice cutting through the room like a blade. "Come here."

I practically ran to him myself; the need to obey his command felt primal. Otherworldly.

Eli glanced up, lazy, smirking. "Well, look who decided to grace us with his presence. You here to join the fun?"

"I said get the fuck over here," Semyon growled. "Now."

My brother had the audacity to chuckle, leaning back in his chair. "Relax. It's just a friendly game. What the fuck is your problem?"

Semyon didn't flinch. The only sign my brother's words hit him was the faintest twitch of his fingers. He was stronger than Eli. More powerful. "That's not your money you're gambling with. And you know it."

The other men at the table began to shift uncomfortably, glancing between Semyon and Eli. One by one, I watched as they mumbled excuses and disappeared into the smoky corners of the room, unwilling to be caught in the fallout of the Kopolov Bratva.

Of Semyon.

Semyon leaned on his forearms, menacing. I watched him, unable to breathe. "You're going to take your money, and you're going to fucking leave. Or you'll deal with me. Not Rafail. Me."

I couldn't help it—I hitched a breath. I had never heard him sound like that before—so cold, so detached. Semyon was a man of his word, and I would hate to see what it meant to "deal with him."

"You think I'm scared of you?" my brother spat.

Semyon tilted his head slightly, his icy gaze unwavering. "You should be."

I gasped. My breathing grew faster, my hands clammy. I watched as the two men stood face-to-face, the air between them charged. Then, without a word, my brother grabbed his coat and stormed past Semyon. Semyon didn't watch him go. Instead, he turned his head slightly, his eyes sweeping the room until they landed on me.

I was frozen in place.

My heart stopped. I couldn't breathe. I couldn't move. I couldn't think.

I didn't want him to see me here. I didn't need to be told he wouldn't approve of me here. But the weight of his gaze pinned me in place, and for a moment, I thought something flickered in his expression—recognition?

Was that... fear?

Then unmistakable anger.

I turned and ran.

"Anya!" His voice rang out sharply behind me.

I ran harder.

THE FIRST THING I notice when I open my eyes is the faint morning light streaming through the curtains. I leap up in bed. I never sleep this late—not so late that the sun is actually up in the sky.

Stefan.

I throw the covers off and run to the door. I remember he locked it last night, but now, when I turn the handle, it opens.

Did I imagine that he locked it?

My pulse races as I look around the room. I glance down at myself and realize I'm wearing nothing. I need to get dressed. I swallow hard, scanning the space, remembering the massive, ridiculously large closet. I look until I find a soft pink robe hanging from a corner near the bathroom. I'll probably have to thank one of his sisters for that later.

I wrap it around me, cinch it at the waist, and quickly run out to check on Stefan. I feel like I've abandoned my baby brother to the wolves. My stomach twists. Where is he? What has Semyon done? What would he do?

He brought me here last night to keep Stefan safe. He wouldn't hurt him... would he? But Semyon has implacable rules, and Stefan is a wild, reckless little boy.

I sprint down the hall, my bare feet hitting the hardwood as I fling open Stefan's door. The bed is unmade, the sheets rumpled and tossed aside as if he left in a hurry. His clothes from last night lay in a pile on the floor, haphazard and careless, just like he always leaves them. He's just a little boy.

What have I gotten my brother into?

My chest tightens when I hear voices downstairs. I take a

deep breath and let it out slowly. I have to stay calm. Why am I panicking?

Maybe because my *entire life* was put at risk? I was forced to marry a man I hate, and now my little brother is caught in the mix. Yeah, no big deal.

I roll my eyes heavenward. I wish Ophelia were here.

I walk downstairs. From here, I can see the huge expanse of his house—sleek, modern, and impossibly large, like something out of a magazine. But the sight that greets me freezes me in place.

Stefan sits on the other side of the open doorway, swinging his legs at the table, sipping something from a cup. Semyon sits across from him.

My heart aches because Stefan looks... happy. Safe.

My god. I didn't know how badly I'd been clinging to some kind of hope, and here it is. At great personal expense, but here it is, nonetheless.

They both look up as I approach, Stefan waving at me with one hand while holding his tea with the other. And Semyon —my cold, terrifying husband.

Except... he doesn't look so terrifying now.

Instead of his perfect suit, he wears a plain white T-shirt and gray pajama pants. Stubble shadows his jaw. His dark hair is ever so slightly mussed, and his glasses perch on the edge of his nose, giving him an almost softer edge.

Superman at rest.

No. No way. He can't do this. He can't sit here, playing checkers with Stefan, eating breakfast like he's some kind of domesticated man who actually cares. Who actually has a heart.

"Good morning," I say, but my voice is sharper and colder than I intended.

Semyon's piercing blue eyes lock onto mine. For one moment, the intensity in that gaze robs me of my breath, and I remember last night's details—every single one of them. His hands. His voice. His promise that we would consummate our marriage. The pain and heat he painted across my ass.

No, it's wrong to think about this with my brother sitting right there. *God.*

Now here he is, looking like an entirely different man, as if I somehow imagined the coldhcarted monster in my dreams.

Is he gaslighting me?

"It's late," I tell him. "I'm supposed to be at the bakery."

With a nod, he explains, his voice firm. "I made a decision. A lot has happened in a very short time. The bakery is closed for the day and will stay closed for the weekend while we figure out what we're doing next with it."

I open my mouth to protest. We don't *close* the bakery.

But he continues. "I have reasons for that, Anya. Don't question them," he says quietly, his tone a calm command.

I hesitate, wanting to hear everything before I respond. "And Stefan has to get to school—"

"Stefan will stay home from school today. On Monday, it'll be business as usual. We have a lot to go over."

"What?" I ask, my confusion spilling over. "No school? But he—"

"You heard what I said," he snaps, turning back to the checkerboard.

Stefan smirks at me. "If he says I'm staying home from school, I'm staying home from school," he says, his tone full of mischief. "Maybe I'll stay home every Friday, and you can't make me go."

Before I can respond, Semyon's voice cracks like a whip." *Stefan.*"

My brother freezes, his smirk vanishing as he looks at Semyon with wide eyes.

"That's your sister," Semyon says, his tone low and dangerous. "And my wife. You don't speak to her like that again. Am I clear?"

Stefan swallows hard and nods. "Yes, sir."

Yes, sir? What? What has happened to my brother, and who is in his place?

I blink, stunned into silence. I've never seen anyone check Stefan's attitude—not even me. And the fact that it comes from Semyon makes it feel even more surreal.

But Semyon isn't finished. "Apologize."

Stefan swallows hard. "I'm sorry."

"It's okay." I nod as my eyes drift to the checkerboard. Stefan's brow is furrowed in concentration as he stares at the pieces, seemingly forgetting what just happened. Semyon sits back, almost relaxed, though his focus is razor-sharp.

It's all... bizarre.

That's the man who locked me in my room last night. The man who spanked me and threatened me. The man I've argued with at every turn because I fucking hate him.

Now he's sitting here, teaching my brother checkers, and acting like he actually cares?

Did I wake up in an alternate reality, or what?

I don't trust it. I don't trust him. But my stomach growls, and I'm in desperate need of a good cup of coffee, so I push through and decide I'm going to take things as they come.

I have to walk closer to Semyon to get to the coffee. I square my shoulders and try not to think about the fact that I'm naked under this robe.

As I draw closer to him, I remember the way he touched me. His low, masculine hum of need. The way it felt having him close and knowing, deep down in my bones, how badly he wanted me.

My body heats. I glance at him, hoping he'll stay focused on the game, but no such luck. His eyes are raking over me in my bathrobe as if mentally undressing me.

Heat skates across my skin.

When I was younger, I'd have given anything in the world for him to look at me like this. But now?

Now, I don't know how I feel about it.

I stand at the kitchen counter and look at the coffee machine in front of me. I've never seen anything like it. It looks like some kind of spaceship—one pull of the bells and whistles, and I might launch myself straight into the atmosphere.

I turn to see Semyon watching me.

"You drink coffee?" he asks.

"Yes, I love coffee."

"But you don't know how to use that."

I blow out a breath. "I'm kind of old-fashioned. I use, like, a French press. That's my favorite way."

Of course, it makes sense that he would have this type of contraption—immaculate, precise, and unnecessarily excellent.

"I'll be right back," he says to Stefan. "You stay right there. This game isn't over." There's a small, playful edge to his voice, but it's still laced with command.

Stefan sits still, taking a huge bite of his pastry. Crumbs spray onto the table and he gives me a grin around a mouthful.

I don't remember the last time my brother grinned.

I face the coffee machine, telling myself *I can do hard things.* I can figure this out.

Before I get the chance, Semyon reaches over. "You use these pods here," he says.

He's standing behind me. I can feel the heat of his chest pressed up against my back, and god, he *smells so good.* I close my eyes as heat floods my chest. We're so close. Just the feel of his warmth next to me and his scent is driving me mad...

"See?" he says, his voice low and almost seductive. Or am I imagining that? "The brown ones are espresso, and the black are coffee. You put them in here and press this button."

"Do I have to, like, tell it what size cup I want or...?"

"No. Each one is calibrated for the exact amount with the right pressure. Espresso shots will be smaller, coffee larger. How do you take your coffee?"

"Cream, milk, whatever."

"Not 'whatever,'" he says, reaching for a crystal-clear mug and sliding it under the coffee machine. "I asked you what you like, not what you'll tolerate."

My heart thumps.

"Cream. I like cream and three sugars. How do you like yours?" I ask because it feels like the polite thing to do.

His lips almost twitch. Almost. "Cream, three sugars."

Is he mocking me? I narrow my eyes at him, but he only shrugs.

"I don't lie, Anya."

I don't think he could if he tried.

I watch as the machine bubbles and clanks, the fragrant smell of coffee filling the air. He takes the finished cup, pours in cream and three sugars, gives it a stir, and holds it between his hands, staring into it before handing it to me.

"Thank you," I whisper, half wondering if I'm thanking him only for the coffee.

With a nod, he makes another cup for himself, and Stefan asks for tea. He likes to pretend he's grown-up, but he's not quite ready for coffee yet.

"Of course. I'll be right there."

I flick the button on the electric kettle and watch as Semyon cleans everything with precision. The pods go into a labeled recycling bucket. He takes a cloth from the sink, wipes a few droplets of coffee off the counter, folds the cloth neatly, and puts it back. He returns the cream to the fridge—immaculate, perfectly arranged, of course—and slides the sugar container back into its exact spot next to the milk.

I watch, half mesmerized, trying not to think about what has to happen between us.

How could someone so beautiful be so cold?

Will it be like having sex with one of those vampires?

Oh my god. Sex. I can't think of that. I need to talk to Ophelia.

Now.

I swallow hard as the kettle bubbles and steam hisses behind me. It's ready. "Here, let me have your cup."

I place a teabag in Stefan's mug and pour the steaming water. But I'm not focused, and the mug slips, the boiling water splashing over my hand.

"Shit!" I yelp, jerking back and cradling my hand. I run to the sink, turning on the cold water, hissing as the burn stings. Before I can grab a towel or think straight, Semyon is there, right in my space.

"Let me see," he says briskly, his voice low.

"It's fine." I clutch my wrist tighter.

"Anya." His voice has that edge again—quiet, unrelenting. Not a question but a command.

I hold out my hand, trembling. I don't want him to touch me again, but I can't stop him. His large, calloused fingers take my wrist with surprising gentleness, turning it over to inspect the red, angry skin.

"You shouldn't be so careless," he scolds, his eyes focused on the burn as he guides my hand under the cold water.

"Thanks for the advice," I snap, sarcasm lacing my shaky voice because it fucking hurts. But it comes out weaker than I intended.

He doesn't respond. Instead, he grabs a clean dishcloth, wets it under cold water, and presses it against my wrist. I hiss at the contact, but his grip doesn't waver.

"You'll blister if you don't cool it down quickly," he says, his voice rougher now.

I glance at him, caught off guard by the tight line of his jaw and the way his brows draw together. He avoids my gaze, focusing entirely on my injury, but the tension in his shoulders betrays something else.

Semyon isn't cold right now. He's not happy but not furious. He isn't detached either. He's just... there. Solid. Present.

Something inside me breaks then. It's been so damn long since I've had another adult I could lean on other than Ophelia.

My breath hitches as his thumb brushes against the inside of my wrist—a faint touch, but it sends heat racing up my arm that has nothing to do with the burn. I hate myself for melting under his gentleness.

"There's a first aid kit in the pantry," he says, breaking the moment as he turns away. "I'll get it. Keep that cloth against your skin."

When he returns, he unfolds a perfectly organized kit, takes out a small packet of burn relief cream, and murmurs, "Let me see."

He stands in front of me, masculine, strong, so in charge.

I show him my wrist and flinch when he smears cream on it before he takes out gauze and carefully wraps it.

"Leave it like this until I tell you to take it off."

For a moment, I just nod. I don't want to argue with him.

"Anya? Are you okay?" Stefan asks from across the room.

"I'm fine," I say, forcing a smile. "You need to be careful with hot things."

Semyon grumbles under his breath but goes back to the table. I watch him and wish I could bring him back.

Stefan moves a checker piece and hops over one of Semyon's. "I'm gonna beat you," he says with a grin.

Semyon rolls his eyes. "I'd like to see you try." On the next move, he jumps four of Stefan's pieces and collects them in his hand.

Stefan's face falls.

I take my coffee and a plate of pastries and walk over to them, rolling my eyes. "Oh yes, Semyon Kopolov, the ultimate checkers tyrant. Crushing the dreams of children one king at a time."

The remark slips out before I can stop myself, but to my shock, Semyon laughs.

It's soft, barely audible, but it's there—a quiet chuckle that rumbles from his chest. His lips curve into a genuine smile.

I freeze, my cup halfway to my lips.

I thought he'd forgotten how to laugh. He looks... different. The sharp lines of his face soften, the cold mask momentarily slipping aside.

For one moment, I see the boy I grew up with. The boy I loved. The boy who broke my heart.

And for a reason I can't explain, I want to see it again.

The thought hits me like a punch to the stomach. What is wrong with me?

I bury my face in the coffee, trying to get a grip on myself. I still have such vivid memories. I wonder if he does too.

"You should always make sure you watch your opponent," Semyon says to Stefan. I've almost forgotten that he's the second eldest in his family, with two younger sisters now. He takes to this role kind of naturally, and I love that. But I can't forget who he is or what he wants. Right now, my brother is safe, and I made the decision I had to, to keep my family together. I suppose... so did he.

I take a bite of pastry and drink the coffee. "My god, this coffee is delicious."

"It's a high-quality brew. Ethiopian beans."

"Well, I'll have to introduce you to the French press," I tell him. "You know our most popular recipes at the bakery are always the simplest."

Why am I telling him this? Like he cares?

"I know. We have a spreadsheet we'll go over later when we discuss it with your new business manager."

I blink at him in surprise.

"What do you mean?"

"I want to build a detailed catalog," Semyon says, his voice steady but focused. "Inventory, profit margins, the items that generate the most revenue."

I blink, momentarily caught off guard. He's actually talking about the bakery's operations? I thought he only cared about the location, just another strategic asset to him. But he's talking about profit margins like he's genuinely... invested.

His gaze shifts to the coffee in his hand. "If you know which item drives the most profit, you can optimize production and reduce waste. The right adjustments could increase revenue by at least thirty percent."

I lean forward slightly, reluctantly intrigued. "You've thought about this a lot."

"Of course," he replies, his expression neutral. "It's a business. Every detail matters." He tilts his head. "What?" he asks when he catches me staring, and it's the first time he seems curious about what my thought process is.

I shake my head. "Nothing."

Thankfully, Stefan is oblivious to the tension between the two of us and eagerly makes his move on the board without batting an eyelash. Semyon shakes his head, lifts his checker, and easily jumps two of Stefan's checkers.

Stefan's face falls, and Semyon leans in. "No. This game is not over. And even if it were, you have to know that I'm not going to take it easy on you. Your sister can mock me all she wants, but I am never going to let you win a game. When you win, you will know that you've won fair and square."

For some reason, it feels like he's talking to me.

They continue to play as my younger brother's tongue pokes out of his mouth in concentration.

"Are you upset that I was poking around in your finances?" Semyon asks with genuine curiosity.

Stefan looks at him and then to me before he focuses back on the board.

"I guess I didn't consider the fact that you'd actually care about the bakery. I just thought you wanted the location."

"Yes, I'm interested in the location, but running a business that's thriving versus one that is barely scraping by is definitely going to be in both of our best interests. My cousin Matvei will help since this is his wheelhouse."

I frown. I don't know Matvei.

I purse my lips and glare at him because how dare he insult me like that?

"You look upset." His brow furrows. "Are you upset? Why?"

He's as methodical with his human interactions as he is with his coffee making.

Jesus. Of course, I've known this about him forever.

"That's my business. My mother began that. And you're insulting me."

"What did I say that's insulting?" he asks, completely oblivious.

"You're mocking how the business is failing."

"I'm mocking nothing. I stated a fact, Anya. Save your pity party for when it actually matters. Right now, I'm going to come in and save your family's bakery. Do you want that or not?"

No, I don't fucking want it, not if it means that I'm beholden to him, but I don't say that.

"It's still my bakery."

Stefan glares at Semyon. "It's still our bakery," he echoes.

Uh-oh. My heart thumps.

Semyon turns his cold gaze to my brother, who doesn't flinch but squirms a bit.

"Excellent." He leans back in his chair, his cold blue eyes sharp. "Then why don't you tell me which item at the bakery is most profitable? What's the return on investment on your basic line of products? The estimated overhead costs—labor, ingredients? Are you profitable or running at a deficit? Have you seen linear growth?"

Stefan freezes, his mouth opening and closing like a fish gasping for air. He looks as if Semyon is speaking a foreign language because, of course, he is.

"Running a business isn't about guesswork. It's about control. Precision. Without that, you're gambling with your livelihood." I cross my arms on my chest as Semyon rises to his feet. He looks down at the board, lifts his checker, and, in one final move, sweeps the rest of Stefan's checkers into his palm.

"Next time, pay attention," he says as Stefan's face falls. "Put the pieces away, please," he says quietly. "After you take your dishes to the sink."

I feel a slight rise in my eyebrows because I never make Stefan put dishes in the sink, clean up his toys, or do anything but his homework. I stare at Stefan.

Have I been babying my little brother?

Stefan stands, takes his plate over to the dishwasher, and half tosses his dish in.

Uh-oh.

I watch as Semyon folds his arms across his chest. A part of me wishes he would stay like this, half-human in his rumpled clothing, but I know as soon as he shaves and puts on his suit, he'll be back to cold and calculating.

"Try that again," he says in a low, stern voice. "Come here, I'll show you how."

Stefan stares and looks at me. I shrug and gesture toward the dishwasher.

Stefan tries again, and Semyon deems it acceptable, but as my brother tries to leave, Semyon catches him. "Not yet. Didn't I ask you to put that game away?"

I watch as Stefan gets that look in his eyes that I am all too familiar with.

Is he going to push back?

I watch as he tosses the checkers into the box. Semyon's lips twitch. "You can do better than that, but I'll let it go for now because you need to go to your room and do what I said."

I bury my face in my cup of coffee.

And then it happens. Stefan snaps. He stares at Semyon with a frown that clouds his vision. "You're not the boss of me," he says, but he says it in a low voice, as if he wants to defy Semyon but isn't quite sure how far to push.

Oh no.

I lower the coffee mug and take a step toward Stefan on instinct.

"You're living in my house," Semyon says matter-of-factly. "I'm married to your sister, and by Bratva law, that means I'm in charge." He lowers his voice. "Understood?"

Stefan looks around and opens his mouth to protest. I stare in horror. *No.*

"You don't have housekeepers? People who clean or something?"

Semyon nods curtly. "I do. But children expect maids to clean up after them. *Men* take care of their belongings and home as a matter of habit. Do you want to be a man or a boy?"

I want to remind him he's only eight years old, but I don't intervene. Not yet.

Semyon continues. "I will be checking, and if you haven't made your bed and tidied up sufficiently, there will be consequences."

I stare at him, aghast. Is he *threatening* my brother?

"Go," he says, pointing to the door. Stefan runs.

I stare at him, at a loss for words. There's a glint of amusement in his piercing blue eyes as he steps closer to me. "He'll be fine. Trust me, I would know."

He was half-raised by his older brother, and I have a feeling disobedience and disrespect didn't fly in that house either.

"I didn't step in because I agreed with you *this* time," I say with a warning frown. Semyon shrugs and steps close, taking my wrist in his hand, his touch surprisingly soft. His fingers trace up to my elbow, and goosebumps erupt over my arm as if waking from a long slumber. When he reaches my shoulder, he gives it a gentle squeeze. I shiver.

"Come with me," he says, his voice low and velvety soft. There's an urgency in his words, and I remember for the millionth time—*this is Semyon.*

The same boy I swooned over, the one who made me melt. The one I can't trust.

I stare, unmoving. Before I can respond, he crooks a finger at me. "You. Upstairs."

Shocking that he wants to leave the breakfast dishes on the table, but it seems urgent.

My breath catches in my throat. Being alone with him is *dangerous*.

My heart thunders in my chest when he follows up behind me and half shoves me in before he slams and locks the door.

Oh my god.

I stare at him when he closes the space between us, grabs my chin, and tilts my face upward.

"You make me crazy, Anya," he rasps, his eyes locked onto mine. I stare into his ice-blue depths as he leans on his forearm, caging me in.

My heart thumps madly in my chest.

It seems like he's warring with himself. "I want you so fucking badly." Cursing under his breath, he mutters in Russian.

I swallow hard. "You hate that you want me?"

His voice is a low growl filled with regret. "No. I hate that I'll fucking ruin you."

I open my mouth to protest, even though I have no idea what I'll say, when his mouth crashes on mine. It's not gentle; it's all-consuming as if he's pouring every unspoken word and feeling into the kiss. His hands tangle in my hair. I stifle a moan at how good it feels when he pulls.

My hands find the broad expanse of his shoulders, his muscles tight and powerful. My arms loop around his neck. I pull him closer so there's no distance between us.

The ground seems to shift under my feet. My silky bathrobe slips loose as his hands skim up my sides. I push against his chest, unable to stop him because I *need* to feel him. I need him to brand me, claim me, mark me with his touch so when I wake alone in bed and remember that *Semyon Kopolov* is my husband, I can convince myself this is real.

"I can't fight you anymore," I whisper, my voice trembling. "Maybe I don't want to."

It feels like I've stepped into the world of adulting, admitting that I want him. I want to feel his hot, branding touch all over my body. I want him to make me tremble beneath him. I want to feel him *in* me.

He groans as my lips graze his skin, and I reach for his waistband. His fingers tighten in my hair, a low curse slipping from his lips as he stares down at me.

"You're so beautiful," he whispers. "My entire world was ordered neat in a box, in a row. And then you came in and smashed it all to hell."

"How romantic."

He groans again, and it feels like victory. He brushes his mouth against mine. Tentatively, I reach for his glasses and gently push them up his face so I can stroke his cheek, unencumbered. I cup his jaw, loving the way his stubble pricks my palm.

He kisses me back.

"I need you," he whispers. "I have to have you, Anya. I'm afraid if I wait much longer, I won't be able to be as gentle with you as you need your first time."

My heart aches as a lump forms in my throat. He's showing a side of himself that might break through every fortress I've built.

"I need you too," I whisper back.

Then he's lifting me. My legs wrap around his torso, his thick length pressing up against my bare pussy. My silk robe does nothing to hide me from him. He's kissing me as if he needs me to breathe again, and I'm kissing him back.

Semyon wants me.

He wants me so badly. He lays me down, taking a moment to stare at me, and I can tell he likes what he sees.

Leaning on one elbow, he explores the length of my body with a touch that borders on worship, leaving goosebumps and heat in his wake—a contradiction that feels so damn right. Brushing his fingers through my hair, he gives it another tug, before he kisses my temple, kisses my lips. He inhales me as he works his way down my body until he reaches my breasts.

Everything in me rises to meet him—my hopes, my dreams, *my body.*

My breasts feel heavy and full, and heat pools between my legs as he laps at one hardened bud and flicks his thumb across the other.

"Do you like that?" he whispers, his brow creased with curiosity.

This is Semyon. Cataloging. Noting.

I can't make peace with the fact that this is the boy I loved—the one I thought I would hate forever. And now I'm surrendering to him. But that was then, and this is now.

"Yes, I like it." I tug his hair. "Do it again."

His hand cracks across the fullness of my ass.

"Ask politely."

Oh god.

"Do it again, please. Please, Semyon."

"Better."

He trails the length of my body down between my legs. "Spread your legs."

I let my legs fall apart, giving him access to my slick heat. I moan when thick fingers find my folds, and he stifles a groan himself.

"Fucking gorgeous," he breathes out.

We're going to do this.

We have to.

I groan as his lips graze my skin. He's just about to kiss my belly when his phone buzzes on the nightstand—a sharp, jarring sound that shatters the moment.

Semyon's entire body grows rigid, his fingers flexing against my thigh as his gaze flicks to the phone.

"It's Rafail."

"Ignore it," I plead, tugging at him again, but I already know he can't. His expression darkens.

"I have to take it," he says to me. "It's law. *Fuck.*"

I clench my fists at the loss of him and turn away when he answers the phone, angry that my eyes blur with tears.

"Yes," he growls into the phone. The momentary calm shatters as Semyon curses, his eyes swinging back to mine. Whatever Rafail just told him impacts me too.

"What? When? Are you sure?"

I scramble to my feet, alarm prickling me. I'm already heading to the closet to get dressed. "What's wrong?" I ask, my voice shaky.

He turns to me, his face a mask of ice again.

"Eli's leaving may be more complicated than it looks."

CHAPTER 13

SEMYON

I KICKED *a loose rock at the bank of the creek, watching it tumble into the water with a heavy splash. It was like the endless noise that lived in my head these days after my parents' death—too loud, impossible to ignore. I thrived on routine, structure, predictability, and the past few months following their deaths had been anything but that.*

Rafail had taken over, the guardian of my siblings, and as the second oldest, I helped. Zoya, the baby, was the one who struggled the most. Yana had her own struggles, different from the rest of us, and Rafail—he held it all together. Me? I was the one who struggled.

I came here to think, to get away from Rafail's constant snarking about everyone having to shape up if they wanted to stay safe and with him. He was petrified of one of us screwing up and him losing guardianship over us. Some days, it felt like the tenuous thread holding our family together was about to snap.

We needed space. I needed to regroup. And I knew I didn't have the tools other people had. I often missed social cues, didn't understand emotion the way others seemed to, and when my world felt like it was crumbling because something changed, people didn't understand that it felt like the plates of the earth shifted, causing my own personal earthquake.

They never understood. When my world was predictable and ordered, the chatter in my head died down.

Here, by the creek, it was quiet. This was where Anya and Eli were my friends, where I could tell them the truth. Where I could be a kid for once.

But it wasn't anymore. That ended the day my parents died.

I heard soft sniffles behind me.

When I turned, I spotted her right away—a tiny, gangly thing with wild hair and eyes that looked even bigger when she was crying. Anya. Eli's baby sister and my friend. She was sitting on the ground, and she hadn't seen me yet, as she hugged her knees to her chest. Eli was supposed to be with her.

"Anya, what are you doing out here?"

My voice was gruffer than I intended. She looked up sharply, sniffled, and muttered something I couldn't hear. I sighed, walking over to crouch in front of her. Emotions were always a challenge for me to figure out, and it was even more complicated when it came to girls.

"Anya, what's wrong?" I asked, trying to soften my tone, though that wasn't something I was very good at doing.

Finally, she raised her head, her tear-streaked face meeting mine with frustration. "Eli said he'd meet me here. He said he was going to teach me how to skip rocks."

Even though I couldn't read people very well, I knew she was lying. Somebody had done something or said something—this wasn't about skipping rocks. "I don't think this is really about skipping rocks, is it?"

She stared at me, and her eyes skated down to my neck, where my first tattoo showed. Something shifted in her expression—recognition, maybe.

"Anyway," I continued, pushing past the tension. "You don't need Eli for that."

She blinked at me, her tears slowing. "I don't?"

"Of course not." I stood up, scanning the bank until I found a few flat stones, then held one out to her. "You just need this —and a little practice."

She hesitated before reaching for the rock, her small hand brushing against mine. "How do I do it?"

"Come here," I said, gesturing to the water. My voice was rough, but I softened it as much as I could. I didn't have time for this—Rafail wouldn't like me wasting time here.

But I wanted to show her.

She scrambled to her feet, her too-big shoes slipping on the wet grass. I crouched low, showing her how to angle her arm and release the stone just right. Then, with a flick of my wrist, I sent it skipping across the surface—once, twice, three times before it sank into the depths.

"Wow," she whispered, her mouth hanging open.

"Your turn," I said, stepping back to give her space.

She tried to imitate my movements, frowning in concentration, but her first throw landed with a heavy splash. No skips.

"Not like that," I said, smirking. "You have to flick it just right. It should hit the surface lightly enough to skip again, not sink."

And she did it. Over and over and over again, she tried, stubborn as ever, until finally, one of her rocks skipped once. She leaped into the air, her laugh bright and unrestrained. It was beautiful. Priceless. I wished I could capture that sound and replay it when the noise in my head got too loud.

"Did you see that?" she said, turning to me, her eyes lit up. For one second, she looked older than her years.

And for one second, I forgot the noise in my head. The only voice was... hers. "Not bad," I said, allowing myself a small smile.

She was tougher than she looked. She picked up another rock and skipped it again. And then another.

"I wasn't crying because of Eli," she admitted after a while.

"I know."

I didn't meet her eyes as I picked up more flat rocks and held them in the palm of my hand. I had figured out that people didn't like it when they were being vulnerable and you looked them in the eyes.

"You prepared to tell me what it was?"

She took a sharp breath, then looked at me. "What would you do if I told you the truth?"

What would I do? What a strange question. "Listen," I said, confused.

"No—" She looked away. "You're too protective sometimes. People are afraid of you, Semyon."

Good. People should be. I was fucking Bratva, coming into my own.

But I needed to know.

"Are you?" I asked, my voice low.

She shook her head with wide eyes. "Afraid of you?"

I swallowed, unsure if I really wanted to hear her answer.

"Sometimes," she whispered. Then she looked back at the water. "And then I remember who you are. Just Semyon. Like a brother to me."

Like a brother to me. Why did that cut so deep?

The sound of voices behind us caught her attention. She looked terrified, her eyes wide.

"Why are you afraid?" I asked, a simmering anger building in my veins. My hands clenched into fists. I leaned in closer, so close our breaths mingled, and I could see the way she drew in a breath. "Who hurt you?"

"It's them," she whispered. "God, it's them. The boys from school. Stupid fucking bullies."

"Anya." I didn't like the fear in her eyes. She was too young, too innocent, too...

"Can you trust me?" I asked her.

She took in a shaky breath. "You're the only one I trust."

Pride swelled in my chest. I stepped behind a tree as two boys came around the corner.

"Did your mom dress you in those rags?" one sneered, gesturing at her clothes.

"I think she got them from the garbage bin." Another laughed, pointing at her scuffed sneakers.

My hands clenched into fists so tightly my knuckles ached.

"Shut up!" she snapped, her voice loud and defiant, but they only laughed harder.

I wasn't going to let this happen.

I stepped out from the shadows. "Excuse me? Do you want to repeat that again to me?"

My voice cut through their laughter, and they froze.

I stepped forward, my eyes locking with the leader of the group.

"We were just joking around," he said, his voice shaky as he took a step back.

"Yeah?" It took effort to keep my voice calm, to stop myself from destroying him right here in front of everyone. Humans were so much more fragile than they knew. I knew exactly where to strike to make his blood flow in rivulets, soaking the earth while he cried for mercy. "Doesn't look like she's laughing. If you're joking, be funnier."

Their eyes darted between Anya and me. I was tall for my age, already built, lean and strong from training under Rafail's watchful eye.

And unlike most, I didn't care whose blood I spilled.

"We didn't mean anything," the boy mumbled.

I flicked the switchblade in my hand, and the blade sprang to life. The group scattered, muttering excuses as they ran.

"Then get the fuck out of here," I said coldly, my voice leaving no room for argument. "You make fun of her again, and you deal with me."

A part of me hoped they would. I'd given them fair warning.

"Semyon," she said in a small voice. "That's what I meant. You can't just threaten them with a weapon."

I met her eyes. "Wasn't a threat, Anya."

She swallowed and opened her mouth like she was going to protest, but then she just finished quietly, "Thanks."

"Anytime anyone threatens you, Anya. Anytime. You come and tell me."

So MAYBE I don't like the idea of my wife at the bakery without me. Even with a guard. She's not *their* wife. I'm the one that will watch her best.

So I set up my laptop in the corner of the shop and watch as she works. I try to concentrate. But how the hell am I supposed to run through encrypted data and try to identify the source of the email he got when Anya's here? She's moving through the space with confidence, tying her apron on with practiced ease. Flour dusts her fingertips as she prepares dough. She softly hums to herself while she kneads it. A stray strand of hair sneaks out from under her bun. Adorable.

Jesus. I have to focus.

She continues to hum, lost in her own world. I should be focusing more on pressing matters, but once customers start entering, fuck it. I ignore the laptop and sip on a cup of coffee instead.

I have to make sure they're treating her well. My wife. She bags up a few rolls for an elderly woman who talks at length about her dog's ailments. Anya listens patiently, even when the lady begins repeating herself. She hands a free treat to a small child in a stroller after the mother buys a cup of coffee. The blonde toddler waves chubby fingers at Anya in thanks. A middle-aged businessman in a suit grunts about the rising price of tea, but when I clear my throat, he thanks her and takes his leave.

Customer after customer comes in. For today, it's just Anya operating the register, but she looks exhausted come midday.

"Break time," I tell her, turning off my laptop. "Take a lunch break."

Her jaw firms as she meets my gaze and clears her throat. "I don't take lunch breaks."

I feign shock, my brows shooting upward. I know she doesn't take breaks. I know everything about her. She works her fingers to the bone and neglects her own needs, as if driving herself into the ground will finally prove to her what no one else ever has. "Do you mean to tell me you don't take care of my wife?"

Blinking, she opens her mouth as if to protest, then shuts it quickly. With a sigh, she looks down at a tablet and swipes it. I close my laptop and go to join her. "I ordered lunch. It'll be here soon. Quick break, and then back at it, if it makes you feel better."

"Right," she says absently, staring at the tablet.

"What is it?"

With a shrug, she doesn't answer at first, but I don't miss the way her lower lip trembles. Then in a whisper, as if she doesn't trust her voice, she says, "Someone left a...really bad review."

I step forward. She doesn't stop me as I take the tablet from her hands. My gaze moves over the words quickly.

Overpriced. Mediocre. Unoriginal. Stick to something else, sweetheart. Baking obviously isn't your thing.

In an instant, I memorize the name attached to the review. Idiot didn't bother using a screen name.

Anya's eyes shine, but she's trying to keep her tears at bay. I hate that. I hate that something as insignificant as a faceless review can affect her so badly. My fingers tighten around the edge of the tablet, then I place it down.

Before she can move, I swipe my thumb across her cheek and wipe the tear away.

"Who wrote it?" My voice is devoid of emotion.

"It doesn't matter," she mutters, looking away.

Someone knocks at the door. Delivery's arrived.

It *does* matter. And I don't forget.

CHAPTER 14

ANYA

I RAN THROUGH THE STREETS, my pulse racing. The cold air bit my skin. I shouldn't have come, but I had no one else to turn to. Eli was in trouble, and after everything—after the way Semyon kissed me—I imagined something between us had changed.

Rodion said I'd find him at the Wolf and Moon, a local pub.

The place was dimly lit and crowded. It took me a few minutes to find him. And when I did, my heart sank to my toes. He sat in the back corner, as if part of the shadows. But he wasn't alone.

She was beautiful in a cruel way that stole my breath—sharp cheekbones, dark red lips, and a figure like a goddess. I felt like a child in my worn clothes, my hair disheveled, flour dotting my top from the bakery. She leaned in close to Semyon, her manicured fingers tracing her bottle, but her attention was all on him.

Of course it was. He was the hottest, most powerful man in the entire place, all strength and power and disinterest. He didn't react to her but sat perfectly still, his expression unreadable. His eyes met mine.

"Anya?"

I stepped forward, the reason for my errand fading as I stared into his eyes and saw something unfamiliar in his gaze—fear. He looked from me to the woman, then back again. I opened my mouth, prepared to beg for his help. Eli was in trouble.

But the woman followed his line of sight and spotted me. Her lips curved down in disdain. "Who's that?"

I swallowed hard. He held my gaze and blinked slowly behind his glasses before he finally spoke. His nostrils flared; he shook his head at me and mouthed 'Go home,' before he turned his attention to his date.

"No one," he said. "That's no one."

IN A MATTER OF DAYS, we've settled into a rhythm. Semyon likes predictability. You could set a clock by him.

He comes with me to the bakery, sits in the corner and works, sometimes takes calls in the back. He even manages the front when I need to take a break. And he always, always makes me take a lunch break.

Stefan joins us after school, where he tells us every single detail about his day and eats a snack before Semyon asks him about his studies and how his classmates are treating him.

But beneath the pretense of normalcy... I'm wondering when he'll make a move, when he'll touch me again, but he's been careful and considerate.

I remember what he said about consummating our marriage. But how can we possibly do that when he's in one room and I'm in another?

A part of me wants that validation, wants to know he really cares about me, that he really finds me *attractive.*

So when his sisters invite me out to get drinks with them, I leap at the chance to get away. I mean, I'm not *really* getting away. We have bodyguards, of course. But when I see the glinting sign above the door in fluorescent lighting, my heart twists.

Wolf and Moon.

Ugh. I remember this place so damn clearly.

Yana proudly sits where her brother normally would, with a glint in her eye and bulge by her side that tells me she's just waiting for someone to fuck with us.

The bar is loud and noisy, but I let myself sink into the chaos. In a world of perfectly ordered events, it feels nice to let loose a little, to let the burn of alcohol soften the edges of my frustration. Yana drinks like vodka's water, her sharp eyes scanning the room. Rodion's wife Ember laughs beside them, relaxed and at ease.

"How's married life treating you?" she asks suddenly, tipping her head back to take another shot. The question is almost too casual. I get the distinct feeling they're on my side, but they want to be sure I'm okay.

I force a smile. "Fine."

Yana smiles sadly. "Liar."

"Hey, come on," Ember says, elbowing her playfully. Her red hair is in a messy bun, her eyes bright. "Let her enjoy her night. She doesn't want to talk about your emotionally stunted brother."

I laugh, but it's forced. Because I remember a night just like this, years ago, only I was a girl and Semyon broke my heart.

"I'm sorry, Anya," Zoya says, shaking her head. "I know it's going to take time. He's not...Semyon's so driven by duty, he somehow forgets that the people in his life are, in fact...well, people."

I shake my head and drown my sorrows in another drink, envious of Yana's high tolerance for liquor, Zoya's calm, and Ember's happy marriage. I'm determined to prove myself. I drink a shot. A glass of wine. Another drink, followed by another, until the memory of the past blurs and I'm laughing right along with the others.

Until *he* stands in the doorway.

"Your husband's here," Ember says, too soon, her eyes twinkling. "I'll be sure to bring those books when we meet." Ember's promised me a few reads to occupy me at the next family dinner.

I hug them all goodbye and take my sweet time walking—or, more accurately, half toppling, to where my husband waits.

He kisses my cheek. I move away, the memory of the night he hurt me vivid. I turn from him, nearly stumbling.

"Anya. How much have you had to drink?"

I shrug. "Lost track."

And fuck you.

He half carries me to the car, swats my hand away when I try to open my own door with a frown, then fastens my seat belt. The cold leather feels good against my heated skin. And still... I want to cry.

The drive is quiet at first—too quiet. The warmth of the alcohol makes my cheeks feel too hot.

"Did you have a good time?"

"Yes. They're excellent company." I hope he hears the note of sarcasm in my voice. "*They* hug me."

I look out the window. I don't care if I sound like a child. The lights feel too bright, my emotions too close to the surface.

"Unlike some people I know," I whisper. My voice sounds slurred, but it cuts through the silence.

"Excuse me?" He exhales. When I look at him, his knuckles are white on the steering wheel. "You're drunk, Anya. We won't have this conversation now."

"Oh?" I ask, with a mirthless laugh. I want to break through his relentless control so fucking badly. "So what? I can't say the truth. You don't even look at me half the time. I'm...I'm no one, remember?"

He stiffens beside me. "So *that's* what this is about."

No, Semyon. That's not what this is about. This is about you ruining my life. This is about you pretending like I'm nothing to you when our past says something different. This is about you sleeping in another bed like I'll taint yours, taking care of me in all the ways you want to and none of the ways that matter.

This is about you breaking my heart.

But I don't say anything to him.

"You don't know who she was, Anya. She would've destroyed you."

I look out the window and shake my head. I don't trust myself to speak.

The car jerks slightly as he pulls over without warning, tires grinding against the pavement. In an instant, he's turned toward me, his blue eyes blazing. He blinks slowly. I swallow, but it feels like a gulp. The slow blink behind the glasses...

"You think I don't want you?" His voice is quiet. Dangerous. "You think I don't feel it every second you're near me?"

My breath catches. The air between us is thick. Charged.

"I'm no one," I whisper.

I don't know how I get there, but I'm in his lap, straddling him. His hands are tangled in my hair. He pulls it back. I'm instantly sober.

"I stay away from you because if I don't, I won't be able to stop." His breath is warm against my skin.

My heart beats so fast I'm dizzy. He's never looked at me like this before... like he's unraveling. Like for once in his life, he can't control me.

I whisper, "You broke my heart, Semyon. Did you know that? I *loved* you." My voice trembles, raw and aching. "And you looked at a stranger, someone prettier, older, more powerful than I was, someone who was everything I wasn't, and you told her I was *nothing* to you."

A hot tear slips down my cheek, then another. I blink, but they keep falling, thick and unstoppable. My breath shudders. "And you...you were my world."

"Anya." His voice cracks, rough with something I can't name.

"And when my mother begged you to stop Eli, to get him out of the danger he was in, you didn't. You didn't help her that day, Semyon, and you could have."

I drop my head to his shoulder. I try to hold it in, but I can't. A sob rips from my throat, and I can't stop it. I wail, gasping against the weight of everything I lost, everything I've carried. I weep for my mother. I weep for the girl I once was. I cry like my heart is shattering all over again. Maybe it is. Maybe a part of me will always be that girl, the one who loved too deeply and only ever wanted someone to love her back.

He grips my shoulders, forcing me to look at him. "Listen to me. I'm done covering for everyone else. Your brother made terrible decisions, and I fucking covered for him. I intervened, over and over, until I couldn't stop the tidal wave. Eli was in too deep. I tried, Anya, even at my own expense.

When you saw me running away...Fuck, Anya. Please just trust me. Please trust that I did what I could."

I stare at him. Semyon is not a good man, but he doesn't lie. I let myself believe he could've prevented her dying, that he could've stopped Eli from his demise. What if all this time I've been wrong?

"And that day at the bar? *Anya.* That was not some random woman but Carolina Korchev. A predator. In Bratva circles, she was a shark swimming in blood, raised in violence, trained to manipulate. She wanted control. She wanted *me.* She would've made you suffer, Anya. She would've hurt you, and I feared I couldn't stop it. *She's* no one, Anya. But I'm sorry. I'm so sorry that hurt you."

His lips meet mine as he holds me to him. I taste the salt of my tears before he releases me and holds me to his chest. I cry until the quiet after the storm rolls in. My eyes are swollen, my face puffy. It hurts to blink.

"Then why don't you want me?"

"Bozhe, Anya." He exhales, his voice rough, almost broken. *"Chyort voz'mi, ty menya svedesh' s uma."*

I'm driving him...insane? *Me?*

"Then why do you keep pushing me away?" I whisper.

Taking my chin in his hand, he brings my gaze to his. "Listen to me, Anya. I've done everything I can to protect you. I want you. I want you more than I've ever wanted anything in my life. When I found out the Irish were moving in, I—"

The Irish?

He shakes his head and clenches his jaw, his voice steady but his eyes blazing. "You're drunk, love. I'm going to carry you upstairs. You're going to have some water and a drink I'll make for you, then I'm putting you to bed."

He leans in and kisses my cheek. "And when you're sober, Anya. We're going to revisit this conversation."

I let him carry me upstairs.

Roll down the covers.

Undress me and help me get ready for bed.

I drink the water he gives me and take the meds, before I close my eyes and sleep.

CHAPTER 15

SEMYON

I STAND in the middle of the grand living room of our family estate. This house, ironically nicknamed "The Cottage," hums with activity as our family gathers. My eyes drift to Anya, chatting with Rodion's wife, Ember. They're sitting on a loveseat, just far enough apart to remain polite, but I notice every movement. Anya's back is straight, her eyes flicking to me every so often, but her smile at Ember is genuine. It's relieved. Ember isn't like the rest of us. She wasn't born into the mafia and barely understands this world. But she's loyal to my brother, and that's enough.

Last night, I tucked Anya into bed. Made her drink water with electrolytes and take pain relievers. She slept hard, and right when I went to talk to her, Stefan woke up for breakfast and Rafail called.

"We have information about Eli."

I've waited this long for my wife. But I won't wait much longer.

Rafail paces by the window, his hands buried in his pockets, dressed as always in a bespoke suit. His wife, Polina, is seated nearby, scrolling through a tablet with Yana, my sister. When Anya and I arrived earlier, the greetings were quick—just little waves and smiles—but I noticed the way their warmth touched Anya. Zoya, my youngest sister, immediately took Stefan under her wing.

"I'm baking cookies in the kitchen," Zoya said with a big smile, crouching to Stefan's level. "Want to help?"

Stefan had looked to me for permission. I gave him a small nod.

Good. He's learning.

After I checked on his room and how well he'd followed my instructions, I told him he did a good job. His little face lit up with pride.

Anya doesn't belong here. She's fire in a world of ice. So while I'm fine with Stefan following Zoya to the kitchen, I make Anya stay where I can see her.

Always within my line of sight. I won't ever forget the way she looked at me when she told me I broke her heart.

I'll make it up to her.

Rafail turns to me, his expression grim. "The Morozovs demand payment," he says. "And there's word that the Irish are pressing in on our territory."

The Irish. My god. In recent years, the Irish have grown in strength and number, commanding all of the eastern coast of Ireland but strengthening their connections in Boston. Their tendrils reach deep into the underworld of Europe and North America, and every goddamn one of us knows it.

"What does that mean for us?" Polina asks.

"It means," I say, stepping closer to Anya, "that everyone needs to be accounted for. It means our enemies will exploit any weakness." For one brief, passing moment, I almost call Zoya back to us, so I can assure myself that she and Stefan didn't walk to the kitchen and straight into a trap.

I turn back to Rafail. "And what about Elizar?"

I can feel Anya's eyes burning into me. I wish she trusted me the way she did when we were younger.

We'll get there.

Before he can respond, the front door bursts open. My uncle and aunt stride in; their presence is an immediate reminder of the rot that sometimes infects even the closest families. Eduard's gaze narrows on Anya, and Irma walks in on a wave of blonde hair and perfume.

Their son Matvei enters behind them. He and his brother Gleb grew up alongside us. Strong, dependable, and unwavering in support of our family, it's been a thorn in his side that his nuclear family lacks the same loyalty.

Broad-shouldered, with a quiet intensity, Matvei knows the ins and outs of Bratva life better than most.

Matvei nods to me. "Semyon, we have to talk," he says quietly. "Later."

My grandfather catches my eye from across the room. He's seated in an armchair, and when he winks at me, I'm not sure what it means. Subtle body language has never been my strength.

"This is a delicate situation," my grandfather says, his wise gaze settling on Anya. "We protect our own."

"Always," Rafail growls, standing to his full height, his fists clenched. "Matvei, show us what you found." Grainy footage fills the flat-screen TV on the wall.

Eli. His face is bloodied, broken, his nose at an odd angle, red lacerations on exposed skin.

Something tightens in my chest.

Eli was my friend.

I married his sister.

We thought he betrayed us. I took her as payment. And now...

I cross to Anya and rest my hand on the back of her neck. I'm not sure what it's supposed to accomplish, but I've seen Rafail do it, and it always seemed to help.

"Where did you get this?" I ask. "Was it a plant? Did someone send it to you?"

"My inbox," Rafail answers.

The footage continues. A pair of hands wraps duct tape around Eli's mouth and shoves him into the trunk of a car.

"I don't understand," Anya says, her voice breaking. "What does this mean? Someone tell me." Her eyes meet mine as she utters one whisper. "*Semyon.*"

My heart tumbles in my chest. All she has to say is my name in that tone, edged with desperation, and I'll do anything, fucking anything, for her.

"It means we've been operating under the assumption that your brother ran," I say quietly. "But he didn't. He was taken. This is a message."

"Or a plant," Matvei says, his massive arms crossed over his chest. He's loyal to our family to a fault, constantly questioning motives and truth.

"Why?" she demands, shaking her head. "Why him? He got into so much trouble with so many people. I can't even tell you how many threats came to our door..."

She flattens her palm against her chest. My fingers on her neck tighten.

If only I'd known. If only I'd paid attention.

"I didn't know," I say softly, my voice steady.

"Neither did I. I knew he was gambling, but I thought he ran. That's why I... I thought he'd left his phone behind to avoid being traced."

Yana taps her chin thoughtfully. "Or maybe he was planning to run. But someone got to him first."

"Wait," Anya says, her eyes narrowing on the screen. "Go back. The first few seconds, there's something I thought was just a blur, but—I want a closer look. Please."

Yana rewinds it.

"Look closer," Anya says as Yana zooms in on the footage. "Can you zoom in further?"

A flash of a hand crosses the screen—a fleeting image almost too quick to notice. But when Yana pauses the frame and zooms, we see it clearly: a shamrock tattoo with a drop of blood beneath it.

"The Irish," Rafail says, shaking his head. "I knew it."

"You were the one who brought this filth into our family," Eduard says, his eyes narrowing on me. "They aren't Bratva. They aren't family. And now, because of this bullshit, our family's at risk." He points an irate finger at Anya. "She—"

"*Enough.*"

I don't raise my voice with Eduard or anyone, but I let my eyes sweep around the room, making sure every gaze is locked on me.

No one will ever make my wife feel like less than again.

No one.

"I don't care who Anya was affiliated with before we took our vows. I don't care who you care about, where your allegiances lie, who you question, or what you think is going on here. But I want to make something very, very clear." I narrow my eyes, my voice cold and sharp as steel.

"Anya is my wife. *My wife.* And you will treat her with the same respect you owe anyone in this family—no, even more so because she has given up more to be my wife than any of you have for your roles. She wasn't born into this world, and you know it."

Anya watches me, her eyes wide and soft. Something in me aches.

Irma's eyes flare with indignation, her lips pressing together in a tight, bloodless line, but she's smart enough not to push me. Not now.

Eduard fumes but doesn't speak. I continue.

"I'll take her back to her home and comb through everything her brother left behind."

Rafail nods, his gaze sweeping across the room. "One week. During that time, we go about life as if everything is normal. But no one—fucking *no one*—goes anywhere without a guard. No unnecessary risks. Everyone will be under observation in case we need to track anyone, and all of us will report back here every night for dinner."

I blink at him in surprise. The last thing I want to do is to haul Stefan and Anya back here for dinner every single night. But before I can voice my protest, Rafail holds up a hand.

"Stress like this will tear our family apart, Semyon." Rafail fixes his sharp gaze on Rodion next. "You know this as well as I do. And our family has been through too much to risk breaking apart now."

Rodion smirks. "You gonna check our homework too? So you're making us report to family dinner like a dad?"

"Watch it, Rodion, or that's exactly what I'll do," Rafail snaps.

Rodion, despite being one of the most ruthless men in our group, falls silent, though there's a glint of humor in his eyes.

"And make sure Vadka is included," Rafail adds. Vadka, Rafail's best friend, is loyal to the Kopolov Bratva to the bone but has more pressing needs when it comes to family. Not related by blood, Vadka's married with a child and no longer spends as much time with us as he did before. He's always the first to go home.

Though his situation has changed, his loyalty to us has *not*.

But Eduard and Irma, who remain quiet, are another story. Their younger son Gleb betrayed us and paid the ultimate price, and while Matvei stands firm with us, I don't trust his parents for a second.

"Excellent," Grandfather says with a dry chuckle, his eyes gleaming as they move to Anya. He's learned the art of not allowing the intensity and stress of the ups and downs of Bratva life to steal the light from his eyes.

"I look forward to coming back together like this." He turns to my wife. "Anya, love, if we're to have dinner together every night, like in the old days, will you bring some of those delicious rolls your mother used to make? Do you still make them?"

His eyes gleam with an almost childlike excitement.

Anya can't hide the weight of everything we've discussed pressing on her, but she smiles benevolently at my grandfather. "I make *everything* my mother taught me," she says warmly. "I'll bring whatever you want."

Rafail's stoic mask cracks slightly, a faint smile tugging at his lips. He runs a hand along the beard on his jaw. "*Anything?*"

"Anything," Anya confirms with a nod. "Do you have a favorite, Rafail?"

"He has a special place in his heart for *medovik*," Polina says.

"Ooh, yes, my mother's honey cake is famous. We brought a sampling home yesterday but can bring more soon. Semyon seemed to enjoy them." I smile.

Rafail's brows dart up. "You mean to tell me Semyon ate... *pastry?*"

Rodion whistles. I drag my finger across my throat to tell them to shut the fuck up, but they predictably ignore me.

Anya looks at me with a blank expression on her face. "No?"

"A pastry. For breakfast." Rafail shakes his head as if she just announced we bought a pet unicorn with a purple mane.

Anya looks bewildered. "What's the big deal?"

To her, it's only pastry. To my brothers, it's something entirely different.

"Nothing's the matter, really," Rafail explains to her. "It's just that Semyon's a creature of habit. I haven't seen him eat anything but a breakfast with perfect macronutrients, including fifty-five grams of protein, since he was eighteen years old. Cheat days? Semyon doesn't *have* them."

Why are they going on about this? "I had no idea this was such a revelatory thing. I can change my mind."

Rodion snorts. "Apparently, for the right pus—"

"Finish that sentence," I warn him darkly. I will kick his ass right here, right now, and make him apologize to my wife in front of everyone. He clamps his mouth shut and shakes his head, turning to Anya.

"Sorry, it's not you. It's just—" He pauses. "No, it is definitely you, but I mean nothing by it."

Anya stares at me. I shrug.

My grandfather rises to his feet while unsteady on his legs. "If you'll excuse me, I need a nap," he says, walking out. "It was a pleasure to meet you, my dear, and I'm very much looking forward to spending more time together."

They all begin to scatter.

Polina clasps her hands under her chin. "Do you have any American-style pastries?" Polina lived in New York, where the Romanov family resides.

Anya nods. "We have New York-style cheesecake, which is particularly popular."

"Oh." Polina breathes. Anya smiles at me shyly.

I take Anya's hand. "We have work to do. Let's go check in on Stefan." I turn to the others. "Six o'clock."

It's just Anya and me. Something just happened in such a short time, and I'm unsure of how I feel. Those emotions don't typically come to my mind.

"So we have to go to my house," she says, biting her lip.

I don't want to go back to her house. I want to take her home to *our* place, lay her down, and show her in vivid detail how much she means to me. But duty calls.

My hands tighten. There are a few things I have to control within the world, in my power, to make my wife happy. I hate the idea of bringing her back to that shithole riddled with negative memories.

"We'll go together and make it a short visit. But yes."

"We have to find Eli," she says in a rush of words. "I want this done as quickly as possible. If he isn't to blame, Semyon... god..."

I nod in agreement. "The sooner we go, the better." Her family home is likely under watch. I'm well aware this could be a setup.

"Is Stefan okay here for a little while? My father won't be home if we leave now."

"Of course he is. I trust my siblings with my life."

She nods, takes in a deep breath, and releases it slowly. "Let's do this."

CHAPTER 16

ANYA

I STAND in the stunning Kopolov family kitchen, mustering up the sternest voice I can, which doesn't hold a candle to Semyon's.

"Stefan, you listen to Zoya and any of the other people here," I tell him, petrified that my brother is going to do something reckless and the Kopolovs won't be too happy about it. I know how Rafail is. Jesus, I know how Semyon is.

"He'll be fine," Zoya says with a smile. "Won't you? We'll make popcorn and watch a movie."

Stefan gives her a side look. "Do you watch superheroes?"

"I love superheroes. Spider-Man is my favorite."

Of course she would love Spider-Man with his self-deprecating ways and nerdy teenage awkwardness. I love that. I give Zoya a little smile. "Superman's mine."

If Semyon understands the reference, he doesn't let on.

I don't like being separated from Stefan. We've been through so much in a short amount of time, and I worry about what it's going to do to him. But then I watch him with Zoya, and I see him smiling. When I look at Semyon, there's something about the steadfast way he watches all of us that brings me a small measure of comfort.

"Where are you going?" Stefan asks, his eyes darting between Semyon and me. "With my sister?"

My heart. My fierce little protector. Semyon gives him a little smirk, almost a smile. "We have some information to find, and we believe some of what we need is back at your home. Is there anything you want us to get for you while we're there?"

"You're going back home with her? I'm coming."

Oh, Stefan.

I shake my head. "You can't. It isn't safe right now. You need to stay here where you're protected."

"If it's not safe for me, why is it safe for *you?*"

Stefan gets that glint in his eyes, the one he always has when he wants to fight and gets himself into trouble. Semyon steps forward and bends down so that he and my brother are at eye level.

"Your sister is safe because she's with me."

And I feel it in my bones, carved into my heart. He means it. He means every word. A lump rises in my throat, and I'm not sure if it's because of my brother's protection or... my husband.

I used to feel safe with him. But then he changed. Or did he?

And for the first time, I wonder... Maybe *I* was the one who changed.

Maybe our circumstances did. Because right now, standing in the kitchen with the boy I loved by my side, I wonder if there's a small part of my heart that doesn't love him still. After all these years.

"Let's go," Semyon says, reaching for my hand and lacing my fingers through his. Our palms meet. I have to draw in a breath.

"Semyon, if Eli was taken—"

"Yeah, I know," Semyon says wryly. "If he survives this, he'll fucking kill me."

I can't help but smile.

"Remember that time?"

"The time he found us soaked to the skin in the shed. All I was trying to do was keep you warm." He shakes his head. "Yeah, I remember that."

I thought Eli was going to *murder* Semyon. I'd never seen him hit anybody before, but he landed a right hook squarely to Semyon's jaw.

And I knew Semyon could fight—I'd seen him in action, and the vicious, calculating way he moved gave me nightmares. But with Eli, he didn't even raise a hand to defend himself.

My brother didn't believe him. I screamed at him to stop and dragged him off of Semyon.

"Did he hurt you?" Eli asked.

Hurt me? Hell, yes, he hurt me. But not in any way that my brother would understand.

"We talked about that on more than one occasion," Semyon says with a wry half smile as we head outside. He never really smiles in a way that reaches his eyes. Always guarded. Always distant.

"Did you?" I ask him curiously.

"Yeah."

Semyon opens the car door. I reach for the handle of the car on autopilot, not processing what I'm doing, when a low growl makes me freeze.

Oh. Right. I don't open my own door when he's around.

He reaches for the door to unlatch it, opening it for me. "That was a close one, Anya," he warns. "Do you really want to have that talk if you disobey me?"

I squirm as a delicious thread of need claws through me.

I'm warming to it.

"What do you have to search back at your home?" he asks me, changing the subject as he slides into the driver's seat. His car is impeccable, immaculately clean, and not a speck of dust. I note everything. The way it starts right up, the gas tank is full, no flashing lights on the dash indicating it needs to be serviced.

I don't know why I'm focused on these details now. It feels like they matter.

"I'm hoping we can access his computer and the phone that he left behind. My father will be out."

Semyon's jaw tightens as he pulls onto the road and begins to accelerate. "I knew your father before he was an alcoholic. I knew him when he was sober."

I look out the window. "Yeah. Me too."

We don't speak for long minutes. "What time does he usually come home?"

"Later."

I glance at the clock. We probably have two hours. My nerves rise the closer we get to home—no. Not home. I don't live there anymore. There's no small measure of relief when it comes to that.

I don't want Semyon to see the shit I grew up in. It's nothing he hasn't seen before, but now that I'm married and know what *his* home looks like, I'm embarrassed.

"You're wringing your hands, Anya." I'm not sure if he's expecting a response when his large hand comes to rest on my knee and gives me a gentle squeeze.

I didn't realize the way I was nervously tapping my knee, clearing my throat, and tugging at a lock of my hair. Did he actually notice those things too?

His hand slides slowly on my thigh, flexing. I remember the kiss earlier. I remember when I was a girl how badly I would've done anything to have Semyon's attention like this. To have him touch me.

"You kissed me once," I say quietly.

"Jesus," he curses.

I blink at him in surprise. "What?"

"Anya, honey, I held myself back so "many fucking times,"
he says, shaking his head.

I want him to say it again.

"I was obsessed with you, but you were too young for me,
and my world was too dangerous."

I look at him sideways and move his hand further up my leg.

"And I'm old enough now?"

"Yeah, baby, and you're as fucking dangerous as I am."

Baby.

Me? Dangerous? He cuts his gaze to me, those beautiful
blue eyes hidden behind his glasses. "Do I look like the kind
of person who exaggerates?"

Thump.

My heart.

I distract myself on my phone when a text comes in from
Ophelia.

> **Ophelia**
> Um, you know the other day you got that
> bad review you told me about?
>
> Yeah

Semyon wasn't the only one I cried to.

Oh no. I give Semyon a sidelong glance before I reply.

I narrow my eyes at Semyon. "Semyon," I say warningly.

"Mmm?"

I gulp. "Did you beat up the asshole who left me the terrible review?"

"Well, not *directly*..."

"Semyon!"

He frowns, a crease forming between his brows. "No one treats my wife that way, Anya," he says, as if that's the natural order of things. To him, maybe it is.

No. Not maybe.

I'm quiet for long minutes. "And all this time," I say in a whisper, "I thought you hated me."

"*Hated* you? Are you fucking kidding me?" He shakes his head. "I'm half-tempted to pull this car over right now just to put you over my knee for that."

I stare. His eyes dart to the side of the road, as if looking for a place to actually park. My pulse spikes. The tension between us is palpable.

"Um. Let's save that for later," I whisper. "We have work to do. Also, I'm...sober now."

"I'm aware." I watch as he breathes in through his nose and out again. Finally, he nods.

"I don't hate you and never have. I distanced myself because I didn't want to hurt you." His voice lowers. "There's a difference."

In silence, we turn down my street. He parks the car. "Now, baby, let's get this over with so I can get you back home to myself."

I turn to him and let my head fall to his shoulder.

No one treats my wife that way.

At first, he freezes as if he doesn't remember what to do.

Then he opens his arms. I tuck my head into the crook of his neck, and his arms come around me.

"Do you like that, Anya? Does that feel nice? If it does, I need to know. I need to learn how to... comfort you." His voice lowers to a half growl as he welcomes me closer, his arms tightening. "C'mere."

I blink back hot tears, my voice a shaky whisper. "Yeah. I like this." I smile. "You're doing great. Just like you did the other night."

He strokes his hand down the length of my back, leaving a

trail of goosebumps. "I like that too." He sounds almost surprised.

The moment feels fragile, like a dream I'm afraid to wake from. I blink back the tears and sit up.

We have work to do.

"Let's do this."

"Yeah," he says in a husky whisper. "Let's go. But we can come back to this whenever you want."

I can't help it. I lean in and kiss his prickly, stubbled cheek before I sit back in my seat and let him come and open my door for me.

Then I remember we're going to my home and how I hate that he's here with me.

When Semyon looks around my apartment, I feel something tighten in my stomach. It's not the first time he's been here, but I wonder if he's forgotten—

"You did a beautiful job here, Anya. I remember what it was like growing up, and I can see that you put your touch everywhere."

I could be hormonal, but I think that might be one of the nicest things anybody's ever said to me. There are very few people in this world who know your history—your siblings, your parents, a childhood friend. But Semyon... he's one of them. He knows. It's one of the reasons why I've never been able to trust him.

"Thank you," I say, turning my back to him so he doesn't see the tears shining in my eyes. What is wrong with me? I'm an emotional basket case.

"I remember every detail of this place, and I can see how hard you've worked."

I don't even know if Semyon has a clue what he's saying to me or how it's making me feel. He's so detached, so clinical.

I don't think he sees things the way other people do, and hell, if that isn't one of the things I love most about him.

"His phone is in my bedroom."

Semyon frowns and shoves his hands in his pockets but doesn't respond. He trails behind me, taking in every detail as if staking the place.

When I get to the room, I open my top drawer filled with what my mother would've called my "unmentionables." I pull it open and rifle through the soft satin and lace in shades of pink, white, and black... one of the few things that did *not* belong to my mother. These are all *mine*.

I like wearing sexy underwear and bras; they make me feel pretty, special—almost like I have a little secret no one else knows. Ophelia's family owns a clothing business, and whenever they discounted items, she'd bring me in. I'd pick out something here and there, and her father would exchange them for loaves of bread and muffins instead.

"It's right—" That's when I see Semyon staring. I freeze midsentence and give him a curious look. "What?"

"I take it back," he says in a rough whisper.

"Take what back?"

"I told you not to bring your clothes back. That drawer... Fucking empty it. I want to see you in every one of those when we get home."

I stare at him, my hand embedded in the drawer of silk and satin undergarments.

Is he serious?

"All right..."

"Do you have the phone?" he asks, his voice tight. He looks around my childish bedroom, which hasn't changed much since he knew me. I still have the rickety bookshelf with my favorite books, the faded pink duvet, and the second-hand furniture my mother painted white. A room frozen in time.

"It's in here," I say, wondering why he's suddenly gone rigid, his look murderous. "What's the matter?"

My pulse quickens with the intensity of his gaze.

"What's the matter?" he growls. "If you don't get me out of here, I'm going to—" He bites his words off and shakes his head. "I've wanted you for so goddamn long. I've held myself back, Anya, and I don't know how much restraint I have left in me."

I blink, his words sending a shiver down my spine. "You... you've wanted me?"

His eyes meet mine, and for a moment, one single moment, the years between us disappear. It's just Semyon, my childhood dream crush, and I'm just his best friend's sister.

"Always," he whispers. "But not like I do *now*. Not when you were too young. I buried it, kept my distance. Kept you safe. But now there's no fucking reason for me not to lay you on that pink bed and ruin you."

I stare at him, our mission forgotten. My hatred for him a

distant memory. I stare at the only man I've ever loved and say what I know will break his tightly held restraint.

"Do it."

A thrill runs through me when he snaps. He lifts me in his arms, and my legs wrap around him, my arms around his shoulders. His thick cock pulses between my legs, and my sex throbs. I ache for him, even as I fear what it will feel like.

His lips brush the shell of my ear. "I saw the way your face fell when we came in here. Today will be the last day you ever darken these doors. But I want your last memory of this place to be one you cherish, Anya. One that's burned into your memory and erased all others before it."

I blink back tears. I'm a wreck. My arms encircle his neck. "Semyon, you already have."

His eyes meet mine, and this time, they aren't cold but engulfed in flame. "Strip, baby, and spread your legs. I want to taste you."

With shaking hands and my heart racing, I tug off my clothes. His hands meet mine, helping me. Impatient. My need grows.

"Hands by your side, Anya." He nudges my knees apart with his.

I do what he says obediently despite my pounding heart. He slips off his glasses. Folds them. Tucks them next to my leg on the bed. Sinks to the floor and drapes my legs over his shoulders.

Oh my god.

The next thing I know, his eyes are closed, and he's inhaling my fragrance with a groan as if he's going to lose his self-control. Something about my stoic, possessive, utterly controlling husband losing his mind at my scent alone makes me want to cry.

He plants a kiss to my sex, and my hips jerk. His eyes meet mine with a wicked glint, holding my gaze as the tip of his tongue sinks between my folds.

Oh. Dear. *God.*

I've never felt anything like this in my life. I feel vulnerable and excited and so damn wet. I want more of him, but at the same time, I want to hide.

He licks again with the flat of his tongue. The sound of his groans fills the room.

Pausing, he laps at my inner thigh. "You drive me fucking insane," he growls. "*No one* makes me lose control but you, Anya. *Only you.*" His tongue finds my clit as he traces my entrance with his fingers. "*Khristos,*" he says on a moan. "You're so fucking wet. This is what I want, love. I want you wet for me before I take you. I need to make sure that you're ready for me."

My head falls back, and I'm lost to sensation again. He licks down the length of my slit, spreads my legs, and pokes his tongue in my core. I squirm as delicious heat trickles through me. I moan, letting myself go, lost to pleasure that only Semyon can give.

My god, it feels *so good.* My eyes flit by the bookshelf, still filled with the books I read as a little girl.

I know then that he's right. My memory of this place will never be the same. I'll be forever changed because of Semyon—because of what we're doing on my pale-pink bedspread in my terrible apartment that holds nothing but bad memories for me.

I'll remember this.

Us.

I'm so turned on that every stroke of his tongue pushes me closer to the edge.

"How does that feel?" he asks, and I realize then he *wants* direction.

"Yes," I whisper when he suckles, and when it's too much, I rake my fingers in his hair. "Oooh, easy. Yes, yes, like that."

The flat of his tongue presses before he sucks again and circles my clit.

I can feel the first spasm of pleasure coming, my need increasing, my ability to hold self-control gone.

"Come on my mouth, baby." His hot breath brands my inner thighs. "Come on my tongue. I want to hear you. Let yourself go, Anya."

My hips jerk, my breath is a moan, a scream I don't recognize escapes my lips, and then I come. My climax is so hard I'm boneless, pleasure wrecking every cell of my body. My vision blurs, my pulse races, electric waves of pleasure washing through me and erasing all else.

He licks me to perfection, and when he's done, and I sag onto the bed half spent, he drags the back of his hand across his mouth and meets my eyes with a wicked, rare smile that makes my heart flutter in my chest.

"You liked that," he says with obvious pride.

"Armph," is all I can say. I'm incapable of actual words.

I watch him in a daze as he unbuckles his belt and tugs it through the loops. Then he unfastens his pants and pushes them down, his thick cock springing free.

I want him inside me so bad I'm practically salivating.

A nervous flutter tickles across my chest. I've never seen a man this close before, not like this. Ophelia and I have giggled over videos and pictures and things we read online, but this—this is next level.

He still wears his T-shirt, but it clings against the planes of his muscles as if the fabric worships him like I do.

"I'll do my best to take you slow," he begins.

"Please don't," I say in a whisper. "Please."

"Jesus fucking Christ," he growls before he leans his weight on me and presses the head of his swollen cock to my soaking hot center. I hold my breath, but he only shakes his head. "Breathe, Anya," he says, bending his mouth to my neck and kissing me there. I giggle because it tickles, but it still makes me wet. "Spread your legs. Relax. Don't tense up; you can't tense up."

His voice is so soft and gentle it's hard to imagine why I hated the man I thought of as being so cold.

He slides the head of his cock inside me, and I let out a moan.

"Did that hurt?" he asks, trembling with the effort of holding himself back.

I shake my head. "A little."

"Alright, baby," he whispers in my ear. "Let me make it better."

The first thrust brings both pain and pleasure. *So much pleasure.*

Too much. Too good.

My pulse races. I was unprepared for the way this feels. My arms encircle his neck. He stills inside me, the walls of my pussy hugging his cock. "Are you all right?" he asks quietly in my ear.

I nod. "I'm so good," I whisper back. "But you need to move, or I might die."

I'll do anything to see the corner of his mouth quirk up again like that. The fleeting smile feels like a victory. My cold strategist disarmed. He obliges, pulling back before thrusting in again, a slow, deliberate rhythm that makes me whimper as pleasure unfurls inside me.

Each movement pulls me in deeper as he thrusts, building a rhythm of pleasure and pain.

"Anya," he whispers.

My nails bite into his shoulders as my world shatters into brilliant shards. My climax blinds me, overwhelms me, wrecks me. He pumps into me, spilling his hot seed with a groan as we come together.

His forehead meets mine. Our breaths mingle, and our fingers entwine.

Vulnerability flashes in his eyes before he blinks it away, but I see it. I savor it. I cherish it.

The man hidden beneath the cold façade... scarred, burdened, but so capable of what terrifies him more than any enemy ever could.

With a kiss to my shoulder, he cocoons me in the pink blanket.

A door opens outside the room.

"In here."

CHAPTER 17

SEMYON

ANYA PANICS and holds the pink duvet tighter around her.

"My father," she hisses. "Semyon!"

"Get dressed," I tell her, drawing a gun. I open her bedroom door and close it shut behind me.

It's a small place, so I'm immediately in front of Lazar, Anya's father. He didn't come alone.

"What the fuck are you doing here?" Lazar snarls. "Kopolov. I thought giving you my daughter was enough."

"Anya and I came here to pick up some of her belongings." I level my cold gaze on his associates—one short, older man with a potbelly, his jowls swinging when he turns to look at Lazar. The other is balding, thin, and frail, but for the cold promise in his eyes. He leans on a cane and looks at the two of us with mild curiosity, the way one might survey an animal caught in a trap. Behind them, strapping bodyguards are stationed, all armed.

I don't fucking care. I know exactly how I could take them all down. I scan the room and take stock of the exits, the guards, and the weapons on my person and at hand. My instincts sharpen. I'd kill every last one of them to get my wife out of here unscathed.

The one with the cane would be the first to go. Bastard looks like he has one foot out the door to hell already. Quick and easy—a shot to the knee would cripple him instantly. The potbellied one? Slow. He wouldn't last ten seconds in a fight. The guards might prove to be a problem, but I can tell by the way they're slouched and hold their weapons lazily that they may be armed but sloppy. Their stances are too loose, their gazes unfocused. Probably fucking high. I'd strike fast, disarm the closest one, and then use his weapon to eliminate the other before they knew what hit them.

My hands twitch at my sides. I could protect her. I *would* protect her—no matter how much blood I had to spill in the process.

If it comes to that. It better not. She belongs here as well as anyone. I wonder if she heard him. She doesn't know he arranged for her marriage long before I gave her the illusion of consent.

"Did you set us up?" the man with the cane demands, glaring at Lazar.

"Of course not. I had no idea they'd be here."

I draw in a breath and stand up straighter. "He's telling the truth. We came to retrieve a few of Anya's belongings." We have no idea who was involved in Eli's supposed abduction. For all I know, it was Lazar's doing. He certainly seems to think of his children as bargaining chips.

The door to the bedroom opens, and Anya steps out, fully dressed, her hair tucked into a neat bun at the nape of the neck, elegant and poised. You'd never know I just took her virginity on the soft pink duvet.

I liked the way she looked wrapped up in it, my very own little present.

"What the fuck are you up to?" Lazar snarls at her. I turn to face him, blood boiling in my veins.

"Speak to my wife like that again, and I'll cut out your tongue."

No one moves.

Lazar's voice is a dangerous slur. "You dare to come into my home and threaten me?"

Why does everyone always think it's a threat?

I tip my head. "You dare to speak to a queen of the Kopolov Bratva with disrespect?"

He takes a step toward me, but I cluck my tongue and shake my head. Since I've mentioned *queen of the Kopolov Bratva*, none of the other men move. I'm well within my rights to punish him for disrespect, and their interference could start a war. Every move is careful, calculated.

One of the guards cracks his knuckles and steps closer. "Lay one finger on her," I warn, my voice deadly calm, even as I'm mentally pulling the trigger. "And I'll cut off your fucking hand."

The room goes silent. Good. They know I'm not bluffing.

"Now, is there a reason why you're here?" I keep my gun trained on them.

"I had work here to do."

"Work?" Anya says, shaking her head. "There's nothing here for you to work on. Why don't you leave and let us finish? Then you and your cronies can do whatever you want here." She holds her head high. "Stefan and I won't be back, so you can finally live in filth like you've tried to make us do."

He takes a step toward her, hand raised. "You think just because you're married, you can—"

I have his shirt in my fist in seconds, his stale breath in my face as I shove his bony body against the wall with a sickening thud. I lean in and bare my teeth, holding myself back with effort. "I'd walk through fire for your daughter. I'd go to hell and burn for her. There's nothing I wouldn't do for that woman, and if that means putting you in the ground to make sure she never fears you again, I'll do it." I let out a breath, my pulse ragged.

"The only reason you're still breathing," I pause, letting my words sink in, "is because I don't want her to blame me for both of her parents' deaths."

Anya makes a sound like a whimper behind me.

A man in the hallway steps in as if to intervene.

"Semyon!" Anya shouts behind me. Someone grabs me from behind, but I quickly break free and knock the guard to the ground with a single punch. Another charges from behind, my boot slamming into his chest with a well-aimed dropkick. He drops like a stone.

Before anyone else can move, I grab the man with the cane and wrench him forward, pressing my gun to his temple. The room goes deathly quiet. My assumption that he was the ringleader is spot on.

"You think you can walk in here and pull this shit?" I hiss, my voice low but deadly. My gaze sweeps over the remaining men. "You should've known better. Touch me, and we start a fucking war. Over what?" I jerk my chin at Lazar. "This fucker?"

The man in my grip is shaking now, his cane slipping from his grasp. He doesn't dare to even make eye contact with me. "Tell them what happens when people fuck with me," I snarl.

His breath stutters. "We didn't— We didn't know—"

"No?" I dig the barrel of the gun harder against his temple. "You know now."

The tension hangs in the air like a blade. One wrong move, and they're done. It'll be their last.

"Get your people the fuck out of here," I command. "Before you give me a reason to finish this."

"Yes, yes, of course," he says, nodding. "We'll leave now. Everyone out!"

At my glare, they scramble to obey. I don't lower the gun until the last of them is out the door.

Anya stares at me when they're gone, her lower lip trembling.

"Well, that was intense."

I give her a grim smile. "Welcome to my world, queen. Let's go. You have the electronics packed?"

She nods wordlessly. "Yeah. In a bag in the room."

I blow out a breath and pull out my phone to give Rafail a quick update. I slide my gun away.

For now.

"You need anything else, take it now. Oh, and Anya?"

She pauses, her eyes wide as she stares at me with something like newfound respect. Or is it fear?

"We're taking that pink duvet home."

CHAPTER 18

ANYA

MATVEI MEETS us in the kitchen when we arrive back in The Cottage. He's sitting at the table, dunking large cookies into a glass of milk across from Stefan, who imitates him. His eyes are wide as he watches the huge, obviously powerful man sitting across from him. I imagine Stefan feels he's met a real-life superhero.

Ha. Little does he know.

But something about the wild look in Matvei's eyes makes me put my hand on Stefan's shoulder.

Matvei smirks. It doesn't make me feel any better.

"You find what you needed?" Matvei asks Semyon.

"That and a little extra bonus," Semyon says with a wry smile. I cringe, frozen in place at the idea of Stefan knowing what happened with my father back there.

I can still feel the tight grip on my heart when Semyon defended me and promised to hurt my father. I half wish for just a moment that he was around when my father hurt my mother.

No. That would've been terrible.

Gloriously vindictive but terrible.

Maybe then I wouldn't have felt the need to blame him for my mother's death. I close my eyes when a rush of emotions chokes me.

Sometimes it feels like a betrayal to my mother to forgive him so quickly. But maybe I was wrong. Maybe I misjudged.

Semyon looks at Stefan and then back to Matvei. "I'll fill you in later." He hands the computer and mobile over to Matvei, whose eyes instantly light up with excitement, grinning like a kid handed his dream toy. Matvei leaps from the table and hurries to a barstool by the kitchen counter, practically bouncing on his feet. He eagerly arranges his setup, not wanting to waste a minute.

"We've been busy," Stefan says with a belabored sigh. I pinch my lips together and nod sagely. "She made me peel potatoes and carrots and wouldn't give me any cookies until I'd eaten a bowl of soup." He makes a face.

Zoya smiles at him from the stove, where she stirs a large pot. "Oh, I know, I'm so mean. You only asked for seconds to be polite, right?"

Her eyes twinkle at my brother, making my heart ache.

God, I'm so damn wound up.

"It's good for you," Semyon tells Stefan while looking over Matvei's shoulder. "Manual labor puts hair on your chest."

When Stefan takes a surreptitious look under his shirt, I stifle a snort.

Matvei stares at the screen, Semyon looking on. "Motherfu—" Semyon backhands Matvei, who quickly shuts up. Stefan stares wide-eyed.

"Sorry, yeah. Listen, I'm going to need way more time with this. These are heavily encrypted," Matvei says, shaking his head. "But something tells me—no. No, I won't say anything until I know."

I stare, my belly sinking to my toes. "Days?" I lick my dry lips. "But if—if my brother's in any danger, I—"

"I'm fine," Stefan says with a grin, taking another cookie from the plate in the middle of the table. Oh, thank god he's young and self-focused enough he didn't consider the fact that *my brother* meant anyone but him. I don't want him to know anything about Eli. Not now.

But for some reason, my eyes are watery, and my throat feels tight.

"Anya," Semyon says gently, his icy-blue eyes behind his glasses fixed on me. "I know you want all the information you can get immediately. But I promise, he can't be in any immediate danger. If they're using him as leverage, they'll need him healthy. He may be uncomfortable for a little while, but he'll live."

I nod. It makes good sense.

Semyon glances at the clock on the wall. "Mandated family dinner in an hour." Looking to Zoya, he begins to roll up his sleeves. "What can I help with?"

Zoya directs him to stack dishes and puts Stefan and me to work with salad prep. It smells delicious in here.

We lapse into a warm, comfortable silence while Zoya stirs and seasons a pot on the stove. Stefan helps Zoya, and Semyon and I stand side by side chopping.

A part of me feels like a traitor for enjoying anything the Kopolov family offers.

And a part of me aches because of how deeply I've longed for the familiar comfort of family and home... just like this.

Semyon walks over and leans close, his voice low and smooth, a playful smirk tugging at the corner of his mouth. "I didn't know culinary skills were part of your extensive resume. I thought your talent ended with baking. Should I be worried you've got other talents with a knife that I should be wary of?"

I arch an eyebrow at him. "Only if you're worried about being sliced to perfection like these veggies. I'm particularly skilled at using mandolins and choppers. Do you need a demonstration?"

"Is that a threat or an invitation?" he whispers in my ear, his voice laced with hope.

"Yes," I whisper back.

My panties dampen. I clench my thighs together, a flood of arousal at the memory of what we did in the tiny bed in my childhood bedroom. His hands in my hair, his mouth between my legs, his tongue delving in and out with tantalizing perfection.

Oh god.

How can I let the memory of absolute ecstasy threaten my loyalty to my family?

Semyon chuckles under his breath, and a thrill races through me.

"Careful, little Anya," he says softly, his voice dipping low. "You keep testing me, and I may have a few things to teach you myself."

My mouth is dry, and my pulse races excitedly.

I shouldn't want this so badly. My brother's right there. I'm his sister.

It's Semyon.

My husband.

Our hands work in tandem, but the electric tension between us buzzes.

"Ahhh." Matvei shakes his head, his fingers over the keyboard flying. "Come to papa, motherfucker."

Semyon throws a carrot at him and hits him square in the back of the head. Matvei groans and mumbles an apology.

"Hey!" I snicker and wince at the same time. That did not feel good. "You have good aim."

His eyes meet mine, and he shrugs. "I never miss."

Rodion comes in and asks Stefan if he wants to play catch

while the others set the table. I can't tell if he's just trying to be nice to Stefan or trying to get out of work.

As the others bring food out and set the table, Semyon's breath is hot in my ear. "Tell me, little Anya. We're going to have dinner with my family. Do you still feel me inside you? Can you feel my cum leaking out of your pussy?" My eyes flutter closed, shutting the world out as I'm lost to sensation. "Tell me, Anya. Because I can still taste you."

I nod, my cheeks flushing hot.

Can I still feel him? *Hell, yes, I can.*

Everyone seems to come out of the woodwork. Tall, elegant Yana—her husband conspicuously missing. I've been told she made her brother promise not to involve him in their work. Zoya, flitting from table to kitchen until Semyon finally puts his hand on her shoulder.

"There are enough people here to help set that table. Stop doing it all on your own."

She gives me a bashful smile.

"He's right," I say gently to her. She looks like she'd run herself ragged for them, and she's the youngest one. I still remember when she was a child. How old is she now? I know she's gone to university.

We set the food on the table while Matvei has a quiet word with Semyon, and I go to the front lawn to bring Stefan in.

"Dinner is ready," I call out.

A part of me doesn't like that we have to come here every night while Rafail sorts his shit and does whatever he has to, but another part of me is happy to see Stefan have a family. Family dinner. When was the last time we did that?

Stefan shakes his head. "I don't want to come in. I'm not hungry," he says defiantly.

Ugh. I do not want to have a confrontation with Stefan right now. "Stefan." My voice is a warning, just as Semyon steps up behind me.

"She wasn't asking. Do what your sister says," he says simply before he turns and walks away, fully confident my brother will listen. Stefan comes in like a scolded schoolboy at the end of recess.

It's almost infuriating how effortlessly Semyon gets people to fall in line. I guess that kind of authority comes naturally when your reputation does most of the work.

I'm tired during dinner, barely holding on through some of the conversation. Semyon sits next to me. Leaning over, he whispers in my ear, "You look exhausted, Mrs. Kopolov. I wonder why?"

My cheeks flush, and I bury my face in a large glass of wine, which definitely doesn't help my exhaustion.

Stefan digs into the food with gusto despite his earlier refusal to admit that he was actually hungry. When his plate is empty, Semyon wordlessly gives him another.

I open my mouth to protest. He never eats this much, and I feel as if I'm a burden to them. Semyon places a hand on my arm.

"There's plenty of food to go around, Anya," he says quietly in my ear. "That's not something you need to worry about here." He nods at Stefan. "Stefan, take your elbows off the table, please."

Stefan sits up taller, his eyes wide. I take another sip of wine. Flustered. Grateful.

Confused.

Semyon snakes an arm across the back of my chair. His nearness makes me tingly, especially when he leans over to whisper, "I will never forget today. And I look forward to putting you to bed tonight. You're so tired."

And then he kisses my temple. "I'll help you sleep."

"I bet you will," I murmur, my cheeks flushing. The way his voice brushes against my skin is like a ghost of a promise. The warmth of his words sparks an unfamiliar flutter deep inside me.

Slowly, the ice begins to melt.

"Stefan," Semyon says with quiet correction when my brother leans across the table on his elbows again. He demonstrates sitting up straight. My cheeks burn with embarrassment. But Semyon, calm with his ever-cool composure, steps in like he's already claimed authority over my brother.

It both grates on my nerves and fills me with warmth. I can't explain it.

"I could've handled that," I whisper under my breath. "You don't have to take over every time with him."

Semyon's lips twitch, and his eyes burn into mine. "I know. Of course you can," he whispers back, his breath warm on my ear. "But I enjoy watching you get all worked up. Keeps things... interesting, doesn't it?"

I find I can't quite suppress a small smile. He knows how to push my buttons. All of them.

"We'll skip dessert. I've had enough of the family dinner thing. I want to take you home," Semyon whispers. "I bought your brother a tablet loaded with every streaming service I could find. He can watch anything he wants. He's had a full day, hasn't he? Food. Exercise. Hard work. I think he needs a little downtime." His long, thick fingers brush over my hand. I'm fixated on the tattoos on them. Why is that so hot? "Don't you think?" he asks quietly.

I want to push him, test him, play along. "I think I'd like dessert."

His gaze darkens on me. "I'll get you anything you want."

"But I want the double chocolate pie Yana made."

"Right," Semyon says, but I can feel the tension radiating off him in waves, that barely-leashed energy that makes my thighs clench, that makes me want to push him until he snaps. Yum. "Here's the deal, baby," he says, his voice low and rough. "You can sit your ass here and eat that dessert. And when I get you home, I'll strip you, lay you over my knee, and paint your pretty ass red so you'll feel me every time you sit for the next fucking week. How does that sound, little Anya?"

My pulse pounds so loudly I barely hear my own voice when I whisper, "You said I had options. What's behind door number two?"

His lips curve into a slow, dangerous smile. Filthy promises shimmer in them, the kind of things polite girls pretend they don't want. I like when his eyes heat like this instead of that piercing coldness I can't control. Who am I kidding? I like all of them.

"Door number two," he says in a low whisper, his voice husky, "we skip dessert. Bring it with us. You say goodnight. I take you home, feed you dessert and then spread your thighs and let me eat *mine*."

My pulse kicks into overdrive, heat pooling in my belly. It's so wrong that he's talking about this stuff right here in front of his family, in front of my brother. Not that any of them can hear him, but it's still not right that he's painted a vivid picture of him between my thighs.

His hand moves from the back of my chair, sliding just under the table, his fingertips grazing across my thigh. Oh my god. I breathe heavier, and when Rafail goes to refill wine glasses, I lift mine to him naturally, hoping he doesn't notice how flustered I am. I shift in my seat as Semyon's hand moves up to an obscene place on my thigh. Heat pools, and my pussy throbs. I'm torn between embarrassment and need.

"You're so pretty when you're aroused," Semyon whispers in my ear. "That pretty pink flush to your cheeks..."

I glance around. Everyone is still caught up in their own conversations, apparently unaware of the tension between the two of us.

"All right, but I like dessert," I whisper. "Can we still have some back at the house?"

His eyes gleam. "Anything you want."

My mouth opens to retort, but I'm interrupted by Stefan. "I want pie," he says. "Can I have pie?"

I smile at him and slowly push Semyon's hand away from me. "I would love a slice of pie."

Semyon's lips thin. "You've made your decision," he says, his voice just soft enough to stay between the two of us. "Enjoy that pie while you can still sit."

I smile at him, my heart racing. I think back to when I was eighteen—young and naive. Semyon was older, powerful. I could never explain it, but the way he'd get stern with me always sent inexplicable heat through my body. Now the thought of him like that again—commanding, unrelenting, in charge—makes anticipation and nerves coil inside me. My cheeks flush as I focus on serving Stefan a slice of pie, though I'm acutely aware of Semyon's eyes on me. His gaze feels like the ghost of a touch.

Tonight will be... memorable.

"How long do you need with the computer?" Semyon asks Matvei.

He shakes his head. "At least a week. There are major firewalls to break through. I've made some progress, but it's like the first crack of an egg. Nothing's really happened yet. The more I can crack through the surface, the further we get.

"I've found some interesting information so far," he adds. "But I'll leave that for you to see later. I don't want to say anything until I have more."

"Anya," Yana says curiously, pulling my attention away from Semyon. "We have a pretty big event coming up in a week."

I remember when I was younger how it seemed Semyon was always going from one event to the next. He lived larger than life, and I was so jealous. His world seemed so much bigger than mine.

"Everyone's expected to be dressed up for it. Zoya and I are going shopping for dresses. Maybe you can join us?"

As if she knows exactly how things work here, her eyes meet her brother's. Semyon sits back, his arms crossed over his chest, his eyes narrowing slightly behind his glasses.

"That's fine," he says. "But each of you will have two guards on you."

Yana opens her mouth to protest, but Zoya just stares him down.

"Six guards?" Yana says incredulously. "Are you serious right now?"

"Serious."

"Semyon's right," Rafail adds, his voice firm. "We're on the verge of a war. We don't know where alliances stand. We'll take no chances."

Then, shaking his head, he mutters, "You're lucky he's even letting you go out at all."

A war... we're on the verge of a war, and my family is at the epicenter of it. I look at Stefan, gleefully eating his pie with gusto. He has no clue what's at stake, that Eli could be in danger.

But we have to keep things safe. For him. For all the children here. For all the future generations.

Semyon's hand flexes on my thigh.

I don't have to do this alone.

CHAPTER 19

SEMYON

I HAVE WICKED plans for my wife when we get back home, but both she and Stefan pass out on the ride. They're exhausted. I can't bring myself to wake her.

She looks younger when she's asleep, the crease between her brows relaxed, free of that worry line between her eyes. I wish I could soothe it for her. I wish I could make it better.

I don't know how to do this—how to be what she needs. Sometimes I wonder if I'm even capable of it. Emotions, connection... it's like a language I've never learned, one I can't comprehend. Every time I think I'm getting closer, she pulls away, and I'm left questioning if I'm destined to fail at this. But I can't give up.

Exhaustion weighs on my chest, my eyes heavy when we park. My eyes feel like lead, but there's no time to rest. Answers about Eli are just within our reach. If he's been taken, we'll have to find him—but that's only part of the battle. If he finds out I've taken his sister...

I'll cross that bridge when I get to it.

I wish I could tell her every circumstance that led to her mother's death. I still remember that conversation we had in their kitchen when she pounded her small fist on the table, her voice trembling.

"You cannot drag him into this," she said, her eyes shining. "I won't allow it, Semyon. I know who you are. I know who your family is."

Anya has her mother's eyes.

What she didn't know was how deeply in debt he already was. She had no idea how many conversations I'd had— begging, threatening—doing everything I could to keep her brother out of my family's business. Out of everybody's business.

Rafail wouldn't engage with him just because he knew what it would do to their family. But we weren't the only Bratva outside of Moscow.

Anya will need to know the whole story eventually. All she remembers is her mother begging me to keep her brother out of the Bratva and me turning my back on them. And that's when it all fell apart. Six months later, Eli was drowning in debt. Her mother confronted me, desperate, begging. Tempers flared, and then... she collapsed. A heart attack, just like that. No warning. We couldn't save her.

None of us could.

Anya blamed me. Hell, I would've blamed me, too.

She stirs awake and looks around, disoriented. There's a faint line on her cheek from where the seatbelt pressed against her skin. Cute.

"We're home?" she asks in a small voice.

Home. She called it home. An unfamiliar warmth spreads across my chest.

"Yeah, we just got here." Silence hangs in the air between us. "I know how tired you are. I can carry you in and come back for Stefan—"

She shakes her head. "I can walk. I'm not comfortable leaving him out here."

She has no idea how extensive the security is around my house, how damn near impossible it would be for someone to get on my property, let alone pose a real threat to us. But I respect her decision.

"Let's get him upstairs."

I feel her eyes on me as I lift Stefan into my arms for the second time. I wonder what she's thinking. I wonder why her breath hitches a little as she leans against the car and watches me.

"Why don't you grab the pie that Zoya sent home?" I jerk my chin toward the back seat. She follows silently behind me as I carry Stefan up to his room. It's tidied from earlier, in a haphazard work of a young boy. But he made an effort.

I lay him on the bed, and Anya helps me prepare him for sleep. We remove his shoes. We work quietly. I lift him while she turns down the sheets. Our eyes meet over the sleeping form of her little brother as I lay him back down, and she tucks him in.

This woman is going to be the mother of my children. I couldn't have chosen better.

But do *I* have what it takes to love a child? Can I think beyond my own needs? I know the challenges I face. I know who I am and the whispered voices that call me the Ice King.

Could I really, truly love another human?

I look down at the sleeping form of her brother. I barely know him. I wouldn't say I love him... yet.

But could I?

We close the door quietly behind us, and I walk her to her bedroom.

"I don't want to sleep in my bed tonight," she says with a yawn, not meeting my eyes.

"Good," I whisper. I reach for her and turn her to me, then slide my palm down to the small of her back and draw her near. I kiss her forehead and lace my fingers gently behind her neck because it seems she likes it when I do that. "Because I want you in my bed. You're tired right now. Get some rest. Then we'll talk."

"You were only teasing about punishing me, then?" she asks, her eyes dancing with mischief.

I shake my head. "Did I sound like I was teasing?"

My dick's instantly hard at the thought of her squirming over my knee.

CHAPTER 20

ANYA

Nervous excitement flutters in my belly.

It feels like a step toward intimacy, sharing space with him. Even in my state of exhaustion, I'm aware of the details, how his room is an extension of his personality—structured. Minimalist. Meticulously organized. Every element of the room is deliberate and precise, from the ebony wood to the steel and glass accents. Even the high-quality linens in understated neutral shades.

There isn't a single personal touch in the entire vast expanse. The whole room is austere, just like him, but the recessed lighting filters in warmth.

"Did you move my things in here?" I ask curiously when I note the white toothbrush, pink bathrobe, and slippers in here that he had in my room. I give him a curious look. "You knew I was coming."

"I expected you would eventually," he says. "But no. Those aren't the same. I had duplicates bought and brought in here." He shrugs. "In case you wanted to go back and forth."

I open my mouth to respond but forget what I'm going to say because he's... undressing. My gaze lingers on his inked hands, captivated by the way they move—steady. Deliberate. There's something about them that makes my heart turn in my chest. He didn't have those tats when he was a boy. No, the tats and scars were the heralds of his moving into power, reminders of a journey he's walked, shaped by pain and brutality. Those hands have lived a lifetime of battles, and he isn't yet thirty.

"Get ready for bed, Anya. You need sleep. We've had a long day."

It feels like I've had a long *month*.

Year?

Lifetime?

But he's right. I do need to get some sleep.

He shrugs out of his shirt, then folds it before he places it in a hamper with dirty clothes. I've never seen anybody fold clothes before tossing them into a hamper, but it's on point for him.

Alright. If he can get undressed in front of me, I can play that game.

When I shrug out of the dress top that was my mother's, it feels as if I'm shedding a part of who I am—my childhood, the memory of my mother. I chose a few of my favorite items from the clothing left in the closet before we left my former home. This top... I can still remember she wore it the day we opened the bakery. I pull it over my head, and just to appease him—and see if he notices—I fold it before I put it in the hamper.

His gaze grows molten.

"I'm keeping that."

"Of course you are."

I turn away, pretending I didn't see the way his desire flares and his dick tents his pants. *Ha.*

Next, the zipper of my skirt. I drag it down, my back toward him. It's old-fashioned, I know, but it was also my mother's, so I love it.

I miss her. I miss her so damn much. I ball it up and toss it into the hamper.

He flinches.

Was it the sudden movement or the balled-up clothing? No wonder one of the first things he taught Stefan was to clean his room.

I stand in front of him, wearing my panties and a bra—pretty, well-fitted garments he's obviously imagining taking off.

I swallow hard.

"We don't have time for this," he says in a low growl.

"Getting ready for bed?" I ask innocently. I am so tired. My eyes feel heavy, but adrenaline courses through me, reminding me of what happened earlier today. "Somewhere to go?"

He narrows his eyes on me and licks his lips.

"You know what I mean. I'm trying to be responsible, Anya, and not fuck you every minute of the day like I want to. But believe me when I tell you, I am far from having exorcised that demon."

A thrill courses through me. My nipples harden.

"I can help with that." My mouth waters when I look at the hard planes of muscle, the stunning ink. When I take a step closer, his Superman-like gaze pins me in place.

I shouldn't do this. But when I reach him, and he slides his hand to the small of my back before he cups my ass, I forget why.

His large, rough palms grip my ass, and I slide one leg up, anchoring myself over his hip. When he buries his mouth in the nape of my neck, my head falls back, and I gasp for breath. He laps at my skin with the flat of his tongue, and my clit throbs with the memory of where he placed his mouth earlier.

I throw my arms around his neck and squeeze, needing more pressure and less, more tongue and mouth—more, more...

He suckles my neck and bites my collarbone. I moan with pleasure. Palming my pussy, he presses with the heel of his hand. I grind against him, so close to climax. I feel like a teenager. What the actual hell is going on here?

"On the bed," he rasps. "Take those off and get on your hands and knees. Grab the headboard, Anya."

Oh god. That'll make me vulnerable. Exposed.

Isn't this what I wanted?

I obediently take off my bra and panties, crawl onto the bed, and grab the headboard. I spread my legs, aware of him approaching me from behind.

"I know you're probably sore from earlier," he whispers.

I shrug, not wanting to admit that I am. Where has my sense of self-preservation gone?

He slowly takes off his glasses and folds them. Oh god, I've already come to learn that means he's about to get busy. "Doesn't mean I can't put my fingers in you and finger-fuck you while I lick your pussy again, does it?"

My pulse skyrockets. I shake my head, my mouth dry. "Suppose not," I say, stifling a giggle.

"But first, your punishment, Anya."

"Wait a minute, I—"

He holds my lower back under his palm while he lifts the other one and slams it across the fullest part of my ass. I clench, but the pain quickly morphs into pleasure, and I already feel wet heat growing between my legs.

"You like it when I punish you."

Heat floods my core. I let out a soft, desperate mewl.

"I want to fuck this pussy so bad. Not now. You need time to heal. I won't hurt you, Anya." He slaps my ass again, hard. "Except to do this."

"I'm fine—" I whine, which earns me another hard spank.

"No. I'll make you come, baby, but with my fingers." I stifle a scream when he bends, bites the place he spanked, then licks it.

"Eventually, I'll take you here," Semyon says, pressing his thumb to my asshole. Oh my god. I am *definitely* not ready for that. "I need to ease you into that. I will," he promises.

"Open for me, baby. I want to taste you again. I want to bury my nose in your pussy and lick you until you scream."

I want that too.

I do what he says, and he arranges himself beneath me. My grip on the iron bar of his bed makes my knuckles white. I gasp for breath when he licks my clit and shoves his fingers into the slick heat of my pussy.

There's a hint of pain at first before he makes it better, rocking his fingers in and out of me. I know he finds just the right spot when a wave of pleasure makes my clit ache. He uses the slightest touch of his teeth on my sensitive flesh, teasing, licking and sucking before he pulls his mouth away, cups my ass in his hands, and says in a low rasp, "If you move away from me, I'll punish you by bringing you to the edge and leaving you there. Is that what you want, little Anya?"

I shake my head, my mouth dry. I want *him*. I want *everything*.

He licks my clit and plunges his fingers inside me. My hips jerk, my body riding the tension, but I don't move my hands.

"Good girl," he growls. "That's my good girl."

He pumps his thick fingers in and out, his thumb teasing my asshole before he flicks my clit with his tongue. "My fucking god, you taste divine." He groans, then plunges his tongue into my core, fucking me with it. It feels so good. I don't want it to stop, but I can already feel myself hurtling toward release—quickly, uncontrollably.

"Beg me. Beg me to eat your pussy until you come on my face," he growls between my legs. *"Beg me*, Anya."

"Please." My voice is a hoarse whisper. "Please—"

He's still beneath me, still holding my ass in his palm.

"You can do better than that," he says in a low, teasing growl. "I know you can. Can't you, baby?"

"S-Semyon... make me come," I plead, trying harder. "I want you so badly. Please."

"Better. You're getting there."

He pumps into me again, fingers deep inside. I climax, clenching hard around him. My clit throbs, and I'm coming so hard I can't breathe. I jerk my hips on his mouth, relishing the feel of teeth and stubble and tongue—harsh, soft, perfect. He licks and suckles me until I'm spent, absolutely wrung out with pleasure. I collapse onto the bed, exhausted, as he lies beside me, still hard.

"I want you in me again," I whisper.

"Not now," he says. Rejection settles heavily across my chest, but I nod. I need to be good. I can do this.

But it doesn't feel right. I like him inside me. I like knowing he wants me, that he needs me. I ache to be filled by him again.

I've always remembered his voice as cold, his eyes distant. But when he turns away from me now, his face is tortured. My vision blurs from exhaustion.

"Sleep, Anya. It's time to go to sleep."

My eyes are closed, but I'm still awake as I feel him moving around the room. Undressing me. Brushing my hair. A warm cloth between my legs. I fade into sleep.

THE ROOM IS *dark but familiar.*

"Semyon, please."

The words claw at my chest. My face pales as I suddenly see her. My mother. She's standing, gasping. I go to her, but I can't reach her. No. No, this isn't how she died. Why is she here now? Why is this happening?

I reach for her, but the more I try to get to her, the farther away she moves. Semyon stands in the doorway, shaking his head.

"Help her!" I scream. "Help her!"

She clutches her chest and falls to the table, crying out to me.

"Anya... take care of everyone. Watch out for your brothers."

She falls from the chair to the floor. I scream for Semyon again, but he doesn't help. He turns and walks away without looking back.

I WAKE IN A COLD SWEAT, my heart racing. I scan the room in a panic. It takes me a minute to remember where I am.

Cold. Austere. Black and steel.

Semyon's room.

My husband.

I'm alone.

I close my eyes as tears well up and spill over.

"I'm sorry, Mama. I tried."

I squeeze my eyes shut, willing sleep to come, but I'm wide awake now. I wonder where Semyon has gone. The memory of our earlier lovemaking is shadowed by all that's passed.

My mind races, sliding pieces and memories together.

I've told myself for years that Semyon could've prevented Eli's fall into ruin. My mother begged him to help. If Eli hadn't fallen, my mother never would've died. She never would've...

I shake my head. *I can't think about that now. I can't.*

Semyon says it wasn't his fault. I held onto my hatred for years, let it poison me. It festered and boiled until I had a true villain to blame for my misery.

But Semyon isn't to blame.

I have to trust him. Trust that what Semyon said about Eli is true—that we can find him, that we can bring him back. But even if we do...

What happens next? Eli has made terrible decisions. He's dangerous. But he's my brother.

I throw off the covers when my stomach growls. Dinner was a long time ago.

I'm not much of a nighttime eater, but right now, I'm ravenous.

I slide into a fluffy pair of slippers and walk out of the bedroom, headed to the kitchen. I know he has to have something to eat here, even though I've barely moved in. I remember what Rafail said earlier about tracking his macros and protein. Makes sense.

I stop at Stefan's room, and when I peek in, he is still dead asleep. But no Semyon.

Has he left? Was I so dead to the world I didn't hear a thing? Apparently so.

I make it down to the kitchen and do a quick perusal of the cabinets. While I do find cases of protein shakes—ready-made and large jugs of protein powder, I also find a few things I didn't expect to see: packages of cookies, unopened. Cheesy crackers, unopened. Several cases of soda pop, all unopened. Foil-wrapped chocolates.

I smile to myself and look around the small pantry. Did he buy this for my brother and me?

Maybe one of his sisters did.

I open the fridge next and find it well stocked with plenty of food. I make myself a quick sandwich, put it on a little plate, and sit in the tiny kitchen nook. This is a large room, and beautiful, but it doesn't look like it gets much use.

When my appetite is sated, I want to find my husband.

My husband. I'm not used to calling him that yet or even thinking of him as that, but I can't help it. A part of me kind of likes it. Younger me would've clicked her heels for joy.

I load my dish into the dishwasher, brushing stray crumbs into the trash bin and wiping down the counter. I make sure not to leave a mess—I know Semyon appreciates order. I like that about him, though I'm sure there will be a day when his perfectionism drives me up the wall. For now, it gives me a strange sense of calm. The clean, uncluttered counters, the bright glow of the meticulously organized fridge, the subtle scent of fresh linen in the air... it all carries an understated luxury that makes me feel at ease. Makes me feel safe.

I don't find him in the living room or in the study or library —whatever that room is. I half expect that behind a closed door, I'm going to find a dark secret, a hidden passageway, someone in chains, or a map of underground networks—not because this place necessarily has an air of mystique, but because of its largeness, in a way that seems to encapsulate something more than what appears to be.

"Can't sleep?"

I nearly scream and jump as I turn around to find Semyon sitting at a table in the corner of one of the large rooms.

"You scared me."

"You scared *me.*"

Of course he looks completely unperturbed, which means that scaring him maybe—maybe—bumped his heartbeat up a notch.

"I was hungry."

"Did you find something to eat?" he asks.

I nod. We don't speak again. He looks down at the chessboard in front of him and makes a move on one side. After a moment of contemplation, he makes a move on the other side as well.

Is he playing chess against himself? Why does that somehow feel symbolic?

I wonder if my presence is welcome, but I'm too shy to ask. So instead, I turn as if I'm about to walk away, just to see what he'll do.

"Leaving so soon?" I smile.

There's something in the tone of his voice that reminds me of our childhood—reminds me who he was. The lonely boy who was forced into adulthood way too soon.

"I didn't want to bother you."

"You're not bothering me."

I pad toward him with my slippered feet and slide into a chair directly across from him.

"I didn't know your house was the home to ghosts."

"There are lots of things you don't know about this house. Or ghosts," he says with a hint of a smirk.

I smile to myself and watch him.

"So, who's winning? You or the ghost?"

His eyes dim, and the hint of a smirk leaves his face.

"The ghost," he says in a little whisper. "Always the ghost."

Semyon leans forward, his fingertips pressed together as he studies the chessboard. "The key is to think several moves ahead. Control the center, predict your opponent's responses," he says, his voice calm but focused.

Is he talking about chess?

I bite my lip, watching the pieces shift in his mind as he contemplates his next move. "Sounds like you're always playing a game," I say softly, tracing a finger along the edge of the board. "Even when it's not chess."

He gives me a faint smile. "Maybe life isn't so different."

I pretend to notice a speck of dust near the corner of the board and flick it away, casually nudging a piece. "Maybe you're overthinking it," I tease. "Sometimes the next move is simpler than you expect."

His eyes dart to where my finger lingers near the knight, realization sparking in them. He shifts his position, his gaze snapping back to mine, bright with excitement. "Brilliant. You're full of surprises," he murmurs.

"Sometimes." My cheeks warm under his steady gaze.

"Do you still play, Anya?"

"Not often. But yeah, I've been playing ever since you gifted me with a chessboard. I just never had the time or enough people interested in playing with me."

His eyes meet mine across the board. Wordlessly, he makes a move.

"Checkmate," I say softly.

I'm leaning closer to him. His eyes are on me. I want him to touch me. To kiss me. But this moment feels sacred, and I don't know if I want to shatter it with the combustive energy that happens when we touch.

"I want to play with you," he says in a voice tinged with so much heat that I don't know if he means my body or the chessboard.

"Is strip chess a thing?"

He laughs out loud. I jump, startled because I don't know when the last time I heard him laugh out loud was. His whole face lights up—an absolute transformation—as his eyes dance, his mouth curves up, and he grins at me.

"Strip chess? It's a thing *now*."

And that's it.

The last trace of ice around my heart melts.

I made him laugh.

Maybe he isn't cold—the Ice King everyone speaks of. Maybe he's just broken.

Like me.

"You look troubled, Anya."

He looks down at the board as if trying to process my emotions.

"I've had...conflicting emotions."

He blows out a breath, maintaining eye contact with me, and finally nods. "I know."

My heart aches. Semyon *hasn't*.

I open my mouth to speak when suddenly the lights go out. We're cast into complete, utter darkness. I don't have my phone with me or a flashlight.

Semyon's voice carries across the darkness. "Seems there's a power outage."

My chest constricts. I don't scare easily, but utter darkness triggers me.

"What do you mean?" My voice is shaky, trembling.

"Are you scared, Anya?" He sounds surprised.

"I don't like being in the dark," I say in a whisper, not trusting my full voice. I might cry. "Stefan—"

"—is sleeping," he finishes for me, utterly calm. "He's fine. We'll go upstairs and check on him if it'll make you feel better. But first, we're going to get a flashlight or candle," he says in a quiet voice. I'm reminded of the older brother who shielded his sisters from so many things. "Before we check on your brother, we're going to secure all of our exits to make sure that this is not something intentional."

If someone came here and cut the power—

"And then," he says calmly, rising. I can hear the way his clothes ruffle and feel warm fingers on my hand. "We're going to take a walk, check a few things, and go to bed— after I'm confident that we're not being sabotaged."

If I were home and the lights went out, I would light candles and put on a brave face for my brother. But I wouldn't ever have to worry about somebody coming into my house or being attacked.

But I'm Bratva now.

"I have candles in every room in this house and a power generator, but I'm not going to trigger the generator yet because it'll make it too easy for anyone who attacked us to disappear. So let's take a look."

He speaks so calmly, without question, as if it's just a matter of course. I don't know how he navigates the room in the dark, but it probably helps that it's unencumbered by clutter, and his memory is flawless.

I follow him, holding his hand. I hear the strike of a match, and candlelight flickers in front of him.

"You look like a ghost," I whisper to him.

"Maybe I am," he whispers back.

The corner of my lips quirks up. He takes the candle and rests it on a flat surface to cast light in the room before he takes out flashlights and hands me one.

We flick them on, and he methodically walks to the different exits. I half expect him to continue going room by room, but of course, he has a much simpler plan. He leads me over to a table, taps on a screen, and within ten seconds, twenty-five different views of access points to his estate pop up. He presses a button, and blue, yellow, and red zones appear.

"What's that?" I whisper to him.

"Thermal scans. It shows me if there's any presence of another body here. See this?"

He points to the bottom right screen. I squint my eyes and peer closer.

"Stefan," he says. "Yes," he answers himself. "It's red, which indicates body temperature. So either," he continues methodically, "a cold-blooded creature has made its way onto my estate, someone has the wherewithal to block their body temp, or it's just a power outage. Let's go up to bed."

He extinguishes the candle and hands me another flashlight. "I'll put this next to Stefan. If this keeps up for much longer, the generator will start up."

My exhaustion kicks in again. I want to sleep, but I feel strange—the adrenaline still coursing through me even as my eyes sag with discomfort and fatigue. I wonder what he thinks in moments like this. It seems so natural for him to slide into the role of protector, to be ready to defend me and my brother. Just like he defended his sisters before him.

"Zoya was always afraid of the dark," he says, and I can't tell in the darkness if he's smiling.

"Was she?"

"She was afraid of a lot of things," he says, resting his hand on the small of my back as we go up the flight of stairs. I don't tell him that I think she still is.

In the bedroom, we head to the right, check on Stefan, and he slides the flashlight onto the bedside table. Stefan is still blissfully asleep, unaware of the power outage.

Good for him.

As we make our way to his bedroom—our bedroom?—the lights flicker back on. It's late at night, so we don't have many around here, but there are a few.

"Well, that didn't take long," I tell him. "Is that the generator?"

He shakes his head. "No, must've been the weather."

I'm glad the power is on because I would've missed an opportunity to ogle him and his tattoos and the hardened muscles of his body. I climb into bed and lift the thick comforter up to my chin. I watch him undress and get ready for bed himself. Then he climbs in beside me.

"Come here," he says in a soft whisper, and he lifts his arm.

I hesitantly move closer, slipping beneath it and resting my head against his chest. He wraps me in a secure embrace, his hold protective and comforting. I drape my hand across his abdomen, letting it settle on his chest, and I close my eyes. Little girl me is *squealing*.

"This feels nice," I whisper. I can't forget what he said earlier and what's happened, but I can enjoy this soft comfort while it lasts—knowing we're safe. Even knowing that if someone attempted to ambush, he would have it under control. I snuggle in, and he holds me tighter.

"I'm not going to be able to sleep like this," he says in a growl.

"Are you sensitive to other people's bodies? Movement? What?"

"No," he says, his voice low and rough. "But if you lie next to me, I'll get hard as hell and want to pin you to this bed and make you mine all over again. And trust me, I will. Make no doubt about it. But right now, I need you to get some sleep." His gaze darkens. "I told you I want to take care of that pretty pussy... let it rest before I wreck you again."

I clear my throat. "If you were trying to turn me on, it worked."

"Woman," he says in a little growl, gently turning me over and spooning me from behind. The thick feel of his erection against my ass makes me smile. But when I close my eyes, sleep feels all too close. I tuck myself under the blanket, the pillow under my head. I've never slept in a bed so big, so comfortable, with sheets so luxurious. I take a peek at his hand, splayed across my belly, and notice a thick scar right alongside the tattoos.

"Where did you get that from?" I ask with a yawn, my eyes already fluttering closed.

"A fight."

When he doesn't offer more, I kind of playfully elbow him in the ribs. "Obviously. Which one?"

"Do you remember that time by the creek? When you were crying?"

My eyes open. I didn't expect him to admit that the scar had anything to do with *me*.

"Yes, I remember it vividly. Why?"

"They came after you again, but you didn't know because you were at school. I did though. I followed them. I watched. One day, one of them made a threat against you."

I swallow hard.

"I made sure that didn't happen again."

My heart beats faster. What does that mean? "Did you kill them?"

"Not *that* time."

He did that. He's admitting that he killed somebody. Oh my god.

"Get some sleep, Anya. You asked, I answered. Now the discussion is over. I want you to rest."

I stare into the darkness. My brother is safe. My family is, for now. I trust Semyon...

Don't I?

CHAPTER 21

SEMYON

THE DAYS PASS, and Matvei feels no closer to getting the truth than he was before. Anya is getting impatient—I can tell by the way she questions things. We go for dinner like clockwork at six every night, and it seems like she and her brother have always been here. She's become besties with Zoya, and she chats with my family as if she knows them.

She does, though, doesn't she? My beautiful wife.

It's getting close to the Romanov ball. They are famous for having these benefits in New York, but now that Polina is situated in Moscow—just outside of Moscow—and her mother spends so much time here, they've decided to extend their balls to Moscow as well. It's a benefit, really, typically an art auction generating several million that they donate to charity. It keeps the Romanovs in good standing, and by association, us.

So I've agreed—reluctantly—to allow Anya to go shopping with my sisters. I'm at the bar with Matvei, Rodion, and Rafail, along with Rafail's friend, Vadka.

"Are you pregnant yet?" Rafail asks, just as he motions to the bartender for another shot of vodka.

"Of course not," I tell him. "What kind of bullshit phrase is that anyway? Men don't get pregnant."

"But they should," the bartender says, her hands planted flat across the top of the bar. I recognize her from somewhere, but it isn't until Vlad speaks up that I know exactly where.

"And why is that?" he asks, his head tipped to the side.

The bartender—Ruth—is Vadka's sister-in-law. He's married to her sister. With a shock of short black hair and eyes that cut right through you, she's memorable. A spitfire. And there are interesting rumors that circulate about her loyalty and ruthlessness.

"Because you men should share the burden of it," she says pragmatically. "It's an absolute shame that evolution hasn't come to the point where you also have children."

"We have children," I tell her, taking a methodical sip of my beer. "What the hell are you talking about?"

"You don't bear them. You don't have to deal with stretch marks, blood, and saggy boobs."

I cock my head to the side.

"...And the labor pains and leaking nipples." She throws her hands up in the air. "I've seen what women go through. It's bullshit."

And with that, she slams the bottle of vodka on the counter. "You can pour your own damn vodka."

"What the hell is that about?" I ask Vadka.

He shakes his head. "Who knows? She's really harmless. Actually, no, not *harmless* at all," he says quietly, shaking his head. "If you're on her good side."

Rodion frowns. "Does she just hate men?"

"Wouldn't blame her if she did," I say, taking another drink of my beer. "We're kind of assholes."

"Speak for yourself," Rafail says, smacking my back.

"You are definitely an asshole," Matvei says to him. "Listen, I hate to dredge up the past, but going through these computer files, I've come across a few things," he says cryptically.

"Like what?" I ask him.

"You all remember that Anissa betrayed our fearless leader," Matvei says, jerking his chin toward Rafail, who grunts into his glass.

"Ended well for me," Rafail says. "I got my wife instead of that traitor."

Matvei's eyes narrow. "And that traitor still betrayed us, didn't she?"

"You weren't supposed to be looking for that information," Rodion says, shaking his head. "You were supposed to be cracking into the computer to get information about the abduction—or supposed abduction or whatever the fuck."

"I know," Matvei says. "And what if I told you that the two things were intricately intertwined?"

"Jesus," I mutter under my breath. "Do you mean to tell me—"

"I don't mean to tell you anything. I want to tell you exactly what it is. This is what I found out." He lowers his voice. "The Irish are heavily involved."

I lean forward, my stomach knotting. He wasn't supposed to find out information about anyone else on Eli's computer. "How involved?"

He shakes his head. "They've been working in the shadows for a while now. *They* were the only ones pushing to secure control of the bakery's location," he explains. "It wasn't about the properties—we know that—it was all about positioning. They knew exactly where to strike."

I shake my head. "And Anissa?"

Rafail stiffens. A few years ago, he was jilted at the altar, and we've been unable to secure the location of the woman who betrayed him. Rafail didn't pursue it after he'd married Polina, but she's been a loose thread ever since.

"She's playing both sides. I dug into communications—she's been meeting with the Irish leadership in secret. The Irish offered her a way out. Protection, financial security—anything to keep her from marrying Rafail. They knew the marriage would strengthen us, that it would unify key factions and block their influence. The whole 'cold feet at the altar' story? Bullshit."

We process all this in silence. I shake my head. "But there's more. Eli's in deeper than I expected. His debt wasn't random, Semyon, but part of their plan. He owes money to Irish-connected interests, and in exchange, he's been feeding them intel. Remember, he had firsthand access to the bakery."

Shit.

I do not want to tell Anya any of this.

"He betrayed his own family?"

Matvei sighs. "Yeah. He probably thought he was just buying time, that he could outsmart them. But the Irish don't play games. They used him."

"And you have proof of all this?"

"Almost." Matvei frowns, tension tightening his features. "I'm still cracking through the last firewall, but this is bad. They've orchestrated everything to fracture us from within."

Cold silence settles between us. The Irish have played a long game.

"I'll keep digging. But be ready. When all this comes to a head... it's gonna get bloody."

"Well, gents," Vadka says, pushing to his feet. "On that happy note, I promised my wife that I would do bedtime tonight, so I need to go."

He pays his tab and leaves.

This is why I never wanted to get involved with a woman, have a family, fall in *love*. All I can think about is Anya's safety. I'm distracted, my loyalty divided.

"That's an interesting development," I mutter. Rafail grunts. Rodion cracks his knuckles. Matvei stares at a tablet as if trying to decide his next move in a game.

My phone buzzes with a text. I immediately hide it so no one else can see.

I smile down at a picture of my beautiful wife wearing a blue gown that hugs her curves in all the right ways. When she turns around in the second pic, her back is completely bare. God. She can't wear that in public.

I tap out a text and send it:

> You can wear that in the bedroom, but I'll spank your ass if you wear that in public.

She sends back a blushing emoji, and I shake my head.

Then comes another picture, this one *even worse* than the first two. There's a strip of red fabric across her breasts, the curve of her lower breasts exposed, and sheer fabric covers the rest. The dress comes all the way up her thighs.

"Somebody's distracted," Rodion says in that same teasing voice. "Your wife sending you nudes?"

"Say that again, and I'll throw you across this bar," I snap.

He holds up his hands in surrender. "Okay, okay, I'm just joking. Relax."

"He's not gonna relax if you keep talking about his wife being nude," Rafail says, smacking Rodion on the side of his head. "Just like you wouldn't if someone was talking about *your* wife the same way."

Rodion shrugs. "It's all in your expression. How else do you explain the way you're looking right now? One second, you're happy, practically grinning at the phone; the next, you look like you wanna whip it across the room."

"Maybe she showed me pictures of dresses she wants to wear to the gala," I snap at him. "So shut the fuck up."

"Wow, she *has* melted the Ice King," Rodion mutters. I growl at him, which makes Rafail's lip twitch and Rodion blanch. He's been on the receiving end of more than one good beating from me and knows he's damn close.

"Open your mouth again," I warn, narrowing my eyes at him. "You fucking—"

"Boys, boys," Rafail says. "Break it up. Rodion, apologize." Rodion's nostrils flare. He doesn't like being made a spectacle of in front of everyone.

"I'm sorry, all right?"

"Semyon," Rafail continues to chide us like we're fucking high schoolers again, "you apologize for taking things too seriously."

"Abso-fucking-lutely not. He was talking about my wife disrespectfully. Like I'd let him get away with that. I'd fucking knock his teeth in."

Matvei whistles low. "Wow. You're right, Rodion. Semyon really has changed, huh?"

"What? What the fuck are you guys talking about?"

"You have feelings for her," Matvei says, looking at me with wide eyes, his jaw dropping. "*You*—Semyon, the original Ice

King, incapable of feelings for anybody. We thought you were a psychopath."

"Who says I'm not?" I shrug.

"It doesn't matter," Rafail says, looking back at me with curiosity in his features. "You *should* love your wife. It will strengthen your bond. It's good for you," he adds. "I love Polina."

I sit up straighter, looking around the room.

Love is good for me? Do I love her?

"Oh god. I love her."

The words feel strange but right. "What does it mean to love someone?" I ask, looking between them. "I wanna know. You guys tell me. What does it mean to love someone?"

"How can someone who's so fucking brilliant not know this?" Rodion asks. "I actually know something he doesn't. Dude, when you love someone, you'd do anything for them. You'd lay down your life for them, protect them. When you're away from them, they take up every thought in your mind. You don't feel like yourself again until you're with them. And then when you are, you become your whole self again."

"Hold on with all that bullshit," Matvei says.

Rafail glares at him, but Matvei nods. "I agree. I've never loved a woman, but I've loved my sister." His eyes grow soft, staring into the distance. "No one like her." His sister was killed in a brutal war ten years ago. He did everything he could to save her but couldn't. His sister was my cousin, and we all mourned her loss.

"I loved Gleb until he became a traitor," Matvei adds. "And my asshole dad and mother."

"They're still family," Rafail responds. "And we're loyal to family."

Matvei's loyal to a fault.

"Love isn't a feeling," Rafail says. "It's not just something in your chest or heart. It's what you do. If you love someone, you do anything for them." His voice drops, and his eyes grow dark. "Anything."

The bartender gives him a curious look, pours another shot of vodka, and hands it over to him. "Well done. I'll call a momentary truce," she says with a wink before going back to serving the bar.

"We weren't fighting, but okay," Matvei says, taking the free drink. He likes a good free drink.

Love.

Holy fucking shit.

I love her.

"You look like you just saw a ghost," Rafail says with a grin. "Jesus, brother, you didn't know you loved her?"

I shake my head. "I knew that I'd protect her, that I was devoted to her, and that I meant every word I said in my vows. But love? No, I didn't... I didn't know I was capable of love."

"Not capable of love," Rafail scoffs. "You were chasing love when you were five years old, always trying to look up a skirt and find someone who would be devoted to you. Then, one day, your whole world came to a screeching halt."

Another text comes in from Anya. I stare at my phone.

> **Anya**
> How about this one?

I look at the screen. She's wearing a soft champagne-colored dress that hugs every curve but covers every inch of her. She has a beautiful little shrug draped over her shoulders.

> **Anya**
> This is the one I'd wear in public.

Her message pings alongside a winky emoji and a picture. A second follows almost instantly. Then a second picture arrives. She's taken off the shrug in this one.

> **Anya**
> And this is what happens when you take
> it off.

My lips twitch in a rare grin. Heat stirs in my chest as I rise from the chair, phone in hand. My voice hardens. "I love my wife, motherfuckers. I'm going home."

Laughter echoes in the room, but Matvei is strangely silent. He frowns at his screen, eyes narrowed in concentration.

"Wait."

"What?" I'm feeling impatient. I need to see her *now*.

Matvei blows out a breath, his shoulders stiff. "Something… doesn't fit. But I need to check one more thing first." He shakes his head. "We're closing in on the truth, but I'll need time to confirm it."

My blood chills. Something is wrong. I pull Anya's location on my phone, my thumb hovering over the screen.

"How long?"

"Soon. Hopefully tomorrow."

The knot in my chest tightens. Anya is waiting. She's worried about her brother, and I know damn well how fragile the peace between us is. The other shoe is about to drop.

CHAPTER 22

ANYA

I SAT *on the stoop of our crumbling home, my chin resting on my knees, trying not to cry. Eighteen wasn't supposed to feel like this. Eighteen was supposed to be special, meaningful. There should have been cake and candles, my favorite treats from the local store, and maybe a book I'd been saving for.*

I'd been planning my birthday for weeks, even saving up a little money from errands around the neighborhood. But it was gone now. My brother Eli found it hidden under my pillow—a really stupid place to hide money. He took it, just like he always did when he needed a quick fix for his gambling.

I felt stupid for hoping this year might be different.

The late afternoon sun hung low in the sky, casting long shadows across the street. My mom tried—she really did—but she forgot dates so often I doubted she even remembered it was my birthday. And she was working today, anyway.

I told myself I didn't care, but the tightness in my chest said otherwise. It's just a day, I told myself. Just a day like any other. And now I'm eighteen.

Ophelia tried to make it special, but she got in trouble at school, and her mom grounded her. She passed me a note in class that said, "Happy Birthday! Your boobs look so much bigger today."

It made me laugh and smile at her, but later, I found myself secretly staring at my chest in the mirror, wondering if they actually did look bigger.

I told myself I didn't care that no one else paid attention to me today. No gifts, no celebration, nothing. My stomach growled, and I wrapped my arms tight around my legs, pretending it was just another normal day.

I was so lost in my thoughts I didn't hear the footsteps until they were right in front of me.

"Anya."

I blinked, startled, and looked up to see Semyon standing there. He held a simple white bakery box in one hand and a package wrapped in shiny paper in the other.

He looked so out of place against the peeling paint and cracked pavement of my world. Even dressed casually—a plain black T-shirt that hugged his lean, muscular frame and dark jeans—he radiated a presence that made me feel small and unsteady. He wasn't like the boys in my class, the ones who stumbled over their words, made fun of me, or teased me about my boobs. No.

Semyon was a man.

Twenty-two to my eighteen. But it wasn't just his age. He'd been a man for a long time now.

There were rumors about him—how he killed for the Bratva when he was only sixteen, how he was feared on the streets of the city. So feared.

But not by me. I didn't fear him. I still saw the little boy who taught me how to skip rocks by the creek. The cold Bratva enforcer was just a role he played, not who he really was.

At least, that's what I told myself.

"Semyon," I said softly, my voice coming out smaller than I intended. I hoped he couldn't tell I'd been crying.

"Hey." He set the bakery box and wrapped package down on the stoop beside me. My heart began to beat faster.

He couldn't be here for... Did he know?

"Zoya said it was your birthday," he said simply, lowering himself to sit beside me.

He leaned back with his legs stretched out. His tattoos were visible beneath the sleeves of his shirt—dark ink, intricate patterns swirling across his forearms. I suddenly felt self-conscious.

Too young.

"I didn't think anyone knew," I said.

"She pays attention to those things," he said, his tone neutral.

"Um, what's in the box?" I asked, quickly deflecting the conversation.

"A cake," he said as if it were obvious. "Chocolate."

My heart squeezed. "Did Zoya tell you I liked chocolate too?" I teased, biting my lip as heat flushed my cheeks.

His lips twitched. "No. Everybody knows you love chocolate."

Not everybody. My dad wouldn't. I wasn't even sure Eli would. My mother might've known, but only on a good day.

But Semyon? Semyon knew.

He flipped open the lid of the box, revealing a plain chocolate cake with messy icing swirls. There were no candles or decorations—just the word Anya scrawled across the top in crooked white letters.

"It's nothing fancy," he said with a shrug.

"It's beautiful," I breathed out, my throat tightening. I bit my lip to keep the tears at bay. "You didn't have to do this."

He turned to me then, his piercing blue eyes softening. "Of course I did. You're my friend."

Friend. The word hit me like a sledgehammer.

I didn't want to be his friend. I wanted to be something more. But I was just the little sister of his best friend.

He set the wrapped package beside me. "Open it."

I slid a finger under the paper, carefully peeling it away. Inside was a chessboard—not a cheap one from the corner store, but a beautiful, polished set with intricately carved pieces.

"It's gorgeous," I whispered, swiping at my eyes quickly so he wouldn't see.

"*You play?*" *he asked, his voice casual, though I could tell he already knew the answer.*

"*A little,*" *I admitted.*

"*Good,*" *he said, setting up the pieces right there on the stoop. "Because I'm not going easy on you.*"

"*Maybe I'm better than you think,*" *I shot back, teasing.*

He glanced at me, his gaze soft. "Maybe you are, Anya."

We played for hours, taking bites of the cake straight out of the box as we moved pieces back and forth across the board. I lost every game, but I didn't care. He didn't talk much, but he didn't have to. Just having him there, spending time with me, paying attention... It was enough.

When the air grew cold, he finally stood, folding the wrapping paper into meticulous little squares. "I have to get home," he said. "Rafail expected me an hour ago."

"*Hope you're not in trouble,*" *I said with a small smile.*

He huffed a laugh. "I'm definitely in trouble. But it was worth it."

For a moment, he stood there, his gaze unreadable. My heart pounded, my breath caught in my throat. Was he going to... kiss me?

I told myself no, of course not. I was just a girl to him.

But then his fingers brushed my jaw, tilting my chin up ever so slightly. My breath caught. His ice-blue eyes searched mine, hesitation flickering in their depths. And then, before I could second-guess it—before my mind could get ahead of my body—he kissed me.

It was brief, more than a question than an answer. His lips barely pressed against mine, lingering for just a heartbeat before he pulled away. His voice was rough when he spoke.

"Happy birthday, Anya."

And then he was gone.

Before he came, I wanted a book, a gift, attention... now I wanted so much more.

After he left, I sat there for a long time, staring at the chess-board and the remaining cake. I swiped my finger through the icing, licking it clean.

It was delicious.

My heart felt full, and my eyes burned with tears.

It was the best birthday I'd ever had.

"WHAT DID HE SAY?" Yana asks, her eyes twinkling. I roll my eyes. She knows her brother.

Zoya gets a teasing look and holds up her palm. "Listen, I actually don't want details, okay? If he's getting all sexy or flirty or whatever—" She makes a face. "My god. I can't believe I'm saying that about *Semyon*. What have you done to my brother?"

The better question is, what has her brother done to *me*?

"Well..." I say, trying to think of how to phrase it without telling her too much. "He definitely has decided opinions about some dresses."

Yana grins. "Of course he does. So, the red one with the underboob, it is?"

"Yeah, I don't think so." I can't help but smile. What I don't tell them is that I have a feeling that if I wore that one out in public, my ass would match the shade of that dress.

Is that a bad thing?

"I'm so glad he married you," Yana says quietly. "You're such a perfect fit for our family, Anya." She smiles. "Not many people knew what my family went through. You do. And you've been nothing but supportive. Thank you." She leans forward and gives me a kiss on my cheek.

My chest tightens. "Of course, yeah."

I miss Eli.

I miss my mom.

I don't miss my dad because he destroyed everything that was good between us, but I miss who he was before.

But even when my family was intact, I didn't have sisters.

And now I do.

"I think we should get these for Stefan," Zoya says with a grin, pointing to a box of remote-controlled cars. I'm grateful for the change of subject before I bawl like a baby. I might be a little high-strung. "Please, this would be so perfect. I can just see them racing around Semyon's perfect house."

"Or these," Yana says, picking up a box of blocks with shapes that look like castles and dragons. "He loves building things. Imagine the look on his face building his own fortress."

My throat gets a little scratchy, and I look away, nodding because changing the subject didn't help. I'm afraid if I talk right now, I'm going to blubber all over both of them.

I'm not the only one who cares about my baby brother anymore.

Yana flips through clothes on hangers, not meeting my eyes. "You know that Semyon isn't... He has some challenges, Anya. You know that, don't you?"

I nod slowly.

"It doesn't mean he isn't as *feeling* as the rest of us," Yana says. "He just doesn't always know how to express that."

"I know. He tries so hard, doesn't he?" I've watched him. I know he catalogs everything like a scientist, that it takes him time to process reactions of emotions. But I love that he tries so damn hard.

"Of course. And I love that you know that about him." Yana grins. "Do you know the day he married you, I told him off?"

"Did you?"

"Yes. I told him not to treat you like a chess piece in his game. And I meant every word I said." Yana sweeps all of our purchases into her arms and heads to the front register. "Rafail will pay for this," she says with a wink.

I nod, thankful. "What did he say?"

She laughs out loud. "Well, at the time? He said it wasn't personal." She snorts. "Don't get me wrong, he *can* be a jerk."

"Who can?"

Semyon stands behind us, hands on hips. My heart melts a little. He's so handsome, so protective, all scowling and Superman-like. The girl who was waiting on us gets all flustered when he folds his arms, revealing his muscular forearms.

"Maybe you shouldn't eavesdrop on our conversation because it has nothing to do with you," Yana says.

"Yeah," Zoya adds, but she flushes bright pink when he gives her a stern look.

"Maybe what you have to say to my wife has *everything* to do with me." But I can't tell if his eyes behind his glasses are twinkling. "Anya, I'm going to have the girls take these packages home. You and I have work to do with the bakery."

He leans in and kisses my cheek, lacing his fingers through mine. Zoya gawks. Yana grins.

When I look outside, I notice that a car idles by the curb, purring softly.

I wave. "Bye, girls."

They wave and watch as I walk hand-in-hand with him. I'm well aware of the eyes of all the people around us. Zalivka is a small, working class city outside of Moscow. Everyone knows who the Kopolov family is. That means they know who I am too.

"I finished running the financials for your business," Semyon says as he opens the car door for me. By now, I know not to even reach for it. "I'm pretty confident that we can bring it back in the black, but you're going to have to make some changes."

He talks on and on about numbers, distribution, and industrial machinery, but all I can think about is making sure that my mom's special place—that she created with her own two hands—doesn't go down.

I nod, processing.

He slides into the driver's seat, shuts the door, and begins to drive toward the bakery.

"Listen, Semyon, I understand all this, but I need to make sure this does not become an industrial production company, no matter how much money it makes. This matters to me. I want to keep it small."

"We will," he promises.

"But let's be honest. You wanted this location. You wanted me because you want access to the bakery."

Something tugs at my chest, an uneasy feeling I can't quite place.

"We will honor what your mother started, Anya," he promises. "You have my word."

I didn't expect this rush of emotion when I got here. God, I'm a mess today. The memory of Semyon bringing me my first birthday cake, my mother elbow-deep in a bowl of bread flour, Eli snatching a cookie off a sheet so hot it burned his fingers—it all hits me with the force of a tornado, and I shove it down. We're here for a reason.

Semyon gives a quick, assessing look around the place.

"You need new appliances. Those are shit." I stare at the appliances my mother scraped for. He goes on as if he didn't just punch me in the gut. "New flooring, new countertops. New fucking everything. No wonder you aren't selling that well."

"Hey." My hands are anchored on my hips, but he misses it because he's already in the freezer.

"And this is a fucking hazard. Goddamn it, Anya, if you or Stefan got stuck in here..."

I ignore him, heat rising in my chest. I remember what Zoya and Yana told me: He doesn't understand the impact his words have on others. He needs to be told. I get this, but still...

"You said we're opening our doors at regular time tomorrow, right?" I ask him.

"Yes," he says from the depths of the pantry. "God, this is a safety hazard too."

He steps out, holding a massive bag of sugar balanced on one shoulder and a tray of baking supplies in his hand. "Who stacked fifty-pound bags on top of each other like that?" He sets the sugar down with a thud, pulling a massive jar of cinnamon teetering on the edge of collapse. "And why is this on top of the bags? One wrong move, and this is going up in a cloud, and do you know you could actually choke on cinnamon?"

He narrows his eyes as he nudges a half-open container with his foot. "Seriously, you could lose a limb back there."

He doesn't know what he's saying, I remind myself. He doesn't understand that I'm taking this personally, and I am taking every damn word personally. I remind myself again. I put my hair up in a messy bun and tie on an apron, and by the time he returns to me, I am elbow-deep in flour.

"What the hell are you doing, Anya?"

"You just told me we're opening in the morning," I tell him. "Obviously, if we're opening in the morning, I need to have some things proofed for baking. And I have to get here before the sun rises; you know that, right?"

"Not if I tell you no, you won't," he snaps, stepping into my space. The two of us are at such opposing ends right now— me, flustered and flour-covered, and him, looking as if he just stepped out of a men's fashion catalog. He's gorgeous and cold, and I want to throw this dough and muss his perfect hair.

"So this is how you'll play it? You'll be nice for a couple of days, a couple of weeks, and then all of a sudden, you're just going to snap and try controlling me?" I blow out a breath. "I am not a pawn in one of your chess games, Semyon! You can't just toss me aside before someone else calls checkmate. You should know that."

He stops. Stares as if baffled. Does he really have no idea how I'd feel about him storming in here and critiquing *my* bakery, the one I've kept together by the skin of my teeth? "What the fuck are you talking about?"

I look at him, incredulous, trying to remind myself that he doesn't understand—but he's a grown adult. He *should* know exactly what's up.

"You heard me. I said I'm not one of your pawns." Even as I say it, a part of me wishes he'd push back because I want to feel him. I want him pushing me against the wall and taking control back. I want his hand around my throat, a reminder of what he can do to me. I want all of it, and I don't understand why I want so many conflicting things at once.

He's too close to me. There's a magnetic pull drawing the two of us together, one I can't resist any more than he can.

"Is that right?" he says, hands on hips. "You want me to leave you alone, stop controlling things? You want me to walk out and leave you to this, don't you? Tell me, Anya. How'd that work for you before?"

My cheeks flush pink as I press my lips into a thin line.

"Tell me to walk away, and I'll leave you right here to do whatever the hell you need to do with that fucking bread."

He can't hide the scorn in his voice, and I can't hide the heat rising in my chest.

"I thought you liked it when I took control," he says with a smug smirk that makes me want to smack him.

"Not with everything." I can't remove the petulant tone in my voice, but he should know this. I don't care if he needs people to explain things to him. This is basic common decency. This was my family home. My mother started this.

"Makes perfect sense," he says with chilling precision. "Run the bakery into the ground. Go out of business. That's an excellent way to honor your mother."

Oh the *arrogance*. Before I know what I'm doing, I do exactly what I imagined—I fling the bread dough straight at his beautiful face. I hit dead center with an accuracy that makes my heart flip in my chest. Bull's-eye.

Semyon watches the dough that falls to the floor with a plop before he bends to pick it up. He tosses it in the garbage and then washes his hands slowly while my heart beats a frantic rhythm in my chest, and I pretend that I didn't just throw food in his face like a child.

"Do you think your stubborn pride is going to save you?" he asks, his eyes flashing blue fire at me. "You'd rather close the doors of the bakery than admit you need help, wouldn't you?"

He prowls closer to me. I stand my ground as my heart rate skyrockets. I cling to my apron, my fingers grasping at the edges as if, somehow, this thin piece of fabric is going to save me from him.

Nothing will save me from him. Not my pride. Not my family. Not my sharp tongue or wit. *Nothing.*

He takes a step forward, boxing me in against the worktable.

"Maybe I wouldn't have to if you didn't trap me in." The petulance in my tone has softened, but I'm still restless, still simmering with anger. Yet deep down, I can't deny it— he's right. I *do* like it when he takes control. I've been holding onto control for so damn long, clinging to it like a buoy.

But now... it's getting fucking heavy.

"It's not my control you hate," he says with such quiet conviction it almost shakes me. "You're scared, Anya. Just admit it."

I shove him, my palms pressing hard on either side of his broad shoulders. It's meant to say no, to push him away, but he doesn't budge an inch. His eyes darken as his strong fingers wrap around my wrists like steel cuffs. Before I can process it, he spins me, my back hitting the cold steel door of the freezer. My breath catches.

I stay still, not wanting to give him the satisfaction of knowing what he does to me. But when his mouth finds my neck and kisses down to my collarbone, his teeth sinking into sensitive skin, I shiver. It's punishing, a reminder of how easily he can overpower me.

Flour dusts our clothes as we give in to each other. He kisses me, and I'm kissing him back—angry and on fire—but a part of me admits I can't do this alone. I don't want to. I know he's right.

"You might have a point, even if you're an asshole about it," I admit through clenched teeth.

"And you might have a point, even though you're a brat." He tugs my hair and grips my ass hard before he lifts me, turns, and slides me onto the steel top of the worktable. I lose myself to him. I'm tugging on his shirt, eager to put my palms on the hard planes of his stomach as he's unfastening and pushing down my pants.

"Leave the apron," he says in a low whisper. "I want the vision of your legs spread for me, your head tipped back while you come, every time I step foot in this fucking bakery."

My cheeks heat, and I smirk at him.

"That's so fucking dirty."

He lifts a shoulder.

"And?"

I shiver when his fingers tighten around my hips, planting me in place.

"You like it dirty, Anya. You just don't wanna admit it yet."

I'm half-tempted to push him away, to slap him, but the truth is I'm already soaking wet, aching for him. His hands slide up my hips, rough and deliberate, pushing my apron higher until it's bunched around my waist. Cool air meets my skin.

I arch my back, pushing against him. He groans low in his throat, a sound that goes straight between my legs, then cups my pussy with the heel of his palm, pressing to where I ache for him. I meet his gaze. This time, I don't look away from his ice-blue eyes.

"You still think you're in control?" He presses his palm harder, circling. I bite back a moan, aching for more.

"Maybe I am." I don't even recognize my voice. It's so low, so seductive.

Now he's moving again, trailing kisses and bites along my jawline, his stubble rasping against my skin. He shoves aside my panties, sliding his fingers into my wet cunt. I bite back a gasp. He doesn't rush—he's teasing me, ever the strategist, driving me insane. He knows just what moves to make.

"I want you begging," he whispers darkly. "By the time I'm finished with you, you'll forget you ever wanted control, Anya."

His fingers dip beneath the fabric, and I cry out softly, clutching his shoulders as he swirls and strokes. He has me exactly where he wants me. With him, it doesn't feel like weakness. I feel wanted. Powerful.

He shoves his fingers back in my pussy, stroking in and out.

"Fucking hell." I breathe.

His lips curve into a wolfish grin that makes my sex pulse. "You like that, Anya, don't you? Admit it—you like it."

I plant my hands on the flat of the steel table, spread my legs, and nod, beckoning him closer.

"I fucking love it. I want you, Semyon."

His control breaks. I want to touch him, but I'm holding onto the table for dear life. It gives me a sort of power when he slides between my legs, bringing his fingers to his mouth and licking them clean. Oh my god.

Neither one of us wants to yield, but right now, we're equals, giving and taking. Then his mouth is on mine, devouring, and I lose myself in him. He drags my butt to the edge of the table, keeps my legs spread apart, and unbuckles his belt. I sit up, holding myself upright while I reach for his belt, helping him. We can't move fast enough. I'm afraid if I don't let him take control right now, I might change my mind, and I can't do that. I won't.

It takes both of my hands to take his thick, hot cock from his pants and slide it between my legs. My head falls back at the first slow thrust, the tip of his cock at my center. *"Semyon."*

He pushes into me, and this time, it doesn't hurt as much as it did before. This time, it feels so good, so right, as if we're meant to be like this together. I feel like a woman. A full-fledged woman. Not Eli's little sister. Not Semyon's best friend's sister.

Anya Kopolova.

The walls of my pussy tighten around the thick edges of his cock.

"Tell me you like it," he murmurs in my ear.

I bite my lip, not wanting to give him the satisfaction. He pulls almost all the way out, and I moan, reaching for him, arching toward him. I want him back.

"Tell me you want this," he whispers. "Tell me you fucking want this."

"Fine," I grit out. "I want this. I want you. I want us. I want all of it. Fuck me, Semyon."

"That's my girl," he growls. "That's my good girl."

He shoves into me again, and it feels so fucking right. I swear that when his cock hits the back of my cervix, I feel a full-body shudder. Again, he pulls almost all the way out before he slides back in again and again, building a rhythm with friction that makes me want to scream. My fingers dig into his back—scratching, begging, pleading. It's dirty and fulfilling. All I can think of is how much I want more.

He fucks me until I scream his name, until the walls of my pussy clench, and I come, and *he* comes inside me, his hot seed spilling. I lean back, sated, my clit still throbbing when he falls to his knees and removes his glasses.

Oh my god. He means business when he slides them off.

My mouth is open in a silent gasp as he drags his tongue, hard and flat, across my clit. It feels so wrong, so dirty.

"Semyon—" My fingers grip the edge of the table, white-knuckled. I'm panting, moaning.

He doesn't stop but eats me out, suckling me, and I'm on the cusp of another orgasm. I come again—harder—crying out, my hands diving into his hair, anchoring myself for support, screaming. Then I slump back on the table, spent and exhausted.

But he's not done yet.

I watch as he gets a wicked grin and walks slowly, fully clothed, to the refrigerator. I'm too drunk to ask what the fuck he's doing, but I don't trust that smile.

He opens it and takes out a bottle of whipped cream. Usually I make my own, but we keep this on hand for emergencies. I'm boneless, barely holding myself on the edge of the table, when he comes back over to me.

How is he still walking right now?

He kneels, removes my apron, and cleans me up. I watch him drizzling a line of cream across the top of my thighs. "Dessert time."

He sucks the cream off and licks my clit. I'm so sensitized, having just come, my hips jerk, and I shake my head.

"*No. No, too much.*"

But then he slows his roll ever so slightly, touching the tip of his tongue to my swollen, sensitive clit. So softly, so gently. And I want more. So much more. I'm drunk on adrenaline and pheromones. All I can think of is *more*.

He laps at the cream again lazily, hungrily, sucking my clit into his mouth and then pushing me to the edge until I'm swollen, begging, needy.

"Semyon... I can't. I can't!" I scream against the edge of the table. My thighs tremble as the aftershocks ripple through me. I'm so sensitive it feels like every flick of his tongue shoots through me, but he's relentless, taking his time, savoring every inch of me like I'm the most delicious, most decadent dessert he's ever tasted.

"Yes, you can," he says, and I almost believe him because he's so confident, and it feels like he knows fucking everything. "And you will, Anya."

He draws another line of whipped cream along the inside of my other thigh. The cool sensation makes me shiver. The contrast of hot and cold, overwhelming pleasure, mingles. My head falls back. I want so much fucking more. I want him to stop. I don't want him to stop. I'm confused and eager.

He draws a pattern with the whipped cream—a fucking *pattern* like a gridlock across my thighs. His eyes meet mine with molten intensity as he lazily drags his tongue across the cream, lapping me up. I stifle a scream when his tongue meets my swollen, sensitive clit again.

"God..." I whisper.

"Good girl," he whispers back, breaking into a wicked grin. "Are you still fighting me?" He chuckles softly.

I shake my head, biting my lip as another climax builds. "I can't do it again. I can't. It's too much."

"Lie to yourself all you want, sweetheart, but your body tells me the truth."

His voice is slow and taunting, full of knowing. He presses a kiss to my other thigh before diving back between my legs. This time, there's no escape. His mouth is ravenous, hungry, alternating between sucking and soft flicks, keeping me teetering right on the edge. It's building more powerfully than it was before.

My hips grind against his face as my fingers tangle in his hair, yanking him closer to me. I've lost all control, and I don't care. Right now, there's only one thing I want.

He drives me higher and higher until the pressure building inside is unbearable.

"Please, Semyon," I beg without shame. "Please don't stop."

He hums approvingly against my clit, the vibration sending waves of shock through me, before he adds two fingers, sliding into my slick heat with a rhythm that matches the strokes of his tongue. My whole body clenches as his curled fingers hit the spot that makes me cry out.

"I once read an article about a woman's ability to orgasm," he says quietly against my thigh.

Of course he fucking did.

"The women they tested got to sixty-five before they called it a day," he says with a dark chuckle. "We're nowhere near that, Anya. And the article explained how the women could've kept going."

"Looks like evolution got something right," I breathe out.

He chuckles, his voice thick with desire. "Come for me, Anya." His tongue flicks again.

My body arches off the table, and I shatter, a scream tearing from my throat. The world tilts, and all I can feel are waves of pleasure. He doesn't stop until I'm sobbing his name.

"God, Semyon..."

I don't know why I'm crying. It feels like the greatest release and my greatest fears were all wound together in a tight knot, and every time he makes me come, something loosens.

I finally slump against the table, and he wipes his mouth with the back of his hand, his eyes dark with hunger. I know he's far from finished with me.

"You're not done yet," Semyon says, his voice rough. He pulls me into his arms, lifting me off the table. My legs wobble, and I love the sound of his slow chuckle. "I need you on your knees, Anya."

I drop to the floor, eager to return the pleasure he's given me. He's hard again. I run my hands over his thighs. His body tightens, his control slipping.

"Anya..."

I take him deep and suck, my tongue swirling around the sensitive underside of his thick, veined cock, hard again for round two. He groans, his hands tangling in my hair as he guides my movements. I love the power I have over him—

the way his composure looks like it's about to shatter with the next flick of my tongue.

"Fuck," he groans out, his voice ragged. "I'm only gonna come *inside* you."

I hollow my cheeks and take him deeper until he trembles. Just when I feel him start to lose control, his hips spasm, and he pulls me up, spins me around, and bends me over the worktable. His hands grip me possessively.

"Ready for me again?" he growls in my ear.

"Always." I pant, pressing my back against him.

With a hard thrust, he fills me, and we both groan at the sensation. Our mutual pleasure is intoxicating. He sets a punishing rhythm, meeting my thrusts and sparking waves of pleasure through me. Now that I've come over and over, I'm slick and wet, and it doesn't hurt like it did before. I hardly remember when it did. I can take him fully, and I fucking love that.

"Mine," he growls into my ear, biting onto my shoulder as he drives into me.

"Yours," I echo, crying out. My nails claw at the steel table for purchase, finding none.

He reaches around to rub my clit. I'm so ready that I come again, screaming. I've lost count of how many times I've come, but as he climaxes inside me again, I spasm around him, pleasure and ecstasy binding into one. He follows me over the edge, his release hot and intense as he spills inside me. We collapse together, breathless and sated.

"If we had more time..."

"Semyon," I say, disbelieving.

"I fucking would," he says. "We have to go to the house, but I'll have you tonight, Anya. I don't want you to forget that you're mine."

How could I forget I'm his?

He bends down and kisses the tender place he bit earlier. "Get dressed, Anya."

"You're enjoying this."

"Not nearly as much as you are," he teases, pulling me to his chest. "You're *mine*, Anya. All of you. I own every breath, every orgasm, every fucking heartbeat." His ice-blue eyes lock into mine, intense and unrelenting. "Do you understand me?"

I swallow, lost in the intensity of his gaze.

"Yes," I whisper, under his power.

His cum lingers on my skin as he cleans me with the balled-up apron, bends, and inhales my raw, wet pussy. "Mmm," he says in a low, raw whisper. "Delicious."

He licks and suckles again. This time, the orgasm comes quickly on the heels of the last. I'm panting, my limbs suffused with fire. My head falls back as I come with a scream. He slowly laps me through the aftershocks of pleasure until I'm done.

"You're so fucking lucky it's ten minutes before six," he says with a growl.

"No! Almost six? Oh my god. I have to get ready. We have to go—"

"Relax, Anya. I already texted Rafail and told him we'd be a few minutes late."

He stands up, pulls me to my feet, quivering, and gives my ass an affectionate slap. "Get cleaned up. I have some work to finish here, and then you and I are going to dinner."

My eyes meet his. I feel half-drugged. I shake my head and walk to the bathroom when something flashes in my peripheral vision. I turn around and stare.

There's a... camera. Staring right at me.

I never installed a camera.

"Semyon?"

"Mmm?" He's reading something on his phone with a scowl.

"When did you put surveillance cameras in here?"

He shakes his head as cold fear trickles down my spine. "I haven't had time. Not yet."

"But... look."

I barely have time to react before the deafening crack of a gunshot fills the room. I scream, my heart slamming against my ribs as shards of glass and twisted metal scatter across the floor. The camera is obliterated, reduced to nothing but broken pieces.

The echo of the shot still lingers as he lowers the gun, fury darkening his features.

"I'll fucking find out who installed these," he growls, his voice tight with rage. "*Khristos.*" His gaze burns with a cold, lethal focus that makes a shiver skate down my spine.

I stand frozen, torn between fear and awe, at the full weight of his wrath in this small space between us.

"Do you think they saw... what.... Oh god, what we did?"

Of course they did.

His lips press into a thin line. "They'd better play it on repeat because it'll be the last thing they ever see before I cut their fucking eyes out."

I close my eyes and stifle a moan. I am in way, *way* over my head.

CHAPTER 23

ANYA

THE BELL over the entrance to the bakery jangles so hard I look up, startled. I know that sound. That anger. *That man.*

My father storms into the bakery reeking of vodka and sweat, his face mottled and angry, hands clenched like a man ready to strike. I stand behind the counter, fingers curling around the edge of the countertop. Every day I come in here Semyon shadows me, but right now he's in the back, unloading the latest deliveries of baked goods. Turns out he's not a huge fan of me lifting the enormous bags of flour and sugar.

Stefan sits at a table, eating a snack and working on schoolwork. He freezes, his hand suspended in the air holding a pencil.

"Stefan," I say quietly. "Go to the back, please." Thankfully, Stefan is much better at listening these days and quickly scoots behind the counter and to the back.

I turn to my father. "You're not welcome here."

He ignores me, of course. He always does. His bloodshot eyes land on me with disdain. "You think you're too good for me now? Playing princess with your husband? You *owe* me."

I stand my ground. "I owe you nothing. You need to leave."

"The fuck I do." He walks past me and pushes the swinging door to the back open. I know exactly where he's going—the safe, that's tucked away in the back. Have I changed that passcode yet?

I follow behind him. "I told you to leave."

Semyon's nowhere to be found, though the back door's partially open. Stefan, however, stands facing us, his feet planted on the ground and his hands on his hips.

"She said leave," he says bravely, even as his little voice wavers.

"Stefan—"

"Anya said to *leave*," Stefan repeats. My father ignores him, pushes past him, and opens the cupboard where the safe is.

"Don't you dare—"

"No!" Stefan yells, reaching for my father's arm.

Oh no.

My father shakes him off and grabs Stefan too hard. Stefan winces and cries out as my father growls, "You mouthy little shit, just like your sister. I owned this bakery." He shakes Stefan, lifting him straight off his feet, as he raises his palm.

"No!" I scream.

The next moment's a blur of movement and sound. The sharp crack of a body hitting the wall. Stefan falls to the floor, running to me, as Semyon fists my father's collar and slams him against the wall, his fingers flexing as if he's trying to decide how many bones he's going to break. His face is carved from ice.

"Did he hurt you, Anya?"

I shake my head. My voice trembles. "No."

"Stefan?"

Stefan shakes his head. "He grabbed my arm, but I'm okay."

"Put your hands on either one of them again," he says, his voice a low growl, "and I'll break every fucking bone in your body. Slowly."

My father's eyes widen in fear. "You wouldn't—"

"I would. And I'd fucking enjoy it." Still fisting my father's shirt, he marches him to the back door with cool authority. "I don't ever want to see you again." He kicks the door open and shoves my father into the bitter cold, slamming the door behind him, before he turns back to us.

Stefan goes to him first. I stare, stunned. "I told him to leave her alone," Stefan tells Semyon. "Just like you told me to."

Oh my god. *Just like you told me to.* He told my little brother to protect me?

"You did good," Semyon says, ruffling Stefan's hair. His eyes meet mine. "Anya?"

"He didn't touch me," I whisper. I still feel tender and shaken, but then in the next breath, something happens that makes my heart melt. Semyon's hand stretches out to Stefan, palm up. No words.

Stefan's small fingers curl around Semyon's larger ones. Holding his hand. I blink back tears.

Semyon's voice is softer when he says, "Let's go home. Someone has a field trip tomorrow." How did I completely forget about it? I take Semyon's other hand. And it feels... right. Good.

I kiss Semyon's cheek. "Thank you."

He kisses me back. "I'm sorry that happened."

We close the bakery up, and when Stefan goes to get his bag, I turn to Semyon. Wordlessly, he reaches for me. I bury my head on his chest and let him hold me. "I wanted to hurt him," I whisper. "But Stefan..."

"Me, too. And it was *only* because of Stefan I didn't put him through that fucking wall. He's out of warnings, though, baby."

I nod. Good. We won't be bullied by him any longer. "Tomorrow, Stefan is going to the museum."

"And we're heading to the Romanovs."

It feels like waiting for the other shoe to drop. But I immerse myself in the feel of the mundane and predictable when we go home. Stefan showing me how Zoya taught him to chop carrots, Semyon boiling the water for pasta while I set the table. We don't talk of my father.

Semyon stands at the sink with his sleeves rolled up, rinsing a coffee cup for the third time. He's so methodical and always like this –quiet, controlled, fully at ease, and somehow...softer around the edges now.

Stefan heads up for a shower after dinner, and I sit at the kitchen table with my laptop. The bakery bills need to be paid. Semyon's phone buzzes on the counter, the screen lighting up with a name I don't recognize. He looks and nods. "I'll take this call in the office. I might be a while. You went to bed *way* too late last night, Anya. Fix that tonight, yeah?"

He leaves before I can answer as warmth floods my chest.

It's the way it is now. Comfortable. Familiar. I don't ask questions about what he does, unless they directly pertain to me, and thankfully most of the time they don't.

I let myself exhale the tension of the day. I haven't had time to really process what happened, but I can still feel my shoulders up around my ears. I open my accounting software and prepare to find the flashing red notices for the bills that are usually overdue.

Except—they're paid. Every single one. Not just paid for the month, but in full.

Semyon.

My hands shake as I go through my emails, scrolling quickly to see what I need, when I note an email from the school. *Shit.* The field trip permission slip was due today, and I—

> *Transportation secured. Permission forms received. Please remember to send fees in an envelope with your student.*

I shake my head. I know I didn't do this. I stare at the kitchen door, bewildered.

Did Semyon...?

I swallow hard and close my laptop.

I take care of what's mine.

I'm his. Semyon Kopolov's. I walk in a sort of daze to where Stefan's backpack hangs off the hook by the front door. I smile to myself when I remember the times he'd fling it off and let it land with a thud and my husband would calmly remind him that wasn't where his bag belonged before he made him try again. He's learning.

I unzip the bag, expecting to find the usual chaos of crumpled papers and empty snack wrappers, but instead—everything's in place. Tidied. And right there in the front pocket is a plain white envelope, labeled in Semyon's bold, signature slant.

Fees – Stefan Borozov

My heart stumbles as I tuck it back in and zip the bag up. What's that coat hanging next to the backpack? I do a quick check. It's a high-end, bright-blue winter coat in Stefan's size.

I close my eyes, a lump in my throat. I'm so used to doing everything alone. Always the one to keep tabs on details, to plan and juggle, to scrape enough together to make my brother's childhood normal. Who knew that of all the things this man could do to unravel me, it would be this? Not just his dangerous touch or stolen kisses, the way he owns my body and claims me as his wife. No... Helping me bear the mental load.

Of course he would. Semyon's a big brother, Rafail's right-hand man. He practically raised Rodion, Yana, and Zoya right alongside him. Taking care of things is what he does.

I shut off the kitchen light, determined to find him. He may have reminded me to get some sleep tonight, but I need to thank him. In person. Thoroughly.

The door to his office is halfway open, his voice low and husky as he takes the phone call. I barely even hear a word he says. He looks up at me, his expression unreadable but tinged with surprise as I shut and lock the door behind me and casually, slowly, begin to undress.

He shakes his head and bites his lip, the cutest fucking thing I've ever seen him do. My jeans fall to the floor in a puddle around my feet. My top next, followed by my panties and bra. I even pull my hair out of its messy bun and toss the little hair tie to the floor with my clothes. He doesn't speak. His jaw tightens, his throat works, and I can practically feel the heat rolling off him as my shirt hits the floor.

"Anya," he says softly. Warning.

I press my finger to my lips. "Shhh."

I sidle over to him, stark naked. He pushes his chair back and hits *mute,* as someone drones on with locations and numbers and times, something about Dublin and Cork. I slide onto his lap and kiss his cheek.

"Thank you," I whisper in his ear.

"I'm not sure for what," he groans. "But you're welcome."

I kiss my way down to his jaw, down the length of his neck, to where his shirt's unbuttoned at the top. I lick his collarbone. My fingers knot in his hair, nails dragging over his scalp.

With no preamble and a stifled groan, he slips two fingers inside me, curling them just right. A delicious shudder rolls through me.

He stands without warning and stabs at his phone. "I have to go." The phone clatters to the floor as he unbuckles his belt in one smooth motion, and in the next breath, I feel him pressing against me—thick, hard, already leaking into me.

"Do you want my cock, Anya?" he asks. "Is that why you came in here?"

"I always want your cock," I say on a half-whine, aching for him, arching my back to tell him wordlessly to take me. "*Always.*"

He drives into me in one brutal, vivid stroke, knocking the breath from me. He fucks me with relentless thrusts, his grip bruising my thighs, his teeth at my throat. "You're so fucking perfect. You're everything."

His rhythm stutters as he slams into me. My pleasure rolls through me as I ride him. He glides a thumb over my clit, my hips rise. I'm gasping, coming.

"Fucking gorgeous," he growls as he comes inside me. We collapse together, messy and breathless, sweat-slicked and tangled. His forehead rests against mine.

"Tell me you're mine, Anya. I want to hear you say it."

"I'm yours, Semyon." And it finally feels right.

"Don't think you can get away with interrupting my phone calls," he says with a halfhearted slap to my naked ass.

I snort and wink at him. "Whatever you say."

CHAPTER 24

THE GRAND HALL of the Romanov estate gleams. Crystal chandeliers hang like constellations, and gold-trimmed mirrors illuminate everybody here. Some might think the gold-trimmed mirrors are just for show, but I know they give Mikhail Romanov and his brothers a better vantage point around the marble columns in this huge place. Mirrors are helpful—they give you a second set of eyes.

What people don't know about my glasses...

The air hums with murmured conversations, soft laughter, and the clink of champagne flutes. Since I've known the Romanovs, they've been famous for holding these galas. Here, people pretend that we're civilized for a little while.

I fucking hate them.

In a way, it's reminiscent of grand dances they held in ages past, the kind where tension simmered beneath every polite bow and curtsy, where hidden motives and unspoken feelings played out across a crowded room.

Of course Rafail's wife, Polina, loves it. This is her family home, after all. Though she grew up in New York, her roots are firmly planted in Moscow's elite circles. My sisters adore it, too, a chance to get dressed up and mingle, to pretend for a little while there isn't a constant shadow of danger that lurks and follows us. Everyone's on their best behavior at a Romanov gala.

Not me though. There's no need.

There are so many different people here, so many different families, and Anya looks a little out of place and confused. But tonight, she's the only one I'm focused on. She's wearing that champagne gown that hugs her figure and cascades in soft waves to the floor. But like a good girl, she's wearing her shawl.

I'll take that off tonight.

The color sets off her auburn hair, swept up in a sophisticated updo, and her hazel eyes seem to shimmer under the lights. If there was ever a doubt in anyone's mind that Anya has come into her own, they'll be gone tonight. Anya *has* come into her own.

Heads turn as we ascend the staircase together, me at her side in a tailored black suit, my hand resting gently on the small of her back.

"Stunning," I murmur under my breath.

"It is beautiful," she says, looking around. "I feel like—"

"Not the ball, sweetheart."

I love the way her lips quirk, and her cheeks turn pink. She's so cute.

"You clean up pretty well yourself," she says with a wink. I give her a discreet little pinch to the ass. I'm the only one who knows she's wearing a vibrator—remote-controlled, the remote in my pocket. She said I'm kinky and wicked.

She has no fucking idea.

Tonight, I'm the one who has to stay sharp, to keep control. But Anya? She can lose herself entirely—and if I have anything to say about it, she's going to end up screaming my name in our bed before the night's over. I want her so fucking wound up, so desperate for me, that by the time I get her home, she's begging, pleading for me to take her. To ruin her.

Every look, every touch will be a slow, deliberate tease until she can't take another second without me inside her.

"Is Matvei here tonight?"

"Should be. Why?"

With a frown, she shakes her head. "I don't... trust him."

Good. She shouldn't. But she's safe with me.

As we enter the ballroom, a familiar figure approaches. Speak of the devil. He greets us with a courteous nod, his dark eyes darting around the room. But there's an undercurrent of something else. Large events like this draw plenty of locals and their attention. If we're going to get any word about Polina's sister, it'll be tonight.

Anya bristles beside me. I don't blame her. We're pretty sure he's a psychopath.

"Good evening, Anya," Matvei says, his tone smooth, distant. "You look lovely."

"That's enough of that," I say, dragging her away from him. He chuckles, and she thanks him, but her smile is plain and guarded. She told me he unnerves her. She knows he's loyal to Rafail, and I've explained to her that his brother Gleb betrayed us. Matvei is polite on the surface, but there's a hard edge beneath his charm—a quiet ruthlessness she's very aware of. Matvei will stop at nothing to show his loyalty.

Once inside, I'm ushered to a more private area where Rafail and Polina are already having drinks. Anya stiffens when she realizes this isn't a huge crowd but a small, intimate gathering. Elegant food is being served on small silver trays, and drinks are being poured.

"Champagne, ma'am?" a waiter offers.

Her back is tight and rigid as I hit the lowest setting on the vibrator in my pocket. Her lips part, and her cheeks flush as she looks at me, a wicked glint in her gorgeous eyes.

"Two, please," she says, plucking two flutes of champagne off the tray and handing one to me.

"I told you I wasn't drinking tonight," I remind her.

"I know," she says with a little grin. "You're holding the second one for when I'm done with the first." She sips. I hit the higher button on the vibrator to punish her for her sass. She groans softly and hides it behind her flute of champagne.

I shut it off when the champagne is done.

"Semyon," she pleads in my ear.

"Yeah, baby?"

She shakes her head as Polina approaches, elegant and graceful with her long blonde hair and silver gown.

We make easy chatter with Polina as she introduces us to a few more people her family knows. Anya nurses her second glass of champagne. I lean in and whisper in her ear.

"What would I feel if I put my hands between your legs right now?" I flick the button.

"Wet," she gasps. "Hot. *Need*." She's lost the ability to speak beyond one syllable. I stifle a chuckle and embrace her.

"Baby," I murmur. "Put your head on my shoulder." She obeys without hesitation.

"Are you ready to come, Anya?"

"Mmmm."

"Good girl. Let yourself go. Come, baby. No one's here." She maintains the control of a queen as I press the vibrator button again. She shudders, her release hitting in waves. I laugh softly, pulling her into my arms as if her trembling shoulders are from laughter and not a climax in the middle of the room.

I grin to myself. One point for me.

"Good girl," I whisper approvingly into her ear. "I'm so proud of you."

"Oh, really?" she teases, tossing her head back and taking another sip of champagne. I note she's a little wobbly on her feet though.

"Really."

I pluck the flute out of her hand and set it on a nearby table.

"Dance with me," I say gently but firmly.

"You dance?" she asks, blinking.

"I do tonight."

Quietly, she places her hand in mine. I lead her to the dance floor, where only one other couple is present. The music shifts to something slower, more intimate. I wrap my arm around her waist as I pull her close, my other hand clasping hers, steady and warm. I love the way it feels with her here against me.

"You're full of surprises, sir," she murmurs, her voice soft.

I reach into my pocket and pull out a small box.

"You haven't seen anything yet. This is for you."

She looks down at my palm. "But we're already married, Mr. Kopolov. That can't be a ring?"

"I know. Open it and see what it is."

She opens the box with a sly smile and looks curiously at the key inside.

"What's this?"

"The key to your new bakery."

New bakery?

"I told you to trust me. Believe me, you'll love it when it's finished. We'll keep all of your mother's appliances, every beautiful thing she installed in there. The only new additions will be industrial locks on the doors, a much larger fridge, and a different freezer you'll have access to. I intentionally kept the original one though." I shrug. "It might come in handy."

We move through the crowd. Anya's posture is stiff, her fingers brushing the hem of her shawl like a shield. I'm getting better at reading her and knowing what she needs. I don't blame her for being nervous in a crowded place, especially when she's a fish out of water. She shouldn't be nervous though. She's with me.

"You're frowning." Her eyes meet mine, curious.

"I can tell you think you have something to fear here. But you don't. Not with me." I thread my fingers across the back of her neck and give her a gentle squeeze.

She wordlessly pulls closer to me, draws in a breath and nods, giving me the smallest of smiles. It's all I need.

We need a breath of fresh air. I navigate toward the outdoor bar.

"I don't really feel like I belong here," she whispers in my ear.

"I can relate to that. I never feel like I belong anywhere." I thought I was getting better at reading her, but I don't fully understand the softness in her eyes when she looks at me and squeezes my hand.

I lean in closer. "I'm going to protect you, Anya. I always will. But you're stronger than you think." I tuck a finger under her chin and bring her gaze to mine. "Don't forget who you are. If I had my way, they'd be bowing to you when you enter."

One day, they will. They fucking will.

"Kopolov."

My focus sharpens when I see him—Oleg Makarov. Unpredictable. One of the Romanov family's lesser allies here in Moscow, but still dangerous. He exudes an air of authority, his gaze honing in on Anya.

"It's been a while, Semyon," he says smoothly before turning to Anya. "And who is this? Your lovely little wife?"

Asshole.

Anya bristles beside me, immediately on edge. Makarov is ruthless and unpredictable, and I don't trust him.

His eyes immediately narrow on her, and his voice lowers. I don't want her to touch him, but when he reaches for her hand, she sticks her hand out and shakes his— mercilessly.

"Yes. Anya Kopolov. His 'little wife.'" She emphasizes the words, and I love that she does.

He narrows his eyes. "Well, aren't you the brave one?"

"And you are?" she presses, unbothered. Pride surges in my chest.

His eyes flash with amusement—a man like Oleg enjoys pushing boundaries, especially with people like Anya, who aren't seasoned for his world. He chuckles, leaning in too close for my liking. "Someone you don't want fuck around with," he finishes, baring his teeth.

"I don't see what's so brave about stating my own name," she says with a cold smile. A part of me wants to cheer her on. *Attagirl.* Another part of me wants to shove her behind me to protect her.

"Careful, girl," he mutters, "In our world, some people don't appreciate a brazen woman."

Alright, that's enough of that. I put myself between the two of them. "I fucking do. That's enough from you."

The shift in the atmosphere is immediate. The polite mask drops from my face, replaced by something much darker. He freezes as if sensing the threat between us, but since he doesn't seem to be getting the hint, something harsher might be in order. "You have something you want to say to my wife?" I whisper. "You know she and I pledged vows to each other. You also know what that means, don't you?"

I imagine how this will play out—the way I'll take him, my fist hitting his jaw. He'll fall back to the ground, his head cracking against the concrete. And no one will move. Not one single person will bat an eyelash because this is nothing out of the ordinary for my family—for this gathering.

But I don't. Not yet. I decide to behave myself. For Anya.

Until he decides he has something else to say to her.

"You're his first wife, aren't you? Enjoy that. Don't you know what this family does with their wives?" His voice taunts again, this time meeting my gaze. "I'm disappointed in you, Semyon. Would've thought you'd have taught your wife her place by now."

Anya's jaw drops.

I get in his face. "I don't think I'm the one who should be careful," I warn him. "Rumor has it you have some affiliations with the Irish. And they're on the move. Doesn't seem like it's in your best interest to fuck that up, does it?"

"I have no idea what you're talking about," he says, but his cold smile falters. His sharp incisors glint at me. "You moved in on the bakery without wasting any time. Seems like you like to take your wife there too, don't you?"

My fist connects with his jaw. It only whets my appetite. "You son of a bitch!" I snarl and shove him into a glass table that instantly shatters. Glass showers down, and Anya screams. No one even looks our way.

He chuckles, getting to his feet as he brushes his sleeve across his broken lip, smearing blood. "I knew it," he murmurs. "That was a test... and you failed."

I step after him, but a heavy hand falls on my shoulder.

"Don't." It's Matvei, his eyes boring into mine. "It's a distraction. You know what it is. Distracting you from *what* is the real question."

Makarov is gone.

Anya stares at me, her eyes wide.

"No one even looked over here," she says, shaking her head. "You punched him, broke the table and shattered glass, and no one even batted an eye." She gives me a reproachful look. "Is this how you boys always handle things?"

Just when I seem to be making traction in understanding her, she throws me a curveball.

Matvei huffs out a laugh. "This is how we do things, Anya. Every guest here tonight is somehow affiliated with a family that doesn't think twice about making a statement." His eyes track the exits. "Stay close to Semyon."

"Let's get some fresh air," I suggest, pushing away from Matvei to a paved area illuminated by moonlight. It seems to do the trick with my sisters.

Matvei walks away from us, but I don't miss the way his hand goes to his waistband—ready to draw a weapon.

"Can we go home now?" There it is again. *Home.*

"Soon."

I can't shake the feeling that something is about to happen, another puzzle piece falling into place.

I walk with Anya. The garden paths are dimly lit, shadows stretching across the stones. It's quiet here, the distant hum of the party fading into the background.

Something is off. The hairs on the back of my neck prickle. I inhale deeply as if the scent will give something away, but I can't catch it. Instead, I notice the way Anya's eyes flick to the shadows, the slight hitch in her breath.

Whipping around, I'm alert. Anger claws at my chest. First the bakery, now this. In my peripheral vision I note quick movement and a flash of metal. My instincts flare.

"Get down!" I snap, pulling her behind me as a figure emerges from the darkness. The first shot shatters the stillness of the night.

I shove her to the ground, shielding her with my own body as another shot rings out. Pain explodes across my shoulder, but I barely register it, adrenaline surging through my veins. I have to keep Anya safe.

Matvei's huge, looming figure plows through the stillness. He pulls the trigger. Fire bursts from his weapon.

"Are you okay?"

"I'm hit," I say through gritted teeth. "Anya, are you all right?"

"I'm fine." Her voice is panicked. "What happened?"

I draw my weapon and shoot. Fire erupts from my gun and from Matvei's. The attackers scatter, retreating into the night.

I could chase them, but that would leave Anya vulnerable.

"Get them. Get the fuck—get them!" I bark, my voice sharp with fury. I nod at Matvei, but he's a mountain of a man, built for power, not speed. He chases after them, firing as he runs, but the bastards are already disappearing. Gunshots echo, but it's too late.

This was no random attack. It was calculated. Designed to disorient us.

Anya gasps. "Oh my god, Semyon!"

I look down to see blood spilling onto my white shirt, onto the ground, onto my hands. *Motherfucker.*

Anya reaches for me, and my blood smears across her fingers, thick and sticky.

"I'm fine," I growl, scanning the darkness again for any sign of movement. But the garden is silent now, a predator retreating.

"Shit." I shake my head. "Matvei was right. What the fuck was that?"

Clicking heels signal the arrival of my sisters. Yana is first, her gaze sharp and lethal, already assessing the situation.

"Who was it? Where's Matvei?"

"The south exit." I've got the whole damn place memorized. It's always my way. I know the south exit leads to the parking garage, shielded only with tall hedges and a wrought iron fence.

Yana doesn't hesitate but kicks off her heels and springs, her figure disappearing into the night. Fucking wish she had been here instead of Matvei since she's twice as fast.

"Are you okay, Anya?" Zoya asks, calm and unruffled as always. She checks on Anya with a quick glance. I love that my sister looked after my wife first, knowing she's a more vulnerable target.

"I'm fine, but Semyon—"

"He's had worse," Zoya says after a quick assessment. But in the dark, I can't tell if she's only saying it to ease Anya's fears. My vision swims.

Anya shakes her head. "He's bleeding."

Zoya remains composed. "We'll take care of him. The Romanovs will have medics."

"I'm good," I grind out through clenched teeth. I feel impotent, bested, and it fucking pisses me off. They could've hit Anya. Who the fuck was that? "Don't worry about me."

But I can't ignore the way Anya looks at me, her eyes wide and glistening with fear. She's trembling, and something tells me this is more than fear. Something deeper that reaches inside me, tightening like a fist around my chest.

My vision goes dark around the edges. *Khristos.* I'm losing blood.

"I'll be back," Zoya murmurs, retreating with her weapon drawn. "Anya, stay here with him."

"Of course," Anya says, shaking her head. "As if I'd go anywhere." Her lips draw downward in a pout. I'd smile if it didn't feel like my shoulder was going to implode.

"Who would just come here, shooting?" She shakes her head. She hovers, her hands near me as if she somehow wants to anchor me in place. "Oh, Semyon." Our fingers lace together, sticky with blood.

"Someone with ties to the Irish." The pieces are starting to fit together. I need meds so I can focus, so I can slide them all into place and call *checkmate.* "Matvei's instincts were right. It was a fucking distraction. Rafail and Rodion aren't here, so I can fucking guarantee they were at the far end of the estate before they pulled their moves."

What I don't tell her is they would likely know my instinct would be to protect Anya, and Matvei would be too slow for a chase. This was calculated.

Anya frowns. "They came close enough to shoot. I saw something on one of their wrists when he turned to go, something that reminded me of the video with Eli."

Of course. The faction's symbol. The Irish syndicate hasn't been quiet about what they want. Tonight, they finally made a move.

"I can't believe no one's looking," Anya whispers. "You're bleeding out on their patio, Semyon. Shots rang out, and no one gives a damn. What the hell?" She shakes her head, her voice wobbly. "How is this normal?"

I don't know what I can tell her to reassure her. I'm doing my best to stay conscious.

But the raw emotion in her gaze is something it takes me a moment to process. I've never seen it before. She's shaking, yes—but there's something more. Something deeper.

What does it mean? Maybe I have seen it before and never realized it.

For a moment, neither of us speaks. The intensity of her stare makes my chest tighten. The world swims in front of me, and my face feels too hot, the skin too tight. *Shit.*

I give her a grim smile. "Violence isn't enough. Life and death happen in the blink of an eye in our world, and the world just keeps spinning, Anya."

Slowly, the weight of my words sinks in. But I can feel it— her fear isn't just for herself anymore. It's for me.

Matvei returns, panting slightly but composed. He leans in. "Definitely the Irish," he confirms, his gaze flicking to Anya. We listen as he gives us more details, but it's only confirmation of what we already knew.

Zoya returns with Mikhail Romanov, the Romanov family pakhan, and someone I don't know by his side, a young man with swarthy skin dressed all in white. His medic, I'd guess.

"Alright," he says with a tight smile. "Let's get you inside and patched up."

"We're not safe," Anya says. "God, Semyon."

I reach for her hand and give it a gentle squeeze.

"We never were, Anya."

Yana returns to us, triumphant and fierce, dragging a bound hostage in her wake. Mikhail's brows shoot up. Anya pales. The man stumbles, a smear of blood trickling from his temple. Yana has a hand fisted in the back of his shirt, the other clutching a gun pressed tightly against his ribs. She moves as always, with deadly grace.

"Got this bastard sneaking toward a getaway car. Couldn't get the others, but we'll get answers out of him."

I step forward, ignoring the burning ache in my shoulder. Anya shifts nervously, but I wave her off. I'm in control now. "Who sent you?"

"You know who," he says in a drawl, not bothering to hide his thick brogue.

"We've got all night," Yana whispers, smirking.

His jaw is tight, his eyes narrowed as he spits on the ground. "You'll get nothing out of me."

I shake my head. This bastard's responsible for a threat against my wife. My blood boils. "We'll see about that."

CHAPTER 25

ANYA

"He's alright," I say in a low voice, twirling my hair around my finger. It reminds me of when I was younger, hiding in my mom's closet, twirling the phone cord around my finger. Back when phones had cords.

"What happened?" Ophelia asks. "This is crazy. It's like all of a sudden, you're living in a romance novel."

"I don't know. It was like we were ambushed or something. I don't really know what happens in these families," I tell her, shaking my head. "All this time, I thought Eli was mafia adjacent. I didn't think he was fully involved. But it seems like there's a lot I still don't understand."

I glance at the sleeping form of my husband. He refused pain meds, of course, because he had to brave it out on his own. I think the real reason is because he has a hostage to talk to.

The man who once seemed so emotionally distant stirs in his sleep. When he wakes, he looks at me, reaches for my hand, and gives it a squeeze.

"What time is it?"

I glance at the time and cover the mouthpiece of my phone. "Six."

Of course. Semyon is like clockwork. Gunshot wound? A... what do they call it... *hostage* somewhere waiting for his questions? Doesn't matter. Dinner with his family is at six.

Ever since Semyon was injured, Rafail has insisted that we stay in their large family home. Stefan, of course, is over-joyed because Zoya is here. And we haven't missed a single dinner since.

"Semyon?" I say quietly. "You want to go down for dinner? You don't have to."

He sits up and swings his legs off the bed. "Of course I do."

"Rafail told you to stay here and rest."

"I'm fine. It's a fucking paper cut, Anya."

I roll my eyes. Of course he'd say that.

"We have a lot to discuss, and much of it directly affects your safety," he says, insistent. "We're heading downstairs."

I go back to the phone. "I have to go."

"Call me soon, babe. I love you and miss you so much. And when are you opening the bakery back up?"

"Soon," I promise, but it's beginning to sound like a broken record. "Love you."

I hang up the phone. Semyon frowns at me, and I'm not sure why.

"Alright, if you feel up for it..."

"I wouldn't go if I wasn't," he says stoutly.

I brush a stray strand of hair off his forehead and adjust his glasses. His steady gaze warms me, his voice a low growl. "Just because I need a little recovery time doesn't mean I've lost my stamina, woman."

"You better not," I say softly, teasing. I straddle his lap and slide my hands over the breadth of his hard chest. It's not this part of him that's injured. I lean in and kiss him, but only briefly. He hates to be late. *I* hate to be told what to do.

I press my palm against his hard erection as his hands lace around the back of my neck, a warning. I trace the line of his cock, my pussy wet and needy. I slide back and bend, touching my mouth to the head of his cock. "You sure we don't have time?" I ask in a mewl. "I want you, Semyon."

I can't help but giggle at his guttural curse as he fists my hair and yanks my head up.

"Keep doing that, and I'll come in my fucking pants." He shakes his head and adjusts his cock. "Hard to concentrate with blue balls. *Jesus.*"

But instead of pushing me off his lap, he fingers my hardened nipple through the thin fabric of my top. I moan and lean in closer. With a tug, he pulls my top down and palms my breast, his thumb tracing a line over my nipple. My clit throbs.

"There," he says with a satisfied smirk before his teeth graze my collarbone. "Now we're even." He slams his palm across my ass. Lucky me, it was his nondominant arm that was injured. "Now get your ass downstairs. If you make us any later, I'll take it out on your ass after dinner."

I cock my head to the side as if contemplating this.

"*Anya.*" But I'm standing, walking over to the door beside him.

"The sooner I can get to our hostage, the sooner I may have answers about Eli."

I swallow. My mouth is suddenly dry. "I know."

At the dinner table, Stefan has much to say. He's eager to tell us about the cookies he made with Zoya, how well he did in school, the new book he's reading, the new level he reached on his game, and the dog he and Zoya want to get.

Rafail growls at the mention of a dog, but Zoya just giggles.

At one point, Stefan is so excited that he reaches across the table and knocks over a glass of milk. Rafail's stern gaze falls on him, and Stefan blanches, but Semyon calmly rights the glass.

"Pay attention, Stefan. It's alright; accidents happen, but fewer do if you're careful."

Stefan doesn't seem fazed. I'd have been mortified at his age. I think this kind of environment will be good for him. Zoya ushers him out to change his soaked shirt. "Let's go get those cream puffs we made earlier."

"I used to bake with my sister," Stefan says petulantly, glancing at me. "When are we going back to the bakery?"

"Soon," I tell him. "Semyon and I are making some renovations. We'll be there soon."

Stefan leaves, and Zoya follows hot on his heels.

"We need to talk about what happened," Rafail says quietly. Polina's eyes flick to mine. Semyon says she feels responsible for what happened because it was at her family estate. She's not, of course.

"We have a decision to make," Matvei says, his voice dark and his gaze pinning me in place. "Are we sure everyone here can handle the truth?"

I press my lips into a thin line. He means *me*. "I think all parties present understand exactly what they need to," I say with a soft smile.

Semyon nods in agreement.

"We scoured the footage," Matvei continues. "The person present in the video we got about Eli's capture is the one Semyon spotted in the attack, but also the one who got away. It seems he doesn't like to be anonymous. We'll know more when we interrogate our hostage."

"Why are you waiting?" All eyes snap to me.

"The weaker he is, starved and thirsty, the easier it will be to get answers," Semyon answers quietly.

My stomach lurches.

"Who have we identified?" Rafail asks, his eyes sharp and focused on Matvei.

"They call him The Undertaker," Matvei says. "The son of Keenan McCarthy."

"Son of a bitch," Rafail whispers. "He's a deadly shot. Infamous."

I get the distinct feeling there are a lot of things they're not saying out loud—things that may or may not involve me.

My face feels hot, and something roils in my belly. I think of Eli.

The Undertaker?

"Why would he just show up and pull that shit?" Rodion mutters, shaking his head.

"The Irish want us to know they're present but not prepared for full-on war," Matvei says. "Not yet, anyway."

"Of course they aren't," Semyon replies. "We have more allies here than they do."

Rodion drums his fingers on the table thoughtfully. "Which brings me to something I've been thinking about. In America, I had drinks with one of the cleaners for the West Coast cartel. He mentioned meeting with the don from the Boston Italian mafia and a few others."

Rafail nods slowly. "Vadka was just telling me about this. The Brotherhood."

"The Brotherhood?" I ask.

"It's a group of the six most powerful underworld leaders in America," Matvei says. "It's unofficial, but when they join forces, they become unstoppable."

"Do you have something like that?" I ask.

"Not yet," Rafail replies, his voice thick with meaning. "But it's time."

Interesting.

"How do you begin something like that?" I ask, curious. It's mind-boggling to think of all of those powerful people in one group.

"First, we get your brother," Matvei says. "Then, we question him."

Semyon's hand tightens on my knee. *Question him.*

What does that involve? Torture?

My head is spinning. I blink, trying to clear my brain, but it isn't very effective. Semyon's too intent on the conversation with his family to notice. His grip on my knee tightens.

"Are you okay?" he asks. I shake my head.

"I'm fine," I lie.

The thought of Eli being in the grip of somebody called The Undertaker? Excuse me if I need a minute.

"We're gonna take care of this, Anya. You have my word," Semyon says. But when I look at him, his face is unnaturally pale. He's still recovering from a gunshot wound, I tell myself, but...

What have I gotten myself into?

I reach for a glass of water and, to my horror, my hand shakes, and I knock it over, just like my little brother did.

"So sorry!" I stammer, flustered. I jump up from the table, and the chair clatters to the floor. I'm dizzy. The room spins.

What's the matter with me? I feel like I'm going to be sick.

As the conversation intensifies, my head throbs. It feels strange. The world tilts at the edges of my vision, but I push it aside. I can't fall apart. Not now. There's too much—

"Anya."

Semyon's on his feet, reaching for me. It's so strange because it seems like the floor is rising to meet the ceiling. How is this... I'm spinning, falling... then everything goes black.

"No evidence of poison," someone says above me in a grim voice.

"She has a fever. If it goes on much longer, we're going to have to take her to the hospital."

"No, she won't be safe there." I recognize Semyon's voice.

"You'll have to do your best to keep her well-hydrated and rested. It looks like a virus, but it could get out of hand quickly."

I try to open my eyes, but they're so heavy. Too heavy. I close them again.

I watch as my mother pounds her small fist on the kitchen table, pleading with Semyon, begging. My father's lifeless eyes stare ahead, the stale stench of whiskey on his breath. Eli appears next—bound to a chair, bloody and broken. But when I look closer, it's not him anymore but Semyon. Blood gushes from the wound in his shoulder, splattering the floor. I try to scream, but no sound comes.

Then I see Stefan playing outside. He's building a castle with the blocks Yana bought him. Behind him, a large, tattooed figure raises a gun. I try to run to him, but my legs are too slow. I can't reach him.

I gasp. Waking. Semyon is sitting in a chair, and his head has lolled to the side. I take in a quick breath.

He's asleep.

"Semyon?"

My lips feel swollen and my mouth dry as if stuffed with cotton. He stirs immediately, suddenly alert, his glasses slightly askew.

"Are you all right?" he asks.

I'm surprised to find myself in bed.

"I'm fine," I say. I think? "What happened to me?"

Semyon's on his feet, rushing to me. Immediately, his hand grips mine. It grounds me, calms me, even as my fears are rising.

"We don't know. We thought you might have been poisoned, but the doctor says there's no evidence of that. You have a fever, but the doctor said it's most likely a virus."

A fever... right away, they thought poison. I stare at him.

"You were out cold."

I shake my head. "Your clothes are a rumpled mess."

He snorts. "Yes?"

"It's just... unusual for you."

Semyon's voice is rough as he leans in closer to me. "I've been preoccupied." He sighs. I can still see his bandaged shoulder. It was only a surface wound after all, but it bled like crazy and can't feel good.

"He definitely has."

I look up to see Zoya standing in the doorway.

"He's been by your side nonstop. You've been in and out."

"*Zoya.*" Semyon shoots her a look, but she just shakes her head.

"He's been absolutely glued to you, Anya. We've all been worried."

"I think I'm okay," I say, shaking my head, though I'm not entirely sure. I still feel disoriented. My stomach growls.

"Are you hungry?" Zoya asks, tilting her head.

I nod. "Definitely. Any new developments I need to know about?" I ask.

"None that pertain to Eli," Semyon says, though his eyes shift away as if processing something else.

It all comes rushing at me at once. The gala. Gunfire. Semyon was shot, and he had a man he was going to interrogate. We had dinner, and I fainted. I stare. "Did you get answers?"

He doesn't respond right away but steeples his fingers and gets that distant look he has when he's planning his next move on the chessboard. His eyes darken, and his voice drops. Sometimes, I love how intense he is. Sometimes, it terrifies me.

"Some, yes. Either Eli is involved with them and went underground to make us question things," Semyon says, "or they're planning something else."

Semyon stares into the distance, as calculating as always, but I can't shake the weight pressing on my chest. What if Eli isn't just a pawn in their game? What if he's a player too? What does that mean for us? I promised my mother I'd hold my family together, but right now, I'm the one unraveling...

"What would they be planning?" My voice sounds strange to my own ears.

"The best way to get to us," he replies. "First, the cameras at the bakery—"

My stomach twists, and I look away. I know exactly what those cameras caught on film. The thought of anyone else seeing it—

"Then the gunshots at the gala. The video of Eli. The Irish are on the move—we know that much. We also know the girl who betrayed us years ago is in league with them. But we don't know how Eli fits into this puzzle."

I sit back, thinking, as Zoya leaves to get some food, and I process all of this.

I need to be independent, to take care of Stefan, but that need clashes with the growing attraction I feel for Semyon. And even as I fight it, I'm terrified of depending on anyone.

From where I'm lying in the bedroom, the estate seems eerily quiet. The walls seem to hold their breath in anticipation. Outside the door, guards stand like statues. It's like living inside a war plan.

I want answers. I want to know where we stand. I want to know Eli is okay—and that my family is safe.

"There's one thing that troubles me in all this," Semyon admits, leaning forward until his forearms rest on his knees. "Remember, when we find your brother, he's going to know that I married you."

"Yeah, so that's not going to go over very well." I grimace. "He'll never forgive you."

I can still see him going straight for Semyon years ago in the small shed. So much has happened between then and now, but will that change how he feels? And where will that leave us?

"I know."

Eli was his only friend. I steel myself for the next question. I look Semyon straight in the eyes. "Did my father have anything to do with this?" I ask.

Semyon purses his lips and shakes his head. "He didn't when he agreed for you to marry me."

I blink, wondering if I heard him correctly. "What was that?"

"He didn't seem involved when he agreed for you to marry me," Semyon repeats, meeting my gaze. "If he were, I would've thought we'd know then."

I stare. My father... agreed to let him marry me?

What?

All this time, I thought it was my choice, that I'd made the decision to sacrifice myself for my family, and now he tells me... it was preordained?

"You said I had the option of marrying you," I say, shaking my head. Why is he acting so casual when I feel like he's just delivered a bombshell? "And now you're telling me my father was playing this game all along?"

"Yes, Anya. I wanted you to know the truth." He runs a hand through his hair, making it stick up. It's unsettling, his hair standing on edge, paired with his rumpled clothes. "I'm sorry for any way I manipulated you."

He says it as plainly as he might apologize for bumping into me in a crowded supermarket.

This was all a ploy to get me to marry him. A plan to gain access to my family's bakery, fortify it, and strengthen his own family.

His family always comes first, doesn't it?

An emotion I can't describe rises in my chest, but I push it down. I have to deal with the present. *Now*.

It was all a lie. A carefully orchestrated plan. I was convenient but nothing more.

I fell for it.

Zoya knocks gently at the door. Semyon's back on his phone with a scowl while my world is caving in on me.

The walls feel too close, as if they're closing in. I tell myself that I'm not in my right mind—that there's more to the story than meets the eye. I tell myself that I need to stop reacting and that I need to think this through before I make a decision.

I tell myself that I matter.

But the words feel hollow.

Something is off. Too much has happened too fast, and the answers only seem to raise more questions. But one thing is clear—Semyon all but admitted it. My father was involved to a degree, enough that he gave me away before I even knew there was a choice to make.

And now everything I thought was mine feels like an illusion.

Who else has been lying to me? What else am I going to find out next?

Zoya hands me a tray with my favorite soup: creamy chicken and rice, a recipe she learned from Polina. Next to the bowl is crusty bread and a simple salad, along with a large glass of water. A few minutes ago, I was starving. Now I can't think of eating anything, but if I don't, I'll draw alarm from them. So I thank her and take a sip of water and a tentative bite of bread.

"I was worried for you," Semyon says with a little smile, oblivious to my inner turmoil. I squeeze his hand back even as a lump forms in my throat. I won't look at him now, my handsome, heartless Superman.

"Hey. Anya, are you alright?"

From the doorway, Rafail stands, his hands in his pockets.

He looks tired, wearing nothing but his dress slacks and a white T-shirt, his ever-present suit jacket discarded.

No, I'm not all right. But I only nod quietly. "I wish I knew why that happened, but yeah, I think I'm okay."

"I know. Rest and tell us if you need anything." My nose tingles. It's nice to have someone taking care of *me* for once.

Rafail looks to Semyon. "We're ready for you."

The person he has to interrogate is waiting downstairs—the person who has answers, presumably. But he hesitates, his eyes on me.

"Go," I say, and to my relief, my voice doesn't waver this time. It feels like I'm telling him to go in more ways than one.

Go... leave me.

Everything's been manipulated, shaped to fit into the grand design of their empire. And for what? Control. My family's safety was used as a bargaining chip in their game.

The walls feel too close, the blankets too hot. I try to steady my breathing, but all I can do is focus on Semyon's rumpled clothes and mussed hair. The man who has become my tether is now the one unraveling me.

He thought he could control me, another piece on his chessboard.

He rises to his feet. "Anya, rest. I'll be back."

My eyes stay fixed on the bandage wrapped around his arm —a reminder of everything he's endured. A reminder that he's human. I know he's been through hell too.

Fear gnaws at me. What else has he kept from me?

I can't afford to break now.

"Anya?" Zoya's voice cuts through the haze. I blink, realizing she's standing in front of me, concerned.

"I'm fine." I shake my head, forcing a smile that doesn't reach my eyes. "I need some air."

"Of course." She opens a window. Yeah, I need more than that.

"Let me know if you need anything else," she says brightly. "Stefan's done his homework, and he's gone to bed for the night."

"Thank you."

I wait until she's gone, stand, and begin pacing. My mind feels like a tangle of memories, promises, and betrayal. My instincts tell me to follow Semyon, to ask for answers, but I stay rooted to the spot. And if I go to him, what will I find? Do I really need to see him brutally beat someone so he can interrogate them and get answers? Do I really need to see another bloody scene?

I can't just leave. Stefan is here. But I have to find a way out.

My phone buzzes with a text. *Ophelia.*

Ophelia
We need to talk, Anya. It's urgent.

I respond to her, my heart racing.

What's the matter?

Ophelia
It's about Eli. I have information I have to tell you, but it has to be secret. Can you come outside? I'll meet you outside.

I look out the window to where armed guards stand at every exit.

Yes, of course.

CHAPTER 26

THE BASEMENT IS cold and damp, lit only by a single flickering bulb. It's our form of a dungeon, but Rafail is too proper to change it. Our prisoner, bloodied and bruised, sits slumped in the chair, his wrists bound behind him. I hope he's close to breaking. I've had a long fucking day.

Sweat coats his forehead, but his half-lidded eyes stay open. Matvei has warmed him up for me.

My voice is low and lethal. I'm out of patience. *"Talk."*

The man coughs, spitting blood onto the floor. "You think you know everything, don't you?" His twisted grin forms despite the pain. "You're fucked too, Kopolov."

Yeah, that's not up for debate. Appealing to my human side is a waste of time.

I take a slow step forward, my hands clenching into fists. I hardly expected him to just open his mouth and tell me everything.

"You may want to rethink your approach to survival," I warn him.

He doubles over, coughing, the sound wet and ragged. He has broken limbs and broken ribs. Blood dribbles from the corner of his mouth.

"Oh, I'm already dead. You know that. Don't fuck with me."

"But you have family," I say casually, pushing my hands into my pockets and walking closer. I'm not bluffing, and he fucking knows it.

His eyes harden. I glance at the notes Matvei gave me. A wife. Kids. I lean in closer. I didn't become who I am by being merciful.

"A wife. Kids. Who are all defenseless right now, left all alone with no one to protect them." I shake my head. "Isn't that a shame?"

I punch him across the jaw. The crack of bone echoes in the silence. He smiles at me, his teeth smeared in blood.

"You thought you could control her, didn't you?" he rasps. "The poor little baker's daughter. But the joke's on you, Kopolov. She's the one who used you."

I freeze, the blood in my veins turning to ice. He's going to say anything to manipulate me—I know this. And yet...

"What the fuck are you talking about?"

"Anya and her brother," he gasps, coughing again. Blood splatters on the floor. "They played you. You married her—

yoked yourself to her family. And now you've handed control of your empire over, bound it to her loyalty, without even realizing it. You're just like everyone else. A disgrace to the Bratva."

A roar builds in my chest. I grab him by the collar, yank him from the chair, and slam him against the wall. His head snaps back, and I hear his breath hitch in fear. Good.

"They didn't fucking use me."

He sneers and laughs—a low, evil, chilling sound.

"Oh, you're wondering now, aren't you? Wondering why she agreed so easily. Why you haven't been able to find her brother. You think you're in control, but you've already lost it. Lucky you get to fuck pretty pink pussy on your way to hell."

I slam my fist into his face again and again until his head lolls to the side, and he falls to his knees. I shove his chest and push him to the floor, kneeling on him. My breath comes in harsh, ragged gasps. Rage clouds my vision. I stare at his forearm—the mark of the Irish.

"What do you know about The Undertaker?" I growl, changing the subject. I don't fucking care what he tells me about my wife.

"Not telling you anything," he snarls. His sunken eyes burn with defiance. He looks like a man who's already decided his fate.

I grab him by the shirt and slam him to the ground. His head hits the concrete. I punch him again and again. I have so many weapons at my disposal—knives, tools, implements of torture—but I want to punch someone. I want to use him as a punching bag. I want to vent my aggression, my anger, my fury. But every time I punch him, I just want more.

One thing Anya doesn't know about me—or anybody in my family—is how fucking bloodthirsty we are. If she knew, she never would've agreed to this.

"Why don't you ask your wife," he taunts. I punch him again, this time hard enough that his eyes shut.

Fuck. He's passed out. Maybe dead. Both the same to me—I'm not going to get anything from him now.

I get to my feet and kick his ribs one more time. The satisfying crunch echoes before I pull the gun from my holster, cock it, and press it to his skull. His brains splatter everywhere. I shoot until his face is a bloody pulp, his body unrecognizable. Then I kneel next to him, take out a knife, and slice off the mark of the Irish from his flesh.

I stand, wiping my hands on my pants, and turn to the guard who watches me. Fear crosses his eyes.

"Wrap that up and send it to the fucking Irish."

I go to leave.

The next person who owes me answers is my wife.

But when I get back to the room, she's not there. Her tray is untouched, as if she hasn't even eaten a crumb.

Cold, familiar dread seeps into my veins.

Why don't you ask your wife?

Has she betrayed me?

My greatest fears. I pull out my phone, dialing Matvei. He answers right away.

"Have you seen Anya?"

"No," he answers. "Why?"

"I can't find her. Have all available men search the grounds. *Now.*"

"Dude, are you overreacting? Maybe you have a fever, and it's getting to your head. Semyon, it's been a long few days. Jesus, man, get some sleep."

"I just told you my wife's missing, and you tell me to get some sleep?" He's lucky he isn't standing in front of me now. I'd throat-punch him.

I call Zoya next.

"Where's Anya?"

"Anya? The last time I saw her, she was in bed. I told her Stefan went to bed and thought that she'd get some rest herself. I left her resting. She isn't there?"

"No." I'm slipping. Of course I knew that. Why didn't I think of that?

But when I pull up the surveillance footage on my phone, it's blank.

What the actual fuck?

I go to dial Rafail, but the signal is blocked. I can't make a fucking call. I'm forced to wander my house like it's the goddamn dark ages.

"Anya!" I yell, the desperation in my voice impossible to hide. "Anya!"

I do a mental inventory of who's home. Rodion and Ember are back at their place. Stefan and Zoya are here, Rafail's family. Yana.

She's the closest one. But when I go to her door and knock, there's no answer.

Fuck.

I try again, but as I turn down the hall, a door behind me opens. Yana stands in the doorway, her eyes blurry, wearing sweats and a T-shirt.

"Semyon? Are you alright?"

"No. I can't find Anya. The surveillance footage is blank, and I can't make any phone calls."

Yana is instantly awake.

"Fuck," she says, turning to tug on boots and pulling a gun from her bedside table.

I hear the pounding of her footsteps as she finishes getting dressed. I'm already running.

I head outside, barking orders to the guards and asking questions. No one's seen her. The estate is locked down in minutes, but without our ability to communicate—

If she did betray me...

I'll find her, no matter what. I have to.

CHAPTER 27

ANYA

I WANDER THE GROUNDS, navigating my way as quietly as I can through the areas least likely to be under surveillance. Zoya taught me. While they have guards and cameras everywhere, the service entrance by the kitchen used for staff and deliveries doesn't have the same heavy guard presence as the main entrances. The perimeter fencing near dense shrubbery leads to hidden pathways only Zoya seems to know about. It seems the youngest sister has had reason to want privacy and found a way to make it happen.

Ophelia has to talk to me, and if it has anything to do with my brother—I can't risk the Kopolov family finding out.

I never wanted this to be a choice between my family and theirs. I close my eyes as a rush of heat floods me. I need to stay awake, sober and ready, but my strength feels like it's at an all-time low.

I know the danger, but my friend needs me, and I don't feel like I can trust myself right now.

I call Ophelia, but her phone rings and rings, and she doesn't answer. I text her, but there's no response.

What the hell?

I stare at the gate and mentally go through the motions. I know exactly how to get out of here if I have to, but I can't leave my little brother. My throat catches.

I've just started to feel like I have a family.

I text Ophelia again.

I'm here. Where are you?

Why does Ophelia have news about my brother?

"There she is."

The low, dark Irish drawl behind me sends shivers down my spine.

I spin around to see a man wearing a mask, sitting on a bench, and someone is bound to him. I can't see in the moonlight. I take a step forward.

"Ophelia!" I yell into the darkness, but the man sitting there shakes his head and chuckles. His laughter sends a shiver down my spine.

"What did you do with Ophelia?" I put steel in my voice but can't help that it shakes.

"Your friend is safe and sound in her bed," he says with a smile I can see through the mask. "She did what she was told, like a good little girl. Unlike some other people I know."

I glare at him and take another step closer, even as everything in me tells me not to.

"Don't worry, your husband isn't coming to get you. He has no idea where you are. He's probably running around looking for you." The man leans forward on his forearms, his eyes meeting mine.

"And your brother is going to fucking love watching that footage I got from the bakery."

My stomach twists into knots.

"You're disgusting," I gasp, covering my mouth with my hand when I realize it is my brother sitting next to him. He's unconscious, his head tilted to the side.

Is he dead?

"What did you do to my brother?"

"He's been sedated," the man drawls. He laughs. "You recognize him, don't you?"

I stare, disbelieving.

Why is my brother here?

"You see, lass," he continues, "your brother and your father had a lot more to do with this than you thought, didn't they?"

He shakes his head.

"Your father signed you away as easily as he signed off your mother's diamond ring. Tragic what people will do for money, isn't it?"

We've all been played. Every fucking one of us.

"What do you want from me?" I demand.

"Oh, just the same thing your brother and father gave me," he says with a smile. "You're gonna go back to your man," he says in that drawl. "You'll pretend that none of this ever happened. You'll run in crying for help and say that your brother is here." He leans forward, his eyes glittering. "Aren't you, lass?"

I stare, unblinking. He wants me to spy?

They'll kill me.

"And then when I ask questions, you give me answers."

"I am not going to be a spy for you!" I shake my head. There has to be another way.

The man clicks his tongue and takes out a gun. He points it at my brother's head.

"That's a shame now, isn't it?" he says. "I would've thought your loyalty lay with your family. After all, isn't that what you promised your mother?"

My heart beats so fast I'm dizzy. He wants me to go back as if nothing happened, spy on my husband, and then feed him information in exchange for my brother?

Why do I have to make a choice? I don't know what to do.

Wait.

"How do you know what conversation I had with my mother?"

"Lass," he says with a wicked grin, "I know a lot more about your family than you think I do. Now tell me. Are you going back and playing the spy, and all will be as it was before? I'll step away, and you'll give me what I need, and no one—not Eli or Stefan or even your precious husband will be harmed."

A shiver races down my spine. *Yet.* No one will be harmed *yet.*

"Then you go back to your man. Pretend everything is normal. Should come naturally to you, shouldn't it?"

I shake my head.

"You're gonna run in and say that Ophelia texted you, and when you came out here, she was nowhere to be found. But surprise! Here's Eli—the fucking traitor. Come back to haunt you." He cocks his head to the side. "Now, do we have a deal, darlin'?" he drawls.

He wags a finger in my direction.

"I can already see the wheels turning. You're thinking you can give me lip service, go back inside, and take your brother with you, aren't you? And you won't answer to me."

He pulls up a tablet and smashes at the screen with one long, inked finger.

"But you see this, lass? That is your bestie, sleeping like a baby." An image of Ophelia in bed, her hands under her chin, fills the screen. "Whatever will happen to her if you dream of defying me? Don't think I have it in me? Maybe you haven't heard of my reputation."

Oh god.

I have no choice, do I?

I have to go back... I have to go back and pretend that every-thing's fine and then feed him information.

I need to stall to get my bearings. "What kind of informa-tion do you want?" I ask him. "It's not like I'm privy to everything—"

He chuckles low.

"Course y'are. The Kopolov family aren't sexists, now, are they? They share their info freely with men and women alike. It's a feather in Rafail's cap he taught his sisters how to fight."

When I don't deny it, he chuckles again. "I'll use your pretty little friend to give me the directions I need. I'll hack her phone. You'll be receiving text messages from me." I stare. So that's how he did it. "Now, darlin'. Do you see this video here?" he says.

The first flash of the screen shows me on the steel table in the bakery, Semyon in between my legs.

My cheeks flame.

"Now, now," he says, shaking his head, hitting pause. "I haven't watched the whole thing. I'm a gentleman, don't you know?"

Sure he is.

"You agree, like a good little girl, and I'll delete this right now and every record I have of it. Now, darlin', do we have a deal?"

"What's in this for me?"

"For you?" He gets to his feet, all trace of humor gone from his face. He spreads his hands wide, a mockery of generosity. "I'll let you live. And your father. And your brothers."

I stare into the darkness, torn. There has to be a way out of this. There has to be.

I want to scream. I'm silently begging for someone to come —Semyon, Rafail, Yana, anybody—but I was the one who got myself out here. I was the one who hid from all of them. And no one's coming to save me.

Maybe that's the crux of it, isn't it? *No one's coming to save me.*

I have to save myself. I have to save my family. And I'm not going to betray the Kopolov.

"Three," he says with a wicked grin, cocking his gun.

"Two."

He whistles low under his breath as if he can't wait to pull the trigger and end my brother's life.

"Okay, okay! I'll do what you say. Please, don't hurt him."

His low, dark chuckle fades into the night. And then—he's gone. Vanished. As if he waved a wand and teleported magically.

I'm alone. My brother is slumped against a bench. And I have to get help.

I run to Eli. I want to shake him and hug him, but the first thing I do is check his pulse to make sure he's breathing. My fingers find his wrist, and I hold my breath until the flutter of his heartbeat beneath them makes me cry out.

"Eli! Oh my god, Eli, what happened?"

If my mother could see him now...

"Wake up," I say, shaking him, but he doesn't budge. "Please, Eli. Please—wake up."

Still nothing.

I hold him to my chest, lift my face to the heavens, and scream. "Somebody help me! Help!" I scream at the top of my lungs.

Floodlights blind me, and I blink, turning my head to the side. Voices. Heavy footsteps.

Semyon's men come running to me.

"I found her! Who does she have? What is it?"

"Semyon, call Rafail! Lock the gate!"

My phone buzzes with a text.

> **Ophelia**
> If you reveal anything to them, your lover
> boy is dead—along with your brother.

I realize, with chilling accuracy, that there is no escape.

His guards surround us, weapons raised.

"Who was here?" They surround me in a circle. My heart aches.

"I told Zoya I needed fresh air. I came outside for a bit of a walk to clear my head. Someone screamed my name and scared the hell out of me. Then—" My voice catches. "Eli."

My brother's back. He's back, and he's alright. I haven't given myself space to process this yet.

They'll have questions. So do I.

I can still hear his cold, bitter voice.

"Eli's here. I heard someone out here yelling, and I came running. And I saw him. I don't know if he's alive," I lie. I better get good at it. "Please, let's get him inside."

I scan the men and don't see Semyon. My heart beats faster. Where is he? I want him, his strong, reassuring presence, but at the same time, I fear one look in his eyes and he'll know what I'm hiding.

CHAPTER 28

SEMYON

For once, I'm glad my brother's bossy as fuck, making us stay here in our family home. I'm relieved to know Stefan's taken care of and doesn't need me and Anya tonight.

We're exhausted, both of us.

The silence in the room is deafening as we get ready for bed. I stand by the window, my fingers wrapped around a crystal glass of vodka. I need something to take the edge off and help me sleep.

Tonight, my best friend came back to us, unharmed but dangerous. Who knows where Eli's allegiance really lies? Tonight, I beat a man to death to get answers. Tonight, I watched my wife collapse and caught her just before she hit her head on the table. I held her in my arms, oblivious to my own pain from the gunshot wound, afraid for the worst.

I've experienced loss so great; sometimes I fear there's a cavernous need inside me nothing can satiate.

When Anya collapsed, I thought the worst.

When Anya was missing, I thought the worst.

When she revealed Eli was home safe, and she screamed for help... I thought the worst.

And now, I'm spent.

Anya's in the small en suite. I can hear the water running as she takes her time. I imagine she's feeling the way I do too. Exhausted. Wary. Uncertain of anything... including me.

The city stretches before me out the window as I sip my drink, but my mind is fixated on only one thing: *Anya*.

The door to the bathroom opens. She stands before me in a tiny pair of shorts with a matching tank, yawning. Adorable.

"You feeling okay?"

"Mmm," she says with a nod. "Fine." I narrow my eyes. It's definitely a lie. "You?"

She shrugs a shoulder and walks to the bed, her shoulders slouching.

Why don't you ask your wife?

"Anya."

"Mmm?" She's in bed with her back to me, curled up, almost like she's trying to protect herself.

I start undressing. "Why were you outside?"

"I told you, Semyon," she says with a yawn. "I needed some fresh air."

I tug off my pants and strip to my boxers before I join her in bed. I slide under the covers and sidle up beside her, spooning her from behind. She's brutally honest when she's vulnerable, and nothing makes her more vulnerable than sex.

My dick presses against her ass. I ignore it and place my hand flat on her belly. My thumb grazes the underside of her breast, barely covered with the thin material.

"I'm so tired," she whispers.

"Me too. It's all good; we just need to talk about today, is all."

"Oh, that's it?" She says with a hint of a laugh. "Which part? The part where I fainted at dinner and still don't know why? Or the part where you acted as if you didn't have a shoulder wound and held me? Maybe the part where you sat beside me in bed all rumpled and disheveled, before you did probably violent things to our prisoner before you ended him? Are those the parts you want to talk about?"

"No."

She lets out a sigh. "I know."

Turning to face me, her eyes are as clear as a cloudless sky, but she can't hide the little wrinkle between her brows. Our breaths mingle. "You want to know more about how I found Eli."

I nod. My eyes want to close. I'm so fucking tired.

"This is what I'm going to tell you," she says in a whisper. "I've told you what I can. Maybe Eli can tell you more."

I stare at her. I want to shake her to get the truth out, but I know it won't work that way. I've built my entire life around control, strategy, and cold calculation, yet nothing prepared me for the raw anger that grips me, knowing there's more to this story and she won't tell me.

Has she betrayed me?

Why don't you ask your wife?

I clench my teeth. "I've given you protection. Stability. I took your little brother into my home, Anya."

She stares at me and opens her mouth, then clamps it shut again. "I know." Her pretty eyes flash at me. "You weren't the only one who's given here."

I grip her shoulder. "My brothers don't believe you. Matvei thinks you're lying. It's too convenient. You pass out. Disappear. End up in the yard where we have no surveillance footage and no access to phone lines?"

She grits her teeth and doesn't speak.

She's hurt and angry—so am I. I have no space for softness, not when she's all but admitting she's complicit.

"You want to pretend we're just going to bury this?" My voice is low, menacing.

Blowing out a breath, she glares at me. I'm fully awake now. "Oh, here's an idea. Why don't you drag me to your basement and interrogate me? Maybe that'll work? If you think I have so much to hide, why don't you use the tools at your disposal?" She shakes her head. "You don't trust me. You haven't from the beginning, have you?"

Her eyes flash with fury.

"You don't get to judge me when you've done nothing but push me away," she hisses. "You think you can control everything, even me."

I exhale through my nose, but my body's thrumming, my pulse racing. In one swift move, I pin her beneath me, my hands pressed on her wrists. I'm stronger than she is, and she can't get away, but I'm the one in her fucking grip. The silence between us is charged with need and fury.

Punishment, possession, and anger twist into one, and I kiss her. I take her mouth. Ravage it. My lips meet hers as I plunder her mouth, owning her, as her hands curl into my biceps, and I ignore the way my fucking shoulder screams with pain. She kisses me back just as fiercely, meeting me blow for blow. Our breaths mingle, our tongues dance. My dick throbs, pressed up to her.

I push her legs open with my knee. "I don't know if I can trust you," I growl in her ear. My grip tightens, my muscles coiled with restraint. I've never wanted to hurt Anya. But I don't trust myself. If I let go, I could break her. No matter what she's done, no matter if she's betrayed me—I will never lay a hand on her in anger.

"You don't trust me?" she throws back in my face. "You were the one who pretended I had no choice in marrying you when the whole time you were planning on doing it with my father. I'm not Bratva, Semyon. I wasn't raised with the expectation that I'd be forced into marriage. You should know that."

I roll onto my back and put her legs on either side of me so she straddles me. I won't hurt her, but I know exactly how to take control. I thumb her nipples until her mouth parts open. "You weren't Bratva," I snap. "You fucking are now."

I pinch her nipples. She screams. I take my thick, aching cock out of my boxers and move a small bit of fabric—the little triangle that keeps me from her—and find her pussy, hot and slick, ready for me. Conditioned, like a good girl.

I slide her onto me, lifting her hips, and she moves, seeking her own pleasure. Her beautiful eyes flash at me, her hair falling across her face. Her hands are planted on my chest. It hurts like fuck, but I don't care.

"Well, that's *obvious*."

I slap her ass hard until she hisses in a breath. I spank her again. And again.

"Behave yourself," I growl at her.

She arches a brow at me, her beautiful lips pursed like a bow. "No."

I lift her, put her on her back, and pin her beneath me. Gathering her wrists in one of my hands, I hold them above her head. "Little brat."

She opens her mouth to sass me again, but I take it with mine. Plundering. Claiming. Our lips clash with our wills. I glide my cock to her entrance and slam into her to the hilt. She arches her back and cries out. Her legs wrap around me, and I thrust into her again and again, my release mounting with my anger. Anya has no skin in this game—unless she's with another man. I lower my mouth to her ear. "Who the fuck is he?" I growl.

"I don't know what you're talking about," she protests, but it's too weak. Too fucking weak. I thrust again, harder, and she cries out, pain mingled with pleasure. Again. And again. And then I pull myself out entirely. "Names, Anya. I want fucking names."

I let her wrists free. Instead of responding, she hauls herself up, grabs the back of my head, and pulls my mouth to hers. She kisses me, her tongue teasing mine. She strokes a hand across my chest. I almost forget my question. I almost forget my name. She grabs my hips and pulls me back inside her. I give her what she wants—another hard thrust, followed by another.

"I was a virgin when I met you, Semyon. Did you forget that?" She smells like dew-kissed daisies. I groan.

Maybe I fucking did.

"The fact that you'd ask me about another man—that you think I would cheat on you? You fucking asshole," she growls. I thrust into her punishingly. My skin is slick with sweat like hers. Again, I thrust. And again. She arches into me.

"Then why were you outside?" I thrust again, pleasure building. I'm not going to let her fucking come. Not until I have the answers.

"Because I wanted to," she says, her eyes flashing with fury. "And now my brother's here. Do you think everybody in this house betrayed you? Is that it, Semyon? You get too close to someone, and it's too much? Can't stand the heat? Too much fire for you? I know how this goes. It's like you forgot who I am, what I've been through as if you think that you're more important than me."

"I've had enough of that sass."

I reach for the pillowcase, tug it off in one swift pull, and fasten the gag around her mouth, tying it tight at the back of her head. She glares at me. I shake my head.

I thrust into her again, and I can't help it—I love the way her eyes grow molten, and she can't stifle the sound of satisfaction deep in her throat. She wants my cock. She fucking aches for me. But when I see her eyes glistening with unshed tears, I wonder. Have I gone too far? Maybe she has been faithful through all of this. Maybe I let the asshole in my head think too much. Maybe I don't trust the way I should.

I lift her up, place her face-down on the bed, knees up, ass in the air. I slam into her until she moans and I'm on the cusp of coming myself before I tug off the gag. I need her to talk to me.

"Face down," I order, my hand hard at the small of her back. She arches into me, her perfect heart-shaped ass wearing my handprint. I bite it. She shudders and screams, melting into me—a silent plea for more.

I fuck her from behind. "You got something to tell me, woman?"

"I've already told you everything," she says, her eyes closed, her mouth parted, half on the edge of climax.

I thrust into her, relishing her moans and the graceful arch of her back. Her pussy clenches around me. I thrust again.

"If I find out you betrayed me, Anya..." I don't finish the sentence. I don't know how to. What the hell would I do if I found out she betrayed me? It's something I can't think of.

She's the only one I've ever allowed myself to be vulnerable with. The only one I've ever wanted.

The only woman I've ever loved.

Her head tilts to the side, her eyes closed as she moans. "But it's fine for you to betray *me*? For you to lie to me? Hmm?"

She's right. She's fucking right.

"I'm sorry," I tell her. "I did what I thought I had to."

She cries out when I thrust again. "Is that going to be a theme in our marriage?"

"I don't know," I say to her with another thrust. *"Is it, Anya?"*

I was a fool for testing her. I was a fool for taking advantage of her. I've seen my family do many things in the name of loyalty and honor, but maybe, sometimes, the ends don't justify the means.

I thrust into her again—and shatter.

She screams my name and grips the blanket beneath us, her knuckles white. My hand reaches out to stroke her, and then she's coming. Screaming my name. Binding herself to me.

It's the most beautiful thing I've ever seen.

CHAPTER 29

ANYA

THE POUNDING on the door yanks me from sleep. My pulse races. Semyon's already out of bed, padding to the door in his boxers.

Bang, bang, bang.

"What the fuck?" He yanks the door open to find Matvei standing on the other side. I can tell by the way his huge shadow fills the doorway. I pull the blanket up over my shoulders.

"Eli's up, and he's throwing a fucking fit down there, wanting to see you."

Semyon nods. "Thanks. On my way."

He shuts the door and turns to me. "I want you to stay here while I talk to your brother."

Right. I toss off the covers and give him a withering look. "Just because you made me come last night, and I was a blathering mess and all, doesn't mean you get to keep me in the dark, Semyon. I haven't done anything to deserve this."

I feel a little guilty because the truth is I *have*. Still, I haven't betrayed him the way he thinks I have. Not even close. I'm going to find a way around the Irish, no matter what it takes.

My phone buzzes with a text.

I ignore it. I could still be asleep. There's no way they have cameras here, right? I have the distinct feeling it's secure as hell here.

What the hell am I going to do?

Semyon walks to get his glasses. "Fair," he finally admits. "Alright, you can come, but I'm the one who leads this, Anya."

I roll my eyes but don't let him see. Whatever. If it makes him feel better.

Semyon's already moving, grabbing his pants, his expression hard. The room's a disaster—our clothes tangled on the floor, the sheets rumpled from our bodies, the air still thick with the scent of sweat and sex. But none of it matters now.

I yank on crumpled yoga pants and a tee—his, I think, tripping over my own feet in my haste to get out the door. He grabs my elbow to steady me.

I raise an eyebrow when he pulls out a gun, loads it, and slides it into his pocket.

"You need your gun? To talk to my brother?"

"We're at war, Anya." The atmosphere in the room feels heavy, oppressive.

War.

We're at war, and where does that put me?

I've never seen so many armed guards in my life. They're stationed in every doorway, cluttering the halls. Upstairs, he said we were at war. Now I *feel* like we're in a war zone.

"Where is he?" Semyon snaps into the phone before he curses and hangs it up. He takes me by the hand, dragging me down a hallway, around a bend, up a flight of stairs, then down another hall. This house is a huge, veritable maze, and I'm not sure if I had to navigate it on my own that I'd ever get out.

Finally, we come to the end of a hall where six armed men stand, their expressions grim. On the other side of the door, Eli screams, his voice ragged and hoarse, desperate. I stiffen. I'm not sure I'm ready for this.

"Move." The men scatter like ants at Semyon's word.

I draw in a deep breath. His hand is on the doorknob before he turns to look at me.

"He's going to be pissed. I have to interrogate him, Anya. I'll let you see him, but if it isn't safe, I'm pulling you out. And you will *not* be in the room when I question him. Agreed?"

I nod, my mouth dry.

He shakes his head. "You'd never let me touch you again," he mutters before he opens the door. We step in, and Semyon slams the door shut behind him.

I expect to see my brother tied to a bed, but someone's taken mercy on him. He's not bound but pacing the room. His face is gaunt, his eyes burning. His clothes hang loose, too loose, his wrists marked from where he was bound. From where I am, I can see angry red peeking out under his collar.

What did they do to him?

The second he sees Semyon, Eli lunges.

"You *fucking* took my sister?" His voice is raw, a growl breaking past his lips as he slams into Semyon, driving him back. "You hurt her? They took me, and the first fucking thing you did was move in and steal her?"

His fists fly, unhinged, like an animal backed into a corner on the attack. He swings wild, fueled by fury, and for a second, Semyon lets him. Semyon, the cold strategist, the man who never relinquishes control to anyone, is letting himself be beaten... *for me.* To give Eli the closure he needs. As if he deserves this for taking his best friend's sister.

"Eli!" I scream. "No! It isn't like that!"

A punch lands hard against Semyon's jaw. His head snaps to the side, but he doesn't move.

"Eli! Stop!" My voice cracks. I grab for his arm, but he's already swinging again.

Semyon moves, grabbing Eli's wrist effortlessly. His expression is calm, but I know that cold look in his eyes. I want to pull them apart, to make them stop, but I can't. Semyon shoves Eli back, sending him crashing into a dresser.

Eli comes up swinging, launching himself at Semyon, his fists flying. A roar tears through the room. I scream as they slam into the wall, grappling, their bodies colliding. A framed print crashes to the floor from the wall, glass shattering. On the other side of the door, fists pound, yelling. Now I know why Semyon shut that door.

Eli swings again but misses, his aim off. Semyon lands a brutal punch to Eli's stomach, but Eli recovers fast. He rams his shoulder into Semyon, and they both tumble to the ground, fists flying. They grunt and curse, rolling while they beat each other. Blood splatters on the floor.

I hate this. My heart is in my throat seeing the two men I love beat each other like this. "Stop it! You're going to kill each other!" I scream.

Neither of them listens.

Eli is smaller and weaker after captivity, but he fights as if he's got nothing left to lose.

And maybe he doesn't. Maybe he fucking doesn't. I swipe at the hot, fat tears that roll down my cheeks.

For once, Semyon isn't in control... isn't calculated. *This is personal.*

They crash into a nightstand, sending a lamp shattering to the floor. They hit each other again and again. They're going to kill each other. They snarl and curse, fighting dirty, fighting mean. I've never seen them fight like this, and something tells me this one isn't going to end.

I look wildly around the room for something to use to stop them when they roll right at my feet. I see Semyon's gun.

I reach for it, cock it, aim for the ceiling, and pull the trigger. Chunks of plaster fall to my feet, dust and debris making me blink and cough. Semyon and Eli stop. Semyon's instantly on his feet, running to me. His hand shakes as he cups my face, fear in his normally placid gaze. "Are you alright?"

"I'm fine," I whisper, choked up at the obvious concern in his eyes.

Eli watches him, wide-eyed.

Semyon's eye's swollen shut, he has a bloody lip, and his wound is bleeding. He lost his glasses somewhere in the mix. He looks younger without them.

Both of them are panting, bloody.

"I'm fine. You fucking idiots!" My hands are planted on my hips. "You couldn't talk like sensible adults?"

Semyon's heaving air, wiping at his split lip. "You done?"

Eli breathes hard on his back, staring at the ceiling. His eyes land on Semyon's shoulder, where blood seeps through the fabric. "Jesus. What'd I do to your shoulder?"

"Oh, just opened up a *gunshot wound*," I snap.

Semyon shakes his head and rolls his shoulders as if it's nothing. "I'm fine."

"My *god*." I shake my head, my nerves completely shot. "Seriously. You two could've killed each other like absolute imbeciles."

Eli's eyes meet mine, narrowed and angry. "Did he hurt you?" He looks back at Semyon, his anger rising again. "That's my fucking sister, you douchebag."

"I'm well aware," Semyon says smoothly. "And, of course, I wouldn't hurt her."

Semyon scoffs, but I can see the tension in his muscles. He lied. He's definitely in pain.

Eli pushes himself up to an elbow. "Why Anya? Of all people, Semyon, my *sister*."

Semyon's eyes flash at him. "Because there are no other women for me, Eli, and there never was."

I stare at Semyon as the truth crashes in on me.

He was waiting for me.

He's planned every move in life just like he plans his moves on a chessboard. He waited until I was grown up—until I needed him—and he had a way to bargain for me.

At another time and place, I'd have been horrified. But now... but now I see the truth.

Semyon Kopolov... loves me.

Eli flinches. I see it, the moment reality sinks in. The bruises, the hollowed cheeks. The way his hands tremble. He's paid the piper too.

I drop to one knee in front of him. "Eli." My lower lip trembles. He reaches for my hand and gives it a gentle squeeze.

"I'm sorry, Anya," he says, shaking his head. "I'm sorry I couldn't stop it I didn't want you mixed up in all this."

I give him a sad smile. "I know, but it's too late for that. I thought you left."

He scoffs. "Left? I might've made some bad decisions, but do you really think I'd leave you and Stefan alone like that?"

Yeah. Yeah, I really did think that.

"Maybe I did."

Eli shakes his head. "I deserve that. I fucked up. Still, you should've run, Anya. Jesus, woman. Instead, you married *him*."

And for some reason I can't explain, I feel like defending Semyon. "It's not like I married the devil incarnate."

Semyon quirks a brow. "Thanks?"

Eli lets out a ragged breath and drags himself to sitting, leaning against the wall for support.

"You're welcome, by the way," he says dryly to Eli. "And you and I aren't done here."

Eli holds his hands, palms up. "I won't fight you anymore." His gaze flicks over Semyon's wounded shoulder. "And you're bleeding through your stitches, dumbass."

Semyon shakes his head. "It's nothing."

"Yeah, yeah, you fucking Bratva hardass."

A beat of silence stretches. They haven't forgiven each other, but are we getting closer to an understanding?

"Are you two done beating the shit out of each other or what?" I ask sternly, hands planted on my hips.

"I'm done," Semyon says wryly. "For now. Depends on what I find out when I ask some questions whether or not I continue the well-deserved ass beating."

Eli shakes his head. "Keep telling yourself that."

Semyon only frowns at him. "You gonna tell me who the fuck had you?"

"As if you need any confirmation."

Semyon's body goes rigid. "I knew it. The fucking Irish." He shakes his head. "Makes no sense why they'd just bring you back, though, unless they had something to gain by it."

Eli frowns. "They want to dismantle your entire operation from the inside out. They took me because I owed them money, but somebody paid them off."

Semyon frowns. "Did they?"

"Yeah. No clue who."

"Still doesn't make sense that they just let you go."

"So yeah, can we figure this all out later, you guys? I think it would be really smart right now if you weren't bleeding out on the floor when you have these discussions?"

Semyon rises to his feet, towering over Eli. "I told you, Anya. We aren't done here." He nods to the door. "Go. I'll come see you after Eli and I talk."

I open my mouth to protest, but his expression brooks no argument. "*Go.*"

Eli pales and swallows hard. "Anya?"

I turn to look at him.

Eli gives me a curious look before he huffs out a laugh. "Wait." He looks to Semyon. "Remember when we used to play chess? And you'd try to talk to me through the moves?"

What the hell is he talking about, and why does that have anything to do with us now?

"Yeah," Semyon says with a nod. "I remember it well."

Eli smiles. "And no one would ever know we had a secret language, did they?"

"Nope."

His eyes swing to mine, and he gives me a knowing look. "It was convenient," he says, talking to Semyon and meeting my gaze. "A good way to talk to each other in secret."

Semyon shakes his head. "Strange time to remember that, but alright."

No. No, it isn't a strange time at all. It's an *excellent* time.

My god.

Eli, you're a genius.

CHAPTER 30

ANYA

My hands shake when I lift the phone and check my messages. I hope I didn't wait too long. What are the rules about this, anyway?

My mind is whirring with the tip from Eli. He was not as unaware of what happened last night as I thought he was. Now all I have to do is play it safe with the Irish and have a not-so-casual game of chess with Semyon.

I hate that he's using Ophelia's number to get to me. It creeps me out seeing the messages under my bestie's number.

> **Ophelia**
> How's your brother?

I know how they'll play this already. They'll ease into a conversation like we're friends before they put the screws to me. I can already hear the deep brogue and see the ruthless eyes.

Fine

Ophelia
And how's your husband?

They're testing me, looking for a weakness.

Boring. Plays too much chess.

Ophelia
Cute. Keep your ears open. We'll be in touch.

The moment the message is sent, I toss the phone onto the bed and squeeze my eyes shut. Where are they? What are they planning?

I need to check on Stefan to assure myself that he's alright. I walk to the kitchen, ignoring every thought that comes up about whatever's going on with Eli and Semyon. Watching them beat each other like that was awful.

I can't imagine how a questioning would go.

I find Zoya in the kitchen, scrolling through her phone. "Hey, beautiful," she says with a bright smile. "You look like hell."

"Thanks?" My voice is hoarse. I lean against the counter, the weight in my chest making it hard to plaster on a smile. "Stefan get off to school alright?"

"Yup. Yana took him today since he overslept and missed the bus." She sobers. "We didn't mention anything to him about Eli. We wanted to leave that up to you."

I give her a small smile. I look to the doorway at the sound of three footsteps—Grandfather, plus his cane. He hobbles in, his gnarled hand on top of the cane, dressed in the same pressed pants and button-down uniform he always wears.

"My, my, if it isn't the loveliest ladies in the house," he says with a wink. "I already saw Yana this morning and said the same thing, so don't think I'm playing favorites."

Zoya shakes her head and smiles at him as she turns to put the kettle on.

"You've had a rough few days, I hear," Grandfather says, pulling out a seat.

I get the teabags while Zoya puts out a simple breakfast of *kasha*, a warm porridge served with butter and honey. My mouth waters.

We talk about simple things, but no one mentions the elephant in the room.

My phone buzzes with a text. I stare at my phone as if it would bite me.

"Are you alright?" Zoya asks with concern. "First you looked like you might pass out again, and now you look like you want to toss your phone out the window."

I give her a wan smile. "I'm alright. I just need to eat."

The door swings open, and Matvei steps in.

"Hey." He makes himself a cup of tea and sits next to Grandfather. "Anya, you know where Semyon is?"

I blow out a shaky breath. "He's with Eli."

Matvei's brows shoot up, which doesn't exactly make me feel any better. "Ah. Right."

He chats with Grandfather about a game he watched while I focus on eating my breakfast and ignoring the buzzing texts on my phone. Just as I push my plate away, the door opens, and Semyon steps inside with Eli.

Zoya draws in a sharp breath. "You two look *terrible*," she says, shaking her head. Matvei narrows his eyes on Eli, likely not convinced he should be in our presence without handcuffs, but Grandfather just sips his tea, his eyes dancing with amusement.

Eli greets everyone with a smile. "Yeah, would love a shower, Zoya."

Semyon, as always, is an unreadable force. "We'll put him up in the guest room on the second floor, the one furthest down the hall." Interesting. The one furthest away from *us*, most likely.

Zoya nods. "I can help, Semyon." She steps over to Eli. "Come on, I'll show you to your room. There's an en suite shower you can use." She throws Semyon a glance. "His... status?"

Semyon blows out a breath and puts his hands in his pockets. "He's a guest, Zoya."

Oh my god. Was she about to lock him up or call a team of guards?

Yes. Yes, she was.

Semyon sits down next to me, and I give his hand a quick squeeze. "I need to talk to you."

His brows lower as he makes a cup of tea. "In a few minutes, of course."

I clear my throat. "Now."

His expression doesn't change, but a flicker of something unreadable passes across his face. "Fine."

Semyon walks me to the pantry and places his hand on my lower back. I melt a little, leaning into him.

I will never forget what he said to Eli in that room.

Never.

I clear my throat. "I want to play a game, please."

A pause. His lips twitch in disbelief. "A... game."

"Yes."

He exhales sharply through his nose, adjusting his glasses.

I can't tell him straight out. If I do, someone on the inside here will know, will rat me out, and we're all fucked.

He exhales sharply through his nose. "Anya, I don't have time—"

"It's chess." My eyes bore into his. I try my best to put the weight of what I need to tell him behind my gaze. If he doesn't understand what I'm saying...

His hands still. He regards me quietly for a long minute, studying me as if searching. I don't blame him.

"Alright, if that's what you need."

"I do."

Leaning forward, his voice drops. "If I play, you'll tell me what this is all about, won't you?"

I clear my throat. "Eventually, yes."

The chessboard is set up in the study, the dark wood pieces polished from heavy use. Semyon sits across from me, his fingers barely touching his pieces when he makes a move. He doesn't rush or speak.

It feels like the chessboard between us is a silent battleground. I can hardly keep my hands from shaking.

Semyon watches me, those ice-blue eyes sharp. Calculating. He's waiting ostensibly for my next move, but I know he's watching me. Reading me.

I pick up a pawn and roll it between my fingers. My throat is tight, my heartbeat heavy.

"You always underestimate the pawns," I begin.

His expression doesn't change, but he's watching me so closely. "Pawns are expendable," he says. "They're sacrifices."

I place the pawn down—not hard, not an attack, but to the side. Out of place. Obviously wrong.

"They don't always move willingly," I whisper.

His fingers still on the table. The air between us shifts as he sits up straighter, and I match his posture.

He's listening now.

I slide another pawn forward. My hands tremble. I keep my expression neutral. "Pawns don't always move the way you expect."

Something darkens his expression. His fingers twitch, hovering over a knight, but he doesn't move it.

I slide my hand to the drawer that houses the other pieces of various games, some colored, some black like these. I find a green piece and carefully put it on the board, covering it with my hand so only he sees.

He picks up a knight. Thinking. He turns it over in his fingers. "No. But they only go where they're allowed."

A chill runs down my spine. He's onto something but doesn't know exactly what yet. I could cry with relief.

I move another pawn. It's a weak move—too exposed. Semyon notices. His eyes flick from the board to me.

"That's a mistake, Anya," he murmurs.

I swallow hard and whisper, "Not if the pawn doesn't have a choice."

His fingers freeze against the rook.

Slowly, he moves his queen—not forward in attack, but sideways. A defensive move.

"There's always a choice."

I glance at the board, my chest tight. I pick up another pawn and set it forward, my words a whispered rush. "Not when you're being watched, and every move you make puts the others in danger."

Voices sound behind us. His aunt and uncle. "I can't believe after all he's been through, they're playing chess," he mutters, loud enough for us to hear him. I roll my eyes.

Semyon goes completely still. He holds my gaze. Finally, he moves his queen forward, blocking my king.

A silent declaration. *No one is taking you.*

I blink, a hot tear rolling down my cheek, and reach for his hand. I give his a squeeze.

"There's too much at risk," I whisper. "You can't play recklessly."

Semyon shifts in his chair, his eyes locked on mine. "And you can't play to lose."

I finally move the knight, a bold move, one that puts me in danger but sets up an opening. My heart hammers.

"If I fall, the rest of the board crumbles," I whisper.

He doesn't blink but moves his rook, cutting off my knight's escape.

"Then I won't let you fall."

I believe him. Oh god, I believe him.

He leans forward with a chilling smile. "That's why we win. No more defense." He moves his queen again, a final shift.

A setup. A trap.

"One more move." He's watching me. "And they're in checkmate."

My chest tightens, something hot and unbearable flooding through me. He understands. He's already planning. Already calculating.

Already preparing for war.

CHAPTER 31

THE SCENT of cinnamon and freshly baked bread gives the bakery an almost nostalgic, homey feel, hiding the tension under the surface.

It's quiet in here, emptied for *this* meeting. I lean against the display case, my arm crossed and my expression neutral. Anya stands behind the counter, wiping her fingers for the hundredth time on a dishtowel.

I casually clear my throat to get her attention.

The Irish have no idea what they're walking into. I know why she's nervous, but she doesn't have to be. I've got this. I've got *her*.

The Irish only think they have control. They don't realize I already have them in checkmate.

"They're in the neighborhood," Anya murmurs, her voice low.

I nod. "It's time."

She pulls out her phone and sends a message. I've got a discreet screen mirroring app on mine, so no one knows I'm watching.

> **Anya to Ophelia**
> The big guns are coming in for a huge treaty. It's today. Be ready.

A full hour passes before the door swings open, and Cillian O'Rourke strides in with six of his men. He's cocky, bold, like he already knows how this will play out.

I feign surprise. "O'Rourke. Nice to see you."

He cocks his head and gives me a grin, baring a gold tooth. Cocky prick. "Speak o' the devil. You were always shite at lyin', Kopolov."

I shrug. He's not wrong. I never saw the purpose.

I move in front of Anya to protect her. She's wearing a bulletproof vest, but it makes me feel better knowing how easily I could strike and slit his throat.

Cillian smirks at me and places an order. To Anya's credit, her hands are steady while she fills his teacup, and I place a cinnamon roll on a plate. "On the house," I tell him with a nod. O'Rourke hesitates.

"Are you turning down my wife's sweets, O'Rourke?" I shake my head. "I remember. Your mother used to bake those Irish apple tarts, didn't she? Shame if you never got to taste them again."

He takes the plate with a scowl as the bell over the entryway jingles, and *they* walk in. Not foreign arms dealers or the force of power-hungry Bratva factions from across the world.

My family.

Dressed sharp. Silent. In disguise. They take their seats, the atmosphere shifting. I walk to the entryway, slide the lock into place, and, just for dramatic effect, turn the *Open* sign around to say *Closed*.

The Irish realize they're surrounded a second too late.

Cillian twitches, reaching for his weapon. *Fucking amateur.*

I move first.

My gun is pointed at him before he takes another breath. The shot cracks through the air, hitting his knee. Bullseye. He drops to the floor, screaming.

The fight is fast. Efficient. I promised Anya it would be, that we wouldn't mar the pretty new floor in the bakery or spill blood on the new tile.

Rafail sheds his coat, rolling his shoulders like he's warming up for a workout, then grabs a chair and smashes it across an Irish bastard's face. The sound of splintering wood barely registers before Matvei moves, muscle and steel, as he takes two down swiftly before they have a chance to react.

Yana and Zoya turn what could've been an ambush into immediate submission. A wrist is snapped, a jaw shattered, and Zoya's blade pressed into the vulnerable flesh beneath an eye. The Irish kneel before us, disarmed and bleeding. Cillian O'Rourke's cocky smirk has vanished.

No more blood. No one dies. We planned it this way: a show of power that leads to negotiation, not flat-out war.

When it's over, the Irish are on their knees. Cillian stares at Anya. "You set us up, you little—"

"Disrespect my wife, and you'll lose that tongue," I warn. I reach for a butcher knife and wield it. Ready. "Hard to eat pussy without a tongue, O'Rourke, mmm?"

He clamps his mouth shut. I don't bluff.

"This isn't a pissing contest, boys." I shake my head. "Now," I say in a conversational tone. "*We talk.* Keenan McCarthy won't be too happy your work was so sloppy, will he?"

Their patriarch is well known for his ruthlessness and fastidious methods.

"You were the ones who came into Moscow. You black-mailed my wife and tried to take what wasn't yours." I shake my head. "We do this my way, or not one of you leaves here alive."

Silence.

Then the sound of slow, deliberate clapping.

I know who it is before I see him. The Undertaker steps from the back in his signature black bespoke suit. His presence shifts the energy in the room. Even his men are terrified.

"You won this time, Kopolov."

Motherfucker was here the whole time. He wanted to see what his men would do. I watch him cross an ankle over a knee and sip from a cup of tea. "Efficient," he murmurs, swirling his tea. "But not as clean as I'd have expected, Kopolov."

I give him a wry smile and nod.

His lips curl, amused, his voice a low drawl tinged with steel. "But I hope you know I'm coming for your sister."

Yana's married, and even he wouldn't tread on Bratva law. Zoya's barely an adult. Rage coils in my chest. I don't react. "We'll see about that."

He winks. "Aye. That we will. Now why are we all here, lads?"

Rafail barks, "Weapons down."

The Undertaker nods. They obey.

I turn back at Cillian. His face is contorted in pain. "This isn't just about bloodshed anymore. It's about power. You have your territory, and we have ours. We could keep fighting, but we don't need to keep bleeding each other dry."

The Undertaker nods, regarding his injured man with interest. "Whatever did you do to earn this punishment, O'Rourke?"

O'Rourke's face is mottled red as he seethes, "Nothing, I—"

"Tried to pull a weapon on our property," I finish, shaking my head like a disappointed parent.

"Aye." His boss nods before he bends to his man and cuffs him. "What'd I tell you about drawing weapons on the Russians, lad?" He slaps the man's cheek hard enough to leave a mark. "You walked in here. Did you expect a welcome party? I ought to shoot out the other kneecap to teach you a lesson, mmm?" With a sigh, he straightens, giving me a "kids these days" shake of his head.

Anya stands stoically beside me, her arms crossed on her chest. My beautiful, fearless wife.

"Let's hear your proposal, Kopolov."

I clear my throat. "We form an unbreakable alliance. A new order. A new way. The heads of each of the most powerful factions vow not to end each other. We fight our enemies together."

He tips his head. Thinking. "And we gain?"

I tip my head. "Survival. A seat at the table."

Nodding slowly, he assesses his men. "This could work in our favor, yes, but only under the grounds of a temporary truce." He finally nods. "Granted."

The Undertaker's lip curls as if amused. Lifting a hand, his men pull O'Rourke to his feet.

"We'll take this deal. For now." He opens the door but turns and winks at Zoya before he leaves. "See you soon, love."

I let him go, but I already know the next time we meet, only one of us will walk away.

I draw her to me. She's still breathing. We're safe... for now.

We'll draw up negotiations and present them to the Irish. We have our work cut out for us, but a temporary truce gives us time.

Anya stares at me. "So that went...well?"

CHAPTER 32

ANYA

It's hard for me to believe Semyon and Eli are here together, chatting over shots of vodka and not beating the shit out of each other. Semyon holds the upper hand though. It's his home, and he's got me.

Eli's got more color on his cheeks now under Zoya's good cooking, but he's still a bit gaunt, his eyes haunted.

"So this is it," he says, shaking his head and looking around the room. At first, I think he's talking about the obvious display of wealth and power in the clean lines of steel and glass and surveillance equipment. The monitors on the far-right wall are at rest for now, but only for privacy. A flick of Semyon's finger on the keyboard, and they'll all spring to life. Eli is observant. He knows.

"Your home," he finishes, his eyes on me. "And you live here, Anya? Stefan too?"

Stefan is peacefully asleep, oblivious to all that's happened. We haven't shown him Eli yet.

Semyon bristles beside me, but I think before I speak. If I could go back and tell little Anya that she'd be married to Semyon Kopolov, that she'd be wearing his ring and sharing a bed, and that he was every bit as devoted as she dreamed about—she'd want to pinch herself.

"Of course I'm living here, Eli. I vowed that I would."

Semyon laces his fingers through mine and tugs me a little closer before he turns to me. "Is that what's keeping you here, Anya?" He's calm as always, but I know him well enough by now to know when he's afraid. He gets this tiny, almost imperceptible twitch next to his lips, and he goes even stiller than usual, his body rigid. Assessing.

I nod slowly. "I would never back down on a vow," I say, but I'm teasing him. I'm trying to come up with the right words to tell him how I really feel.

I'm safe with you.

Stefan is safe with you.

We have a future together because we were born for each other.

I love you.

But before I can speak my mind, Eli clears his throat. "It was meant to be," he finally admits with a sigh. "Though you know she blames you for Mom's death, don't you?"

The air in the room goes still. Semyon turns to Eli. "Maybe it's time you tell her everything."

Eli takes another slow sip of his vodka before he finally nods. I'm not breathing. My breath feels constricted and tight. I've hated myself for wanting Semyon, for being so weak that no amount of logic could rid me of the ache. Of needing him to want me back.

"Anya, I let you believe Semyon was the enemy," Eli says, his voice pained. I watch the blunt tip of his finger trace the edge of his shot glass. "It was easier that way. It seemed you were better off having a target, someone to blame for what happened to us."

In the darkened room lit by moonlight, Eli looks like my mother. He has her cheekbones, the slant of her elegant neck. I swallow the lump in my throat. It only rises again.

Do I want to hear what he has to tell me? The weight of Semyon's rough, warm hand settles on the back of my neck. I can breathe again.

"She begged him," I whisper. "Begged him not to let you get involved."

Eli shakes his head sadly. "It was too late at that point. Our family was in debt thanks to Dad's gambling. He pissed away everything we had, and I tried to stop him. Turning to the Bratva seemed my only choice."

Semyon's fingers tighten. I lean my head on his shoulder.

"Semyon tried to talk me out of this daily. He knew who we were dealing with. He knew how easily things could go sideways." Eli shakes his head. "It wasn't Semyon's fault, Anya. He tried to save her the day she died."

I close my eyes. A hot, fat tear rolls down my cheek.

"Why didn't you tell me the whole story earlier, Semyon?"

"You wouldn't have believed me."

He's right. There's no way I would have. Eli is right, too. It was easier to blame Semyon. I already felt like he'd abandoned me when my family began to unravel and his began to grow in strength and number.

"The day she died," Eli continues, his voice cracking and his eyes glimmering, "Dad was drowning in debt, and I was trying to hold it all together, selling my soul to whoever would pay the most. She blamed Semyon. She begged him to rescue me, and then—her heart gave out. Semyon and I were there. Semyon called the paramedics—he called in everyone he knew—but it was too late."

I was coming home from the bakery when I heard her pleading, her voice rising and falling between the others. By the time I reached the upstairs landing, Semyon shoved past me, his expression unreadable. Eli was holding her—she'd collapsed. I screamed for Semyon, but when he didn't come, I knew he'd run. He was fleeing. And Eli... he lied, telling me what he thought I needed to hear.

My heart aches.

"I didn't want you ruined like I was," Eli says, his voice breaking. "I lied to keep you away from *him*."

He'd seen us that day in the shed. He'd seen the way I stared at Semyon. He knew.

"I'm sorry I couldn't save her," Semyon says quietly, his voice raw, stripped of its usual steel and ice. "I promise, Anya, I tried."

Semyon doesn't look away or even flinch but lets me see him as he truly is—loyal and devoted, holding onto quiet regret he's carried for years. Willing to be the scapegoat.

For years, I've imagined this differently—maybe I'd scream and rail against him, throwing things or even fists, demanding justice for the mother I lost. But now I feel... hollow. And past that well of sadness... a little hopeful.

Semyon's voice is softer this time. Unraveling. "I used to think needing someone made you weak," he admits. "That love was a liability, that it would make you concede control." He huffs out a laugh. "I was right, in part."

"About what?" I whisper. I need to know.

"That love makes you lose control. I'd give anything for you, Anya. I'd do anything for you. The thought of losing you— I'd carve my own heart out, then go back to life without you. Without *us*. And I'll do anything to prove that to you."

I stifle a sniffle. Semyon bared open and pleading hits me harder than I could've prepared for.

"I don't love you the way you deserve," he whispers. "But I swear to god, I'm going to wake up every day and try over and over again until I've got it right... until there's not a doubt in your mind... until you *know*—"

I fall into him, holding onto the only thing that has ever made sense to me. It feels right and natural and so damn perfect when his arms encircle me, and he holds me tight.

"I love you, Semyon. I've always loved you, and sometimes I hated that I did, but I still do."

"And I love you."

When he holds me tighter against him, I wonder if he's the one who fears being left like I always have.

I tilt my head up to meet his eyes. "We're going to put this in the past with everything else that happened. Thank you for telling me the truth."

His fingers find mine.

"God," Eli says with a hoarse laugh. "You guys are going to really rub it in, aren't you?"

I grab Semyon's shirt and fist it in my hand, yank him to me, and kiss him—hard, unrelenting.

"Answer enough," Eli says, cursing under his breath. "You two get a room. Oh, wait. You have a whole house. Guess that's my cue to go to bed."

I bury my head on Semyon's chest. I don't want to be apart from him, even for a second.

"I've got your stuff in Stefan's room," Semyon says. He tells Eli how to get there. I'm amused—he wants both of my brothers under close supervision.

The house is quiet as Semyon and I sit alone. The monitors buzz, waiting for a command. I lay my head on his chest, listening to the steady rhythm of his heartbeat.

I feel... lighter.

He smells of vodka and woodsmoke.

"Thank you," I whisper. I want to go on, to elaborate, but my throat feels tight.

"For what?"

"For trying to help her. For forgiving Eli. For... marrying me."

Semyon chuckles. It's happening more often now, but it still never fails to make my heart swell from the sound of it. "If you think you're the only one who benefits from this scenario, little Anya..." When he tips his finger under my chin, I look up at him.

"Thank *you*," he says before he gives me a brief, chaste kiss.

I smile at him and echo his question. "For what?"

With a sigh I feel deep in my bones, he shakes his head. "For teaching me that I'm actually capable of loving someone. For forgiving me. For loving me."

I thread my fingers through his. Our heartbeats sync.

"Are we still at risk?" I ask. I can still hear the man's words in the bakery.

"Always."

"And Zoya—"

"Will be protected." He says it with an air of finality, and I wonder if he isn't in a little bit of denial over that. But I know how loyal he is. He'll do everything to protect his sisters.

"And Eli?"

"Has paid his debt."

I don't ask any more questions. Sometimes, it's better not to have all the answers.

"Let's go to bed, love."

I go to stand, but he surprises me by sweeping me up in his arms.

"I can walk, Semyon. You don't have to—"

"Carry my wife to bed?" he says in that voice that makes my body instantly warm. "I do. I need to conserve your energy."

My head falls to his shoulder. I close my eyes and let it go. Everything. I let him carry me. Let him bring me upstairs and lay me down, strip me of my clothes, then make me climax until my toes curl, and I can't breathe. Let him claim me. Let him fall asleep beside me in a tangle of limbs and slow breathing until the morning brings a new day.

EPILOGUE

ANYA

STEFAN'S LAUGHTER rings through the house, pure and joyful. I lean against the doorway to the living room, watching as Eli lifts him into a rough hug, ruffling his hair like he used to when we were kids.

I'm so glad Stefan was innocent to all that happened. At least one of us can be. For one fleeting second, I can pretend we're normal, that our family wasn't fractured and broken. For once, I feel... whole.

Stefan is talking a mile a minute, telling Eli everything that's happened while he's been gone. Behind me, Semyon is quietly loading the dishwasher with his trademark efficiency, but I know he's taking everything in. He doesn't speak, not now, but he's there, ever vigilant. My powerful Bratva leader, rinsing juice glasses and stacking dishes.

I swallow hard.

"Semyon, Eli's back!" Stefan announces as if Semyon doesn't know. His innocence is endearing. "Anya, did you see him?"

I smile, hugging my arms around me and taking another sip of coffee. "I did."

Semyon turns to face Stefan and crooks a finger. When Stefan meets Semyon, he kneels on one knee. My fearless Bratva later, kneeling on one knee before a child.

"You've gotten so much taller," Semyon says in his sleepy rumble of a voice. "How old are you now? Twelve?"

Stefan smirks. "Still eight, but definitely taller. I'll be taller than Eli *and* you."

"Then keep eating those vegetables your sister's always harping on you about," Semyon says.

Stefan eyes him seriously. "Even the spinach?"

"*Especially* the spinach."

Stefan frowns. "I'll think about it."

Semyon looks up and smiles at me, actually *smiles*. It's still so rare, and something in my chest loosens.

Stefan returns to Eli and tells him all about the Kopolovs as if it's all been some kind of crazy adventure. I suppose for him, it has been.

"I'm going with Eli back to our house today!" Stefan calls out as I wipe down the breakfast table.

I meet Semyon's gaze. He nods. "They're safe, Anya," he says quietly. Then to my brother, he raises his voice. "Make sure you get your homework done first, Stefan." My throat aches. I'm not doing this alone anymore. "Back to school tomorrow."

Back to everything tomorrow. Dinners at the Kopolovs, which I've come to look forward to. A full day at the bakery, a "re-opening" we've planned in detail. Semyon and I, here in our home together.

We clean the kitchen in amicable silence, both of us lost in a world of our own while Eli and Stefan get ready to leave. Semyon insists they take a full guard with them. Semyon's told me Eli's still not fully in the clear with the rest of his family but thankfully keeps me ignorant of whatever they have planned.

Sometimes I want all the details. Sometimes I don't. For now, I want to know that Stefan and Eli are safe. That's all I need.

It's a lazy Sunday afternoon. I'm still in my jammies at noon, my hair in a messy bun, no makeup on. Semyon is sexy as sin in his gray sweats and white tee.

"Chess?" he asks when the kitchen's sparkling clean.

"Maybe we should play something more low stakes," I say with a wink. "We used to play checkers when I was younger, remember?"

He tilts his head to the side. "I remember everything about you when you were younger."

"Do you?" I smile at him. It soothes me to hear him talk with fondness about my younger years. It heals me a little each time. "Like what?"

He tucks his hands into his pockets with an almost boyish shrug. His glasses have fallen down his nose a bit, and he hasn't bothered to fix them. "You used to chase fireflies by the creek."

That's right, I did. I stare at him in wonder. How could I have forgotten? "You were the only one who could make me smile after my parents died. You'd crack a joke or do something silly. You'd stare at me when I was with Eli like you were half-scared and half-enchanted, and you'd blush a pretty shade of pink when I caught you."

"Oh god." I cover my mouth with my hand and shake my head. "*No.*"

"You did," he says, taking his hands out of his pockets and walking toward me. I look up at him as he nears. He smells like clean, snowcapped mountains and spring air. "You were this shy kid with freckles all over your nose. Innocent. Trusting."

Our toes touch. His knuckle under my chin lifts my gaze to meet his.

"And now?" I whisper.

"And now? I was afraid you had too much light and innocence for my world." Shaking his head, he holds my gaze with his steely blue eyes. "But I'm afraid I'm the one who's been fully corrupted, sweetheart."

"I'm glad you've finally admitted it, Superman."

"Superman?"

"Don't you know that's how I see you?"

An adorable furrow across his brow is the only indication that he's fully confused. "*Me?* A superhero? I'm definitely *not* the good guy."

I brush my thumb along his stubbled cheek. "No? I'm *shocked.* I thought for sure you lived to stop trains from plummeting to their deaths from broken train tracks and helping little old ladies cross the street."

"Nah," he says with a shrug. Leaning in closer, he brushes his lips across my forehead. "Unless they're giving out capes for burning the world to embers to save *you*, I'm fresh out of luck when it comes to heroics. Now. About that strip chess game..."

We settle on lap chess, a "Semyon" strategy indeed. I sit on his lap, playing my part, and he feels me up, playing his. I don't know how he can play backward on the board, but I'm not sure that winning is his ultimate goal here.

"Look, love," he says, gesturing at the board. I lean forward to get a better look, which gives him full access to my tiny sleep top and bare breasts. "I used to think the queen was just another piece to protect the king." He makes a move. "But you've shown me she's the most powerful piece on the board."

I stare, disbelieving. He's left me wide open and doesn't even see that—with a sweep, I make my move.

"Damn," he growls, bending to kiss my neck.

It takes all my energy to stay focused when he thumbs my nipple. "No fair, Semyon. You can't distract me."

I stifle a groan and turn to him. My knees rest on either side of his thighs, my triumph at having finally beaten him fueling my need for him. My body aches to be filled by him, touched by him. I frame his face with my hands as his settle on my hips. Our lips meet, and our breaths mingle.

"Checkmate," I say with a grin.

He looks at the board and shakes his head.

"You win, Anya." He kisses my cheek. "I've never been so happy to lose."

THE END

BONUS EPILOGUE

PREVIEW

UNVEILED: A DARK MAFIA STALKER
ROMANCE

CHAPTER ONE

Matvei

Branding is *not* the same level of pain as a tat, and I don't know why I ever let Rodion convince me otherwise.

But this isn't just my brand. It's my vow to sear my soul Bratva, my promise to give every ounce of my being my Bratva kin.

I sit on a stool, molars locked, my feet hooked under the rungs so I don't topple off. Fucking hell.

"How's that pain, bro?" Rodion, my younger cousin and best friend, stands a few feet away, strategically out of my reach, his arms crossed on his chest.

"'*Feels like ink,*'" I mock. I glare at him. "I'm gonna kick your fucking ass."

It doesn't feel like ink. It feels like penance.

Rafail, the head of the Kopolov family Bratva and my oldest cousin, shakes his head. "He's due," he mutters.

Vadka presses his lips together, a look of concentration on his face. I look away as he presses the brand into my back. I close my eyes and try to mentally transport the fuck out of here, but it doesn't work. The pain is too raw, too vivid. My throat burns from swallowing a scream, the sickening stench of seared flesh filling the room. Someone makes a retching sound.

"What'd he tell you?" Vadka says, doing a piss-ass job of hiding his amusement.

I exhale through my nose. "Said it felt like a tat."

Vadka snorts but keeps his hand still. "You should definitely kick his ass for that, but *you're* the dumbass that believed him. How is a prickling needle the same as a hot iron scarring your flesh?"

If a tat is a paper cut, a brand is severing a limb.

Jesus.

The pain makes sweat dot my brow. I have to take my mind off of this.

So instead... I think of Anissa.

The woman who betrayed my family. The woman who's *mine.*

Anissa fucking Laurent.

The runaway. The ghost. The girl who managed to slip the noose off her neck and vanish into thin air like a goddamn myth. But my mind is a vault of every detail I've gathered across the years I've tracked her.

Sister to Polina Kopolov, my *pakhan's wife.* Both of them pawns in a brutal game of life and death, neither knew of the other's existence. Anissa still doesn't.

She's sometimes blonde, sometimes auburn, sometimes short or dyed black. Her eyes are striking blue, but cold. Always analyzing. Watching. She looks at the world as if it's a threat to her.

I want to be the one who makes her look that way.

Her mouth—full lips that smirk like she knows every secret you've ever kept, smug because she's clever enough to wipe out full identities. And just above those pouty lips she has a birthmark I'm obsessed with. I imagine resting my finger there when I finally have her pinned beneath me.

"The next part is the hardest. *Breathe,*" Vadka reminds me when he lifts the larger brand, so hot I can see steam rising from it in the cool basement air.

"Fuck," Rodion says, paling. Maybe he's the one making the sound like he's about to vomit. I imagine the satisfying feel of my fist connecting with his jaw.

I close my eyes and breathe through my nose. The problem is, it isn't just the pain, but the way the smell of burnt flesh brings back the worst memory of my life, the one I try to bury.

I remember the way the walls of The Cottage basement absorbed the sounds of my brother's screams, the cement floor slick with his blood. I stood, my arms crossed on my chest as cold decision settled in my veins. My brother betrayed us. I had to watch him die. My younger brother, the one I had protected and half raised, the one who I'd give my own life for committed the unforgivable sin of betrayal. He traded his blood for a pocket full of promises from our enemies.

And now, I'm hunting down the girl who made betrayal look easy.

She ran from my *pakhan,* made a mockery of our family, then joined forces with our enemies. Made the whole world think we were weak.

Just like my brother.

Gleb hung in front of us, wrists raw and bleeding from the cuffs—a living warning of what happens when you break the *Vorovskoy Mir,* the Thieves' Code.

"Tell us the three laws you took a vow to," Rafail said. When we were younger, Rafail acted the big brother for all of us. He was stern and unyielding, our guide and friend. Now, he was our *pakhan,* the acting leader of our Bratva, the one who called for the execution of his cousin. My brother.

And I vowed I would watch every brutal, soul-tearing second.

I'd failed my younger brother. It was on *me* to teach him to obey the law of the Bratva. *I* was the one that taught him how to ride a bike, how to smoke a joint, how to fuck a girl well and good and keep her coming back for more. I was the one that bailed him out when he fucked up, but that night—that night I was the one that burned his tats from his flesh before he faced the ultimate punishment for his sins against us.

I took a blood vow when I was eighteen years old. And I'll die before I'll break it.

Just like Gleb did.

The Thieves' Code was ironclad:

The Bratva comes before all else.

Never cooperate with the authorities.

Never, ever betray your brothers.

There's a reason we're feared, a reason why the mark of the Bratva makes women hold their children closer when we pass and grown men tremble.

"We're done."

My eyes fly open. Someone presses a bottle of vodka to my lips. I drink as if I'm dying of thirst. It helps, a little.

I sit up straighter. Every cell in my body seems concentrated on my back, the pain carved into my flesh, throbbing, relenting. I grip the neck of the bottle and take another swig.

Vadka lists off instructions for healing the brand. I only half-hear him.

I spilled my blood and took an oath. Let them brand me. I did what had to be done.

Now, *she's* the next step. My offering. My proof of loyalty.

My obsession.

I grit my teeth and think of her. Anissa fucking Laurent. The runaway. The traitor. My ghost.

The girl who ran away from my *pakhan* but made a fool out of all of us. Rafail has moved on. Thanks to my brother's folly, Rafail married a woman he thought was Anissa, while Anissa ran.

Unpunished.

She's mine. I'm going to own her. Every inch, every breath, every scream. She doesn't know it yet, but she's already mine.

Rafail stands in front of me, feet planted on either side, his arms crossed on his chest. He's dressed in a suit, still wearing his jacket. As always.

"Our meeting's in London on Sunday, Matvei," Rafail says. "I want you there."

Though Rafail is happily married, Bratva men don't forget betrayal. Rafail has not forgotten. He knows exactly why the specific date matters. I meet his eyes and nod. "It would be an honor."

Even as I'm breathing through my nose, my body throbbing in pain, pride surges in my chest. Ink marks the sign of the Bratva, but branding means something entirely different. And Rafail trusts me.

London.

Perfect. My cousin Semyon has orchestrated a proposal, a coalition of the most powerful crime syndicates in the world, seeking asylum. They all assemble in London. Keenan McCarthy's Clan from Ireland, now headed by his son. The Rossis from Boston's Italian mob. The Yacuza, the Cartel. We sought the most dangerous, the most powerful.

Our family represents the Bratva.

"And from London, you're heading to Dublin?" Rafail asks in my ear.

I nod.

Now I know why Rafail chose today for my branding. Word will be released that I've taken the ultimate step of allegiance. My tats tell a story, but the brand means absolute loyalty, proof that I've bled, suffered. Penitence for the crimes my brother committed. A chance to be reborn into Bratva leadership.

Breaking the *Vorovksoy mir* is a death sentence. Brutal, slow, and inescapable.

Anissa thought she was clever, sneaking under the radar and flitting from one place to another, changing her identity. But it doesn't matter if she took an oath or not—she was promised to my Bratva. She ran, and now I'm going to teach her exactly what happens to runaway brides.

She's not just a target or distraction, a pretty little plaything to take the family name. *No.* She's a fucking craving under my skin. I'll chase her to the ends of the earth if I have to.

She never swore an oath, but she ran from a promise. From my family.

That makes her my responsibility, my obsession. My fucking craving. She's not just a runaway bride—she's the girl who made me invisible, and I'm going to burn my name into her skin like this brand is seared into mine.

She doesn't get to run from us twice.

WANT TO FIND OUT WHAT HAPPENS NEXT? ORDER YOUR COPY OF "UNHINGED: A DARK MAFIA STALKER ROMANCE" BY SCANNING THE QR CODE BELOW. AVAILABLE ON MAY 9TH!

Fueled by dark chocolate and even darker coffee, USA Today bestselling author Jane Henry writes what she loves to read – character-driven, unputdownable romance featuring dominant alpha males and the powerful heroines who bring them to their knees. She's believed in the power of love and romance since Belle won over the beast, and finally decided to write love stories of her own.

Scan the QR Code below to receive Jane's Newsletter & be notified of upcoming new releases & special offers!

Be sure to visit me at www.janehenryromance.com, too!